Myra Duffy writes b
best known for her c
Cameron – an ordi
involved in extraordi
Bute provides ins
'contained' setting and the history and the geography of the island are important in providing a background to the action.

Myra divides her time between Glasgow and the Isle of Bute and has family connections to the island stretching back several generations.

www.myraduffywriter.com
or contact her on duffyma308@googlemail.com, @duffy_myra (Twitter) or on Facebook.

THE ISLE OF BUTE MYSTERY SERIES

The House at Ettrick Bay
Long-buried secrets lead to murder.

Last Ferry to Bute
Mysterious deaths at a nursing home and a shady antiques dealer.

Last Dance at the Rothesay Pavilion
Past events cast a shadow over the present as the Pavilion is renovated.

Endgame at Port Bannatyne
The world of filmmaking hides a deadly secret.

Grave Matters at St Blane's
A proposal to build a theme park is the catalyst for violent events.

Death at the Kyles of Bute
The Kyles of Bute Hydro Hotel is again open for business, but someone has murder in mind.

Bad Blood at Rothesay Castle
A party of American tourists is on Bute, but a killer is stalking one of them.

Deadly Secrets at the Standing Stones
A family wedding is not what it appears to be.

The Brydeshill Affair.
A young man is found dead at Brydeshill. But who is he?

Foul Play at the High Kirk
A Christmas Pantomime ends in murder.

When Old Ghosts Meet Dangerous events are sparked off by a chance sighting on the Edinburgh to Glasgow train. (Prequel)

MYRA DUFFY

DEAD DROP AT THE BUTE CIRCUS

Adams and Straiton

First Edition

British Library C.I.P.
A CIP catalogue record for this title is available from the British Library.

For Bill and for Jane

THE ISLE OF BUTE

The Isle of Bute lies off the west coast of Scotland, only two hours from the city of Glasgow. It has been occupied for over five and a half thousand years but rose to prominence in Victorian days when its proximity to Glasgow made it a favoured spot for the wealthy to build summer houses and the not-so-wealthy to enjoy the delights of the seaside in the many rooms available for rent during the holiday season.

The northern part of the island is Highland in appearance, but the southern part is lowland and fertile. Ettrick Bay is on the western side of the island and here the mile curve of sandy beach looks over the tiny island of Inchmarnock to the Sleeping Warrior of Arran.

ISLE OF BUTE
N
Maids of Bute
Kyles of Bute
Kyles of Bute
Kames Bay
Port Bannatyne
Ardbeg
Rothesay
Ettrick Bay
St Ninian's Bay
Mount Stuart
Scalpsie Bay
St Blane's
Sound of Bute

PROLOGUE

There was a gentle swell on the Firth of Clyde, setting the vessels at anchor in the bay bobbing as the clink of the rigging drifted over the water.

Gordon steered his small boat out of Rothesay harbour and set course for the Marina at Port Bannatyne, his mind on a welcome pint in the newly refurbished Anchor Tavern on the seafront.

What a great idea the community buyout had been. It had taken a lot of work but in the end, thanks to the support of the locals, it was now more than a place to have a drink – it was somewhere for the villagers to come together and visitors to experience the hospitality of the island. He'd visited several times recently on trips to Bute and was looking forward to meeting up with the regulars again, to hearing the latest news. He'd made a number of good friends and now he had a boat of his own he'd be part of the sailing fraternity.

As he'd left the Marina at Rothesay the ferry had come sweeping in and a line of pantechnicons bearing the name of Kanzi's Circus trundled off. He'd watched with interest as they lumbered away in the direction of the King George V playing fields in the High Street. Posters advertising the circus were everywhere in town and with the island numbers swelled by the summer influx of visitors during the first week of the Glasgow Fair, they'd be guaranteed a full house every night. He might buy a ticket for one of the performances. It was many years since he'd been to the circus.

It would be another lovely day tomorrow, he thought, turning back to look at the sun slowly sink down behind the Cowal hills in a rose-streaked sky. How lucky he was. Retirement had worked out well for him, given him the opportunity to do what he'd always wanted. He missed Sally, his wife. Of course he did – well, most of the time – but her death had left him a wealthy man. Sally had been so frugal. Always worried about not having enough money for retirement. What good had that been to her? Dead before she could spend it.

He was still a young man – well, youngish. Who knew? He might meet a woman who shared his interests. Sally hadn't been like that. If he was being truthful they'd had little in common, had drifted apart, especially once the children left home. A pang of guilt struck him, but he pushed it away. This was his time now. He'd settled some of the inheritance on the children and they'd been more than happy to see him buy this boat. He was sure he'd get the hang of it if, as planned, he spent the summer sailing around the island.

His daydream was interrupted as he realised with a start that he was travelling towards one of the large yachts moving slowly and erratically across Kames Bay. What was this man up to? Gordon tried to wrest the steering wheel around but he was too close to the other boat to create a gap between them. He tried again but lacked the strength to move quickly enough. This was fast becoming an emergency. An emergency he wasn't equipped to deal with.

He held on tightly to the wheel with one hand while beginning to wave frantically with the other, shouting as loudly as he could. Where were the flares stored? He'd been given instructions when he'd bought the boat but he hadn't paid much attention. After all, what could go wrong in the tranquil waters of the Firth of Clyde, he'd thought? How stupid.

He took a deep breath, trying to control his rapidly increasing heartbeat. Surely whoever was at the helm of the yacht would hear him, would notice his approach, and take action to avoid a collision?

Now he was near enough to see the deck of the other boat clearly. He continued yelling, grabbing the yellow oilskin jacket lying beside him to wave over his head.

There was no movement on the other boat, no sign anyone had heard his shouts of warning. The large yacht dipped up and down on the water but from the way it was behaving it didn't appear to be on a planned course.

Suddenly Gordon realised why the man at the helm wasn't moving. He was slumped over the steering wheel. Had he passed out? This was worse than he thought. He grabbed his mobile phone to summon help. No signal. And he'd no idea how to work the boat's radio. Even if he could reach it in time.

Cursing his bad luck, trying not to panic, Gordon closed his eyes, held on tightly to the wheel and waited for the inevitable crash.

ONE

'You've done what?'

I put down my coffee cup to gaze at my husband, Simon, in astonishment. Perhaps I'd misheard him.

He cleared his throat before saying, 'I did consider discussing it with you, Alison, but I thought you might veto the idea. Come up with some objection or other.' He fiddled with the spoon on his saucer, avoiding looking at me.

This explained the maps and the books on sailing he'd been buying recently. 'It's your money, Simon. You've worked hard to earn it. There's no reason you shouldn't spend it on something you really want.' I hesitated. 'But a boat? You know nothing about sailing.' Then I added, 'Do you?' This might be part of his past I knew nothing about.

'Not strictly true,' he blustered. 'A distant relative who lived in the Lake District had a boat. We spent a holiday there one summer when I was a teenager and he took me sailing on Lake Windermere.'

'How often did you go sailing with him?' I'd no memory of Simon mentioning this relative.

'A few times,' he mumbled.

'Oh, Simon, even if he did teach you how to sail, don't you think Lake Windermere is a bit different from the Firth of Clyde? That you'd need more experience?' Limited as my knowledge of sailing was, I'd a feeling it wasn't as easy as Simon was suggesting. 'I hope you won't run into trouble like that poor man who had a collision in Kames Bay?

How terrible was that?'

He didn't reply immediately but turned away to stare out of the window. Then he said, 'That was an unfortunate accident.'

We were spending the summer in our cottage on the Shore Road in Port Bannatyne. We'd bought it the previous year and after a lot of work had managed to restore this old building to a cosy dwelling. Or rather the builder had as neither of us has any DIY skills. It was small, with only two bedrooms, a living room, a bathroom and a kitchen with a modest extension but perfectly adequate as a holiday home. Most of our possessions were in storage in Glasgow, awaiting a decision about a permanent home on the mainland. They might be there for some time.

After years of working, much of the time overseas, Simon had decided the contract he'd recently completed would be his last. 'I'm not going to take on another commission,' he'd said. 'I want a permanent base. I'm tired of travelling, of being away from home. Early retirement will suit me fine.'

If I were being truthful this plan to spend the summer on the island wasn't helping in our decision making. In fact it was making it more difficult to agree where we should live, especially as we weren't tied to any particular area of the country.

What's more, I suspected Simon might find the pleasures of spending much of his time on the golf course not as exciting as he'd imagined.

Being a writer, I could work from anywhere, though I'd no new project right now. Early retirement would be an opportunity to spend more time together, do some of the things we'd planned. Walk the West Island Way, for example, which was rapidly becoming a distant dream.

And if we did agree to settle on the island for good we could look for a bigger house. The cottage was fine as a holiday home but too small for the long term.

We'd given up house-hunting during the summer. The cottage was comfortable, the weather mostly good since we'd arrived on the island. Plenty of time for such a momentous decision, though from time to time the thought that we'd have to make up our minds jumped into my head.

As a way of reinforcing my warnings about the perils of being an inexperienced sailor, I said,

'What do you think about that accident? The one in Kames Bay, where you'd have thought something like that would be most unlikely.'

'That was different,' he protested. 'There was something seriously wrong with the man on the yacht. He wasn't in control. It was impossible for the sailor of the other boat to avoid crashing into him. A boat doesn't respond as quickly as a car.'

'Mmm, that's as maybe. Perhaps if he'd been a better sailor he'd have managed to save the situation.' I added, 'From what I heard he'd set off with little or no experience,' but Simon didn't pick up on this.

'Whatever happened, Alison, it's no concern of ours…yours.' He emphasised the "yours". He stopped. 'Don't tell me you know either of the boat owners?'

'No, no. Of course not. I only know is what I've read…or heard.'

Simon sighed. 'If you're really so worried about my having a boat, I can resell this one.'

Rather ashamed of my earlier reaction, I said in a softer voice, 'What kind of boat is it?'

He grinned sheepishly, then said, 'It was an

opportunity not to miss. You remember I told you about Damien Loughty? I saw the advert for the boat online and then met up with him in the Anchor Tavern, the new community pub, one night a couple of weeks ago. He brought some photos for me to look at and…'

Holding up my hand to stop the flow of this story, I said, 'Don't worry, Simon. You've already bought the boat so I'm sure it'll be fine. As I said, if it's what you really want then enjoy it.' Yes, he'd told me about his meeting with Damien but I'd paid scant attention.

A look of relief crossed his face and he pushed himself back in his chair. 'You'll love it,' he said, bubbling with enthusiasm. 'Damien showed me lots of photos. It'll be perfect for sailing around the Kyles on a warm summer evening. With a glass of wine in your hand.'

This was beginning to sound more interesting. A picture flashed into my head of a yacht like the ones we'd seen at the Marina at the far end of Port Bannatyne. Of course it wouldn't be as big as some of the enormous vessels overwintered there, but if it had a deck where I could sit back and relax while Simon piloted us down the Kyles of Bute perhaps this was a good idea despite my initial doubts.

'When do I get to see this new toy of yours?' Oops, wrong word to choose.

Simon sounded rather hurt as he said, 'It's a proper boat and it's being delivered tomorrow evening. Damien is sailing it from its current berth in Inverkip.'

'What time will he arrive?'

Simon shook his head. 'Already I've learned that with matters of the sea, there's no exact time, only an

ETA, an estimated time of arrival. Damien said he'd text me when he arrives and we can walk along to the Marina and pick it up.'

I wasn't sure "pick it up" was a nautical term either but then what did I know?

The deed was done and now I was over the surprise I was beginning to look forward to this new venture. Especially as Simon had said my only duty would be to sit back on the deck and relax with a glass of wine. And if the weather held as the forecast promised it would be idyllic out on the water, sailing down the Kyles of Bute.

Would I never learn? I should've known it wouldn't work out like that. Only this time what happened wasn't my fault.

TWO

Next morning Simon was unable to sit still. He kept checking his phone. When there was no word from Damien he went into the garden, pottered about for half an hour, came back in, went out again until eventually he said, 'I'm going for a game of golf. There's bound to be someone at the Port Bannatyne clubhouse happy to partner me for a round.'

'Good idea,' I said, looking up briefly from the book I was reading.

'Unless you'd like to do something else?' He hesitated.

'No, I'm fine here.' I put my book down. 'How about I come along to meet you at the clubhouse and we go for lunch at the Kingarth Hotel after your game? We could have a walk at Kilchattan Bay. Text me when you finish.'

'Will do.' And with that he went upstairs to change, before rummaging in the downstairs cupboard for his golf clubs and setting off, whistling as he left.

As the door closed behind him, I lifted the morning newspaper from the coffee table and went through the kitchen to the garden. An early morning chill had given way to warm sunshine. Although the cottage garden, backing on to the High Road, was compact there was an area at the bottom with a comfortable bench where a large false cherry tree in full leaf offered shade.

I should've realised this wouldn't be easy. Reading outdoors, I mean. I'd started with an article about the problems with holiday flights, pleased we'd decided to spend the summer on Bute, only to be distracted before finishing it. There were too many diversions: the swifts, returned from wintering in the warm south, swooping and diving in the summer air, the shriek of the oyster catchers down by the shore, the noisy seagulls, always on the lookout for a discarded snack.

But one item in the newspaper did capture my attention: the story about the collision between a yacht and a boat in Kames Bay.

The sketchy report gave few details. The debris from the accident had been cleared away and luckily the owner of the boat had been only slightly hurt. There was little information about the pilot of the yacht who'd caused the crash, apart from the fact he was found slumped over the steering wheel when the collision occurred. A heart attack or a stroke was suspected: he'd been airlifted to the mainland and taken to a private hospital.

That didn't stop the rumours. I'd heard several possibilities during my visits to town in the couple of days since the accident and the suggestion that a heart attack or a stroke had been the cause was too simple for most people. The preferred idea was much more sensational. He was a drug smuggler who'd been murdered by a rival gang. But from the little hard information trickling out there was no sign of a struggle on the boat. The unflattering photo in the newspaper was of a seriously overweight man, named as Jonas Gastrell. I felt sorry for the poor sailor who'd collided with him. What a shock. Thank goodness he was only slightly injured and was making a good recovery.

Engrossed in this article, the sound of my mobile startled me. Drat. I'd left it on the kitchen table in the cottage and, dropping the newspaper, I sprang to my feet to hurry to the back door. As I arrived, the ringing stopped. Probably yet another cold call, I thought, and was about to go back into the garden. If it was urgent the caller would ring back or leave a message. But curiosity got the better of me. It might be our son, Alastair, phoning from Canada (as an academic he is vague about details like time difference) or our youngest, Deborah, whose life is often beset by a crisis.

But I was wrong. It was our elder daughter, Maura, who lives in Kent with her husband, Alan, and their three children. Nothing to worry about. Maura is the most sensible of our three children.

I dialled her number. 'Hello, Maura. Sorry I missed your call. Good to hear from you.'

'Hello, Mum. How are you? And where are you?' Her voice sounded flat, so unlike her usual bright self.

Trying to put aside a sudden feeling of worry, 'Enjoying life on Bute,' I said and we exchanged pleasantries for a few minutes until she said abruptly, 'Could I come and stay for a few days?'

This posed a difficulty. 'Maura we'd love to see you all, but the cottage has only two bedrooms and it would be impossible.'

Much as I'd be delighted to have them to stay, there was no way we could fit everyone in. 'I could book one of the cottages on the Kames Castle estate at the end of the village. The children would enjoy it there. Plenty of room for them to run about, work off their energy and be near the beach. They'd love that.'

There was a pause on the other end of the line before she replied. 'My plan is to come on my own. Alan is taking the children to his parents for a few days. They claim they don't see enough of them. I thought it would be a good opportunity to visit you and Dad. Catch up.'

This was strange. Alan's parents live not far from Maura and her family in Kent and if anyone doesn't see enough of the grandchildren it's Simon and me.

Maura said again, 'I thought it'd be a good idea to come on my own. It's ages since I've been back to Scotland.'

This was true. 'Of course. We'd love to see you. And, yes, the spare bedroom is fine for one person. When were you thinking of?' Any further questions could wait until she arrived.

'How about tomorrow,' she said.

THREE

'There must be a reason for this sudden decision to visit us.' Simon stared gloomily into his coffee cup before draining the last dregs.

He was right. We'd enjoyed an excellent lunch in the Smiddy Bar at the Kingarth Hotel and I'd waited until coffee was served before telling him of Maura's phone call and her plans to come to Scotland.

Trying not to sound concerned, I said, 'I'm sure there's not a problem. Perhaps family life is getting to her and she'd like a break. It's hard work with three young children. And in my opinion she went back to work too soon, though I didn't dare say to her.'

'You didn't find it difficult, having a teaching job and looking after three children,' Simon said, putting down his coffee cup and drumming his fingers on the table.

I let this comment pass, though I was strongly tempted to make a snippy reply.

'It's probably nothing to worry about,' I said, trying to sound positive. 'And it'll be good to spend time with her on her own. It's ages since we've seen her without the family, had a chance to chat without interruptions.' Much as we loved our grandchildren they were extremely boisterous and exhausting.

I put my hand over Simon's to stop the annoying noise. He looked up and sighed. 'Trouble is Damien texted to say he's sailing the boat from Inverkip to Port Bannatyne tomorrow evening. Will Maura want picked up from the Airport in Glasgow? Or is she bringing her car?'

'I didn't ask. If she's flying up I can go over to the mainland and collect her. That will leave you free to wait for Damien.'

'You don't understand, Alison. I'll need help with the boat once Damien leaves…'

This was a different problem. What kind of help did he have in mind? If Simon had little experience of boats, I'd even less if you didn't count being out in a rowing boat on the boating pond in Victoria Park in Glasgow as a child. And then my dad had been in charge. Probably because I'd almost capsized us after taking a turn at the oars.

'Damien will surely park it for you at the Marina? By the time he arrives and hands over the boat it'll be too late to go out.'

Simon replied, 'Sunset isn't until around ten o'clock at this time of year.'

'Even so. Not a good idea for a novice to be sailing so late. Better to wait till the next day. '

Simon laughed. 'I think 'berthed' is the correct expression and yes, you're probably right. The boat will be fine at the Marina until we have time to take her out.' His expression brightened. 'In fact, Maura will be a help while she's here.'

He sat back and unfolded the daily newspaper. 'Gosh, there's an update on that story about the guy who caused the accident in Kames Bay. The story has made the national press. Jonas Gastrell. Turns out he was in his late 50s and…heavens, and originally from Chislehurst in Kent. Maura's part of the world. I wonder if she knew him.'

'I doubt it,' I said, trying not to smile. 'Kent is a big county. And some of that information has already been in the local paper.'

Simon seemed not to hear me but frowned as he read on. 'Oh, dear. This report talks about a massive stroke. That doesn't sound good.' He read on. 'That's interesting. Apparently he was the owner of that circus that's arrived on the island.'

'You mean Kanzi's,' I said. 'There's lots of publicity around town. I wonder why he decided to sail to Bute instead of travelling with the rest of the circus company?'

Simon folded up the newspaper before saying, 'No idea, but I'm sorry for the unfortunate sailor…and for the circus folk.'

'That squashes rumours about murder,' I said. Or did it? The trouble with rumours is that they sometimes contain a grain of truth.

We paid our bill and left, chatting about Maura's visit before walking through Kilchattan village and down to the bay to sit for a while looking out over the water in companiable silence.

'Let's go, Alison,' Simon said and reluctantly I stood up. We remained standing side-by-side for a moment, listening to the sound of the water, watching the rippling of the waves lapping in on the sandy sweep of the bay. It was so peaceful here.

The drive back to the cottage was slow, made slower as we encountered a herd of cows being driven from the field to the milking parlour in the farm opposite the Kingarth restaurant.

Beside me I sensed Simon's impatience but I was content to sit and watch as the great beasts lumbered slowly across the road. Yes, the modern world had intruded here as elsewhere but every so often you encountered a reminder of a more leisurely pace of life, a memory of times when we didn't have to live at a frantic tempo. One of the reasons we'd chosen Bute for a holiday home.

The farmer acknowledged us with a wave of his stick as the last of the cows plodded into the farmyard and his dog circled excitedly at his heels.

'We can go now, Alison,' Simon broke into my thoughts and I started up the engine again. As we drove down past Mount Stuart through Kerrycroy and Ascog to Rothesay I kept thinking about Maura's visit and I was glad to reach Port Bannatyne and come to a stop outside the cottage.

'What should we do while Maura's here?' Simon said as we went indoors. 'It would be a good idea to have a couple of outings planned.'

'How about Ardencraig Gardens at Craigmore? I'm sure she hasn't been there.'

'Of course. Maura said she's enjoying creating a garden at their new house, didn't she, and she'd enjoy a day out at Ardencraig. Might give her some inspiration.'

But at the back of my mind, even as we planned various trips, I wondered about the real reason for her visit.

The story of the owner of Kanzi's circus and his yacht slipped to the back of my mind. Simon was right. I'd been involved in enough mysteries on the Isle of Bute. There could be any number of reasons why Jonas Gastrell had decided to sail to the island rather than travel with his circus. None of my business. Now that Simon had retired, I was looking forward to a calmer life, to enjoying summer on the island. Once again I was wrong.

FOUR

Maura arrived with more luggage than I'd have thought necessary for a short stay. As she came through the Arrivals Gate I was struck by how thin she'd become, her face pinched and her coat hanging loosely. Her hair had been cut severely short, accentuating her cheekbones. But though I stole a sideways glance at her from time to time, I said nothing.

She'd caught an early morning flight from London and Simon was delighted when I told him of her plans. 'You'll be back in time to help with the boat, then. Damien says he'll be here by this evening. He'll keep me updated by text.'

'Good to see you, Maura,' I said, trying to control one of the wayward suitcases on wheels as I lifted it from the luggage carousel. 'My car is in the short stay car park so it's lucky you arrived on time.' Parking at the airport has become a nightmare.

We chatted as we walked out of the terminal building but it was mostly about her journey and the difficulties of negotiating the London transport frenzy when 'It's been ages since I've been in town,' she said. 'I'd forgotten how busy the Tube is.'

But when I asked about Alan her reply was vague. 'He's looking forward to spending time with his parents,' she said dismissively. 'And it'll be good for the children to have time with their other grandparents. I thought it would be an opportunity to visit you and Dad for a few days while they're away.'

This struck me as odd. While Alan is quiet and pleasant I didn't have the impression he was close to his parents. Indeed I seemed to remember that Maura had remarked on a couple of occasions that he'd hinted they should move as he felt his parents lived too near them, were too ready to drop in without warning. But now wasn't the time to be quizzing her about her in-laws.

The journey back to Weymss Bay was quiet, the traffic light and as I had to concentrate on the road (perhaps I'm becoming too used to island life, I thought) there was little conversation.

No sooner were we settled at a table in the passenger lounge on the ferry than a voice beside me said, 'Hello, Alison. Been to the mainland?' It was Gladys Jaxman, the owner of the Four Winds Hotel. She sat down beside us.

Gladys was dressed as though for a night out in tight-fitting leopard-skin jeans and a sparkly jumper, her bleached blonde hair secured on top of her head by a large diamanté clasp. I remembered her as a chatterbox and I could see Maura becoming edgy.

'I'm going out for a breath of air,' she said, standing up. 'I love to be on deck as we come into Rothesay. Good to meet you, Gladys.'

As Maura disappeared off to join others in the seating area outside, Gladys resumed her one-sided conversation. By the time I'd listened to stories about her family's exploits and the problems with the hotel "Impossible to get staff these days" we were sailing into the calm waters of Rothesay Bay and towards the ferry terminal.

She jumped to her feet, leaning over to lift her bag from the seat on the other side of the table. 'I must catch up with you properly, Alison. We could meet for coffee?'

I nodded, unwilling to make a firm commitment.

Then as she turned away, she said suddenly, 'Awful about that poor man found dead on the boat in Kames Bay, wasn't it?'

'Dead? I don't remember reading he was dead.' Too late I realised it would have been better to change the topic of conversation quickly rather than be involved in rumour and speculation.

But she was not to be deterred. Before I could reply she went on, 'They're saying it was no accident. He died soon after they took him off his boat. And they've decided it was murder.' She said this with some relish, though she didn't elaborate on who "they" might be and I didn't ask.

If this was true, how had she found out? The newspaper reports had said only that he'd had a serious stroke and had been taken to a hospital on the mainland. Then I remembered how the island network functions – how news travels fast. Perhaps he was dead, but for some reason this wasn't being revealed to the general public. And why would the reports say he'd had a stroke?

Unwilling to comment, I turned away, saying, 'I'll check my daughter knows we'll be docking soon,' just as I spied Maura getting to her feet to have a better view as we came into Rothesay Bay.

Oblivious to this, Gladys persisted, 'Did you pick up who he is? He's Jonas Gastrell, the owner of the circus that's arrived on Bute. Have you heard anything, Alison?' She pulled the clasp from her hair, shook it out and then piled it up again to secure it.

When I said, 'Only what I've read or heard on the news,' she looked disappointed.

There was a pause. Possibly she believed that, given

my reputation, I might have some insider knowledge but was reluctant to say. She was sadly mistaken. And even if I had, I wouldn't have been discussing the incident with her.

Gladys waited. 'I've heard no more than you about what happened,' I said again, shrugging my shoulders.

But Gladys wasn't about to give up. 'I'd an idea as you've been involved in so many incidents on the island, helped solve so many mysteries, you might know something about it. Have more information than the rest of us.' She raised her eyebrows and smiled encouragingly.

This was true. I'd been caught up unexpectedly in mysterious events over my years of coming to Bute – but as an unwilling participant. And always by chance. Those days were over. I'd no more information than anyone else about Jonas Gastrell. And this time I'd heed Simon's warning about keeping away from trouble.

And so, trying to appear uninterested, I said, 'Sorry. I know no more about it than anyone else.'

Momentarily distracted from the conversation about Jonas Gastrell, 'Oh, look,' she said, pointing out of the window. 'There's that cruise ship, The Niobe, anchored out in the bay. I heard it was calling in here this week. Great for the businesses on the island.'

Maura appeared beside me and the voice on the loudspeaker urging all drivers to return to their cars saved me from further discussion about the yachtsman. I'd a dread of being misquoted. It wouldn't be the first time that had happened. Politeness prevailed however and I said, 'Would you like a lift?'

Fortunately she said, 'Joe is picking me up, thanks,'

and she headed towards the passenger exit saying, 'Don't forget about that coffee, Alison. Then we could catch up properly.'

As we drove off the ferry Maura said, 'What was that about?'

Briefly I explained how Simon and I had met Gladys.

'I thought I'd better leave you to it,' Maura said. 'I didn't want to be asked a difficult question about why I was here and contribute to the island gossip.'

As we followed the line of cars down to the traffic lights, Maura pointed to the banner in Guildford Square. 'Look at all the posters for Kanzi's circus. They're very popular – one of the few circuses left.'

And indeed Guildford Square was adorned with a garish banner advertising Kanzi's Circus while smaller posters fluttered on the lampposts. 'Yes. I believe they'll be here for a week before moving on to Glasgow.' I added, 'Though perhaps you're a bit old for a trip to the circus. The girl in the Bute Tool company knows someone who works there as a technician. She says they have a core of permanent acts and then recruit some on a temporary basis to keep the show fresh.'

'You're never too old to have fun,' she said, smiling for the first time since I'd picked her up. 'Something for the cruise ship passengers to enjoy.' Then she said in a sad tone of voice, 'The children would love it.'

I was about to make a remark but then thought the better of it. Until I found out what was going on, the real reason for her visit, best to keep away from the subject of Alan.

Instead I said, 'It's going to be difficult for them now that the owner isn't able to continue,' and I gave her a brief version of the crash in the bay.

‘How awful,’ she said. ‘Was that what your friend, Gladys, was keen to discuss?’

‘You know how rumours spread,’ I said and the subject of Gladys and her love of gossip was dropped as we chatted about the children. Or rather I asked questions to which Maura replied briefly. Perhaps I’d find out more once we were back at the cottage but for the moment she seemed to be content to gaze out of the window as we drove back, only commenting from time to time on how little had changed since her last visit.

‘That’s one of the pleasures of the island,’ I said though I did point out the large metal sign saying BUTE recently installed beside the discovery Centre. ‘A great place for a photo opportunity,’ I said.

Just past the end of the row of shops on Victoria Street I suddenly remembered. ‘I’ll have to stop at the Co-op for bread. We’re almost out.’

I did a quick left turn into the West Kirk car park and slid into a space.

‘I’ll walk across with you,’ said Maura. ‘It’ll give me a chance to stretch my legs.’

As we walked towards the entrance to the Co-op, Maura said, ‘Do you see that man in front of us? I think I recognise him. But I must be mistaken.’

‘Who is he?’ I said, following the direction of her gaze.

‘He was a neighbour of ours for a while.’ She shook her head. ‘But I can’t think why he’d be on the island.’

The Co-op was quiet and shopping took only a few minutes, though we did pick up a pack of doughnuts in addition to bread.

As we reached the self-service till, Maura let out a yelp. ‘I don’t believe it.’ She turned to the tall, rangy man at the next till. 'I thought it was you. What are you doing here?' she asked.

The man spun around, stared, and then laughed in surprise. 'I may ask you the same question,' he said.

'Mum,' said Maura, 'this is Brannan. He was our next-door neighbour when we lived in Bromley for a short time.'

Brannan smiled, displaying a set of Hollywood style gleaming teeth in a tanned face. Whatever his job, appearances were important.

'You won't be able to guess,' he said, a smug look on his face.

Maura put her finger to her lips. 'Let me think. I know you've had lots of acting jobs. Are you still doing that? In something I'd know about?' She grinned. 'Have you been offered a role in a big American production?'

Brannan laughed as he gestured to a poster adorning the wall opposite the tills. 'I've joined the circus,' he said.

Maura took a step back and squeaked a reply. 'You've done what? Don't tell me you're one of the performers?'

'I leave that to younger members like Fabio and Melody Blue. No, I'm the Ringmaster. I was fed up with audition after audition for minor roles on stage and TV that came to nothing and when this opportunity came up I decided to try for it. And got it.' He grinned. 'It's really an acting job – you don't have to do anything except pretend to keep the clowns in order and introduce the acts with a flourish.' He made an exaggerated bow, difficult in the confined space of the self-service tills.

'That's amazing. We'll have to come and see you in your new role,' said Maura as I became aware of a queue of impatient shoppers building up behind us.

'We'll have to move,' I hissed, grabbing my receipt and lifting my purchases.

'You can have ringside seats courtesy of the circus,' Brannan said. As we left the shop together he grabbed a leaflet from a pile sitting on the desk at the entrance and pulled a pen from his jacket to scribble a phone number on it. 'Call me and we can arrange to meet up. It'd be good to talk over old times.' He winked as he said this.

Was that a blush I detected on Maura's face? How well did she know him?

'We have to go,' I said firmly, catching her by the elbow.

As we reached the car park and I stowed the shopping in the car boot she said, 'Gosh, wasn't that strange meeting up with Brannan…and here of all places.'

'Is he married?' I asked as though the reply were of no consequence.

'What a strange question, Mum. Not as far as I know. At least not when we were neighbours.' She considered this for a minute. 'Now you come to mention it, he might be divorced. I've an idea I read an article about him a couple of years back. Some model he was in a relationship with. Why do you ask?'

'No reason. I was thinking if he was married, had a family, it would be difficult for them if he was on the road most of the time with the circus.' This wasn't my motive but Maura didn't pick up. Or pretended not to.

She shrugged. 'I've no idea. But don't many of these circus performers travel with their families? Have a large caravan instead of a house? It's a way of life they enjoy.'

I made a non-committal remark as we set off to take the right-hand fork for the Shore Road through Ardbeg.

We chatted about the weather, the state of the Rothesay Pavilion, 'Looks as if it may never be finished,' the sad remnants of the old pier that had been used for those travelling to the Kyles of Bute Hydro when it was a flourishing Spa. We avoided the one topic I wanted to raise – the real reason why was she here on her own.

'Gosh, the cottage looks so pretty,' Maura said as she stepped out of the car. 'You've done loads. I remember the pictures you sent me when you first bought it. It looked run down. I love the black and white.'

'We did invest a lot of time and energy in it – and money,' I replied, thinking of the many problems we'd encountered in the renovation. Still, that was in the past. Now we were enjoying living here.

Simon opened the door and put his arm around Maura as he drew her inside.

'How good to see you, Maura. We've been looking forward to your visit.'

As she walked into the hallway, Simon lifted her suitcases. 'You've a lot of luggage,' he said, heartily.

There was a moment's pause, then her face crumpled and she suddenly burst into tears.

'Oh, no. What's wrong, Maura?' I said, alarmed at this outburst, stepping forward to hug her.

'I've… left… I've left…Alan,' she said, hiccupping between sobs.

I gazed at Simon over Maura's shoulder as she continued to sniffle. This was the last kind of news we'd expected.

But worse was to come in the days that followed.

FIVE

'I knew there was something wrong,' I said to Simon later that evening as we sat in the living room. 'That this was more than an ordinary visit no matter what she's told Alan.'

After much sobbing and an incoherent story, Maura had gone off to bed. 'I'm sure you'll feel better in the morning,' I'd said. But even as I said this, I was aware how inadequate my words sounded.

And I wasn't sure a night's sleep would help. Whatever was wrong it must have been serious for her to leave Alan on the pretext of a routine visit to her parents.

One ray of light. Damien Loughty had texted Simon to say that due to "Unforeseen circumstances" he wouldn't be arriving until a couple of days later than planned. That gave us a breathing space to consider how best to help our daughter.

'Mmm. Is Maura's marriage really our problem?' Simon sounded glum.

'Of course, it is. She's our daughter.' But I understood his reluctance to become involved.

Simon sighed. 'There's been no indication their marriage was trouble. If asked, I'd have said they were an ideal couple.'

He was right. This had come like a bolt out of the blue. Of our three children, Maura had given us the fewest worries over the years and we'd always had an easy relationship. 'Anyway,' he added, lifting the remote control to switch on the television, 'I'm sure it'll blow over. Let's not think about it till we speak to Maura again in the morning. The late news is about to come on.'

Would it "blow over?" From the little Maura had said we'd the impression this split was more than a tiff, had been brewing for some time. And I suspected there was something serious behind her departure from Kent, something she hadn't yet told us. Simon might be able to put this problem to the back of his mind. I doubted if I could.

As the images of various disasters, home and abroad, filled the television screen, I paid only cursory attention. Was the difficulty so great it couldn't be sorted? Was whatever had caused the rift significant enough for Maura and Alan to divorce? What about the children? And where would they live?

Suddenly my attention was drawn back to the screen. A photo of Jonas Gastrell, standing proudly aboard his yacht, loomed up as the channel switched to local news. There was little more information except to say his yacht was registered in Folkstone. A member of the police force came on, appealing for help.

'If anyone was sailing in the area and noticed anything unusual could they please contact us. Mr Gastrell is currently being treated in hospital but is unable to assist. His condition is life-threatening.' So the rumour that Jonas Gastrell had been murdered was, as I'd suspected, far-fetched. He was still alive but seriously ill. Or was it possible he was dead and the police didn't want to release that news yet? Thankfully as the owner of the boat hadn't been seriously injured he had now been discharged from hospital.

'There must be someone who can help us piece

together details of the accident,' the police officer was saying. 'There were several boats in the vicinity. If you think you can help, please contact us as soon as possible.'

As he finished speaking a phone number and an email address flashed up on the screen.

I became aware of a noise behind me and turned around to see Maura standing in the doorway. 'I couldn't sleep,' she said. She stared at the screen. 'I recognise that man,' she gasped. 'Of course. I didn't put two and two together when Mum told me about the collision in Kames Bay. She didn't mention his name.'

'Really?' Simon looked surprised.

'Alan went to school with his son, Nicolas, and I met him and his son a couple of years ago at a Christmas drinks' party Brannan hosted. I didn't realise he was the owner of Kanzi's Circus. I wonder what will happen now? Possibly Nicolas will take over. Not that he knows much about running a circus from what I've heard,' she added darkly. 'Alan says he was anxious to leave that life behind. Went to work with a big financial company in the city. Though I suppose he doesn't need to be hands-on. He can rely on the performers to keep everything going. And then there's Brannan of course. He seems to have settled into his new career.'

'What do you mean? If Nicolas Gastrell doesn't want to take over from his father will that be the end of the circus?' Simon said.

'Not necessarily. The circus has a good reputation. From what I've heard…' at this Simon rolled his eyes but ignoring him I went on, '…from what I've heard Kanzi's has a group of performers who are permanently with the circus as it travels around

Britain. Other acts are recruited on a temporary basis. Often they're local.'

'Where did you hear this?' Simon asked as Maura said, 'Yes, I realised when I saw the posters in town. They travel all over the country.'

I shrugged. 'It was the only topic of conversation when I was in the Bute Tool Company getting a spare key cut for Maura.'

'I expect someone will have to take over, else the circus won't be able to continue to run performances.' Simon sounded only vaguely interested.

'Is it possible Brannan will do that – at least in the short term?' I said and then Maura and I had to explain our encounter with Brannan in the Co-op.

'Mmm. I wonder if it would work with Brannan in charge. He must have had oversight of the company if Jonas was sailing to Bute rather than travelling with the circus. It's a bit of a mystery. I don't know much about Jonas but the circus seems to have been a great success in recent years. We intended to take the children…before…' She stopped abruptly, turning away but not before I noticed tears welling up in her eyes.

'I'm not sure I approve of circuses,' Simon said, jumping in to cover the awkwardness of the situation, though this might not have been the best thing to say in the circumstances.

I tried to catch his eye, stop him, but he either didn't see me or ignored me as he went on, 'The way they train animals to perform can only be cruel.'

This made Maura smile. 'Oh, that might have been the case in the past, Dad. It's different now. Modern circuses don't use animals – it's all about acrobats and daredevil acts. You can rest easy. There won't be any animal acts at Kanzi's.'

‘Wait a minute.’ Simon lifted the local newspaper and leafed through it before stopping to point to a page near the middle. ‘Yes, here it is. The advert. I didn’t pay much attention. Kanzi’s Circus is on Bute for a week.’

‘Yes, we know.’ I explained about the posters in town.

‘How come I haven’t noticed them?’ Simon frowned.

Instead of replying, I said, ‘You’re right, Maura. If Brannan was in charge that must have been why Jonas Gastrell was sailing to Bute. An opportunity to enjoy his yacht. But I wouldn’t have thought he’d be much of a sailor if he lived in Kent.’

‘He didn’t. The family came from Kent originally – they were travellers before becoming involved with the circus. It’s been in the family for generations. But Jonas didn’t have much to do with the family business until his father died. He has an older brother but he wasn’t interested in taking it on. So Jonas stepped up. A lot of people rely on Kanzi’s circus for their livelihood. There aren’t many circuses left nowadays. I gather it’s an extremely costly business to run. That’s why there’s only a small number of regular employees.’

‘Quite an undertaking if he wasn’t particularly keen on taking on the business,’ Simon said.

‘It’s in the blood, I guess.’ I joined in the conversation. ‘Perhaps he felt a family loyalty. And now he may not be able to continue if he’s seriously ill.’ I didn’t add, Or if he’s already dead.

‘What will happen to the rest of the tour? If Brannan isn’t willing to step in will they cancel the rest of the shows?’ Simon frowned.

‘I think it’s too late to call off the Bute

performance. They arrived a few days ago and set up in The Meadows. They've probably sold lots of tickets and it'd be too costly to cancel.'

'I'm surprised you don't know more about it, living on the island,' Maura said.

'Most of what I've heard has been rumour and speculation,' I said. 'When I popped briefly into a couple of shops in town. The village shop has all the essentials we need.'

Maura seemed to find this amusing. 'Becoming quite the Brandanes then?'

'I don't think so. You have to be born on the island to qualify as a Brandane.'

'And so it all depends on Nicolas being willing to take over?' Simon said. 'What if he decides not to?'

Maura shrugged. 'We can only guess. If Nicolas won't take it over there may be another family member with an interest in it. Certainly it would be a pity to see it fold.'

Simon said, 'Well, it's not of concern to us. Is it, Alison?' Once again this said with a steely look at me.

For once I was able to reassure him. 'Of course not. I didn't know the man or indeed any of the family. And I've no information about the collision in the bay. There's no way I'm likely to be involved.'

Maura frowned. 'Wait a minute. When we met Brannan in town why didn't he mention this to us?'

I shrugged. 'I guess he's trying to keep everything calm until they have a new boss. And probably doesn't want rumours to spread.' Not that his plan had worked.

'Let's hope it's sorted out,' Maura said. 'Someone has to keep the show on the road.'

She turned to go, then said, 'Oh, I meant to say,

you've done wonders with this cottage. It's as lovely inside as it looks from the outside. I remember the photos you sent me – this room was semi-derelict.'

'Yes, we did put in a lot of work – or rather the builder did,' I said, gazing around with some satisfaction at the cosy living room. The colour scheme of soft green and grey had worked well and let us re-use the grey sofa we'd had in our previous house. One item fewer to store. I wasn't too sure about the stripped floorboards – the rug covering them was cheerful but might not be warm enough in winter if we were still living here. Which looked increasingly likely. Somehow the Bute effect had drawn us in and we'd become content to take each day as it came. The thought of house-hunting again filled me with dread. In the meantime we were perfectly happy on the island. Or we had been until Maura's arrival.

SIX

Despite our determination not to interfere in Maura's marriage problems, Simon and I sat up late going over likely scenarios. 'Don't rush ahead as usual. It's probably no more than a tiff. They're both stressed. Alan is in a busy job that often takes him away from home and Maura is left with the responsibility of three children as well as a job.'

'You were away a lot, working in other countries,' I replied but had to agree when he said, 'Not while the children were young.' During those years he'd been head of department in a further education college and although the job could be hectic and often difficult, he managed to be at home most of the time.

'Enough for tonight,' Simon said, standing up and yawning and stretching.

He was right. There was nothing to be gained by endless speculation. Maura would tell us in her own time.

But after a restless night even several cups of strong coffee the next morning didn't make me feel any more alert.

'I'm going for a walk around Kames Bay,' I said. 'You should come. It will do us good.'

Simon declined with a shake of his head. 'I'm going to get in touch with Damien. Check if there's any update on when he'll arrive.' Simon was taking to the idea of owning a boat with great enthusiasm. He'd recently sent off for several charts and they now lay spread out over the kitchen table. A large map of the area around Bute was pinned on the wall, covering the family photos I'd so carefully pinned up.

'It's only temporary,' he'd said when I'd questioned him. 'I'll be taking these to the boat once it arrives. Meantime I have to familiarise myself with the sea routes.'

He spoke as though he were planning to skipper a commercial vessel and I couldn't resist a dig. 'I'm sure the Captain of The Niobe doesn't need as many charts as these.'

But I'd had enough of being indoors, and I left Simon to pore over his maps while I picked up my jacket from the peg in the hallway and closed the front door behind me quietly to set off towards the Marina.

I called in at the shop in the village to buy a newspaper and walked around Kames Bay as far as the little cluster of houses on the far side past the lodge at Kames Castle. The only other person out this early was a dog walker on the beach. I sat down on one of the memorial wooden benches which are a feature of the island, a way of commemorating loved ones. Port Bannatyne village has many such benches and this one was inscribed "For Frank Downen, who loved this view" a sentiment which was repeated on many of the other benches dedicated to family members set at intervals on the grass verges around the Kames Bay.

From this viewpoint, in the early morning sunlight, Port Bannatyne had a continental air, its setting in the curve of the bay adding to its charm. The village committee had worked hard to enhance the appearance of the shops and houses along the front by adding window boxes filled with summer flowers while the lights strung between the lampposts along the promenade would offer a soft welcome as dusk fell. At this time of year it looked especially charming and down by the pier the stone troughs had been lovingly planted with a riot of summer bulbs. Even the quaintly shaped bus shelter at the top of the quay gleamed with a fresh coat of paint.

I sat back and closed my eyes, the newspaper lying unopened beside me, breathing in the unpolluted air. Did I really want to go back to live in the noise and the bustle of a city? Would it not be better to look for somewhere on the island? The cottage was now in a good state of repair so we should be able to sell it easily. I allowed myself to daydream. Where would we go? There were some lovely houses along at Craigmore, with an unrestricted view over the Firth, but might they be too large for two people? Built in Victorian days when the rich merchants of Glasgow sent their families to Bute for the summer, away from the pollution and filth of the city, many were now converted to guest houses or small hotels. And running a small hotel wasn't on my wish list.

As I thought about these villas and the families who had once lived in them, I was seized by a pang of worry. If the situation with Maura and Alan was serious would they separate, or worse still, divorce? Would they sell the house in Kent and divide the proceeds? With the way house prices in the South East had soared in the past few years she would certainly be able to buy a substantial property on the island.

Stop it, I told myself sternly. There was no reason to worry before we knew the facts. But I realised the problem would nag away at me. I had to know more, find an opportunity to speak to her on her own. Determine how serious this business was. Or if, as I hoped, it was no more than a blip.

As I scanned the front page my mind kept drifting and it was impossible to concentrate. Maura and her problems weren't easily dismissed and with a sigh I stuffed the newspaper into my bag and stood up, stretching to ease the ache in my neck. Something else I should investigate if we were on the island over the winter – joining the weekly exercise classes held in the Port Bannatyne hall.

In the interests of making a start on this plan to improve my fitness, I walked briskly back to the cottage where Simon and Maura were sitting at the table in the kitchen having breakfast.

Maura looked marginally better than she had the night before and I reassured myself that it was likely the stress of the journey had contributed to her tiredness.

As I came in he crossed to one of the cupboards, took down a mug and poured me a large coffee.

'Thought I'd have a game of golf this morning,' he said in a hearty voice. 'Unless you've something organised? There's always a fellow golfer at the clubhouse looking for a game.'

He turned away from Maura and frowned at me. Was this a ploy to leave Maura and me on our own for an opportunity to talk about her problems?

'Fine,' I said. 'Maura and I might go to Ardencraig Gardens later.'

Simon hurried off to collect his bag of golf clubs from the hall cupboard and I sat down opposite Maura, deliberately taking time to pour milk into the coffee, adding just half a spoon of sugar. Another attempt at a healthier lifestyle.

We sat in silence drinking our coffee until we heard Simon shout, 'I'm off. See you later.'

‘Did you sleep well?’ was my opening gambit.

‘Not much,’ she confessed.

Another silence. I took a deep breath. There was no point in beating about the bush.

‘What’s going on, Maura? Have you really left Alan?’

She didn’t meet my gaze but stared at her coffee cup. ‘Yes.’

A one word reply which told me nothing. ‘There must be a reason.’

‘Well…there is.’

What was this about? I couldn’t see the mild-mannered Alan as other than a good husband. He worked hard, drank little and didn’t gamble. I remembered Maura telling me that when Alan had begun researching his family history he’d come across one of his great-uncles who’d been the black sheep of the family – an alcoholic and a gambler – and the rest of the family had as a result shunned both. A memory that had affected Alan’s immediate family.

‘There must be a good reason,’ I said. ‘Dad and I had the impression you and Alan had a great relationship.’

Maura shrugged. ‘We’ve not been getting on recently. It’s difficult to explain.’

‘But he’s a good father, works hard and I’m sure he loves you. What else do you want?’

‘That’s it. He works all the time. Oh, he does try to be there for the children, but there’s no me time. I never seem to stop. I have a part-time job which I love but Alan’s been promoted again and I’ll have to give it up.’

This I didn’t understand. ‘Why? Surely there are excellent childcare facilities in your area? And couldn't Alan's parents help with any emergencies?' (Make themselves useful for once, I thought, but didn't say so).

'Noah has had an ear infection recently and couldn't attend nursery until it had cleared up, which meant I had to take time off. Alan was sent to France on business so he wasn't available to help.' She shrugged. 'It seems simpler to resign.'

'Even so. This is no more than a temporary problem surely. Before long all three children will be at school.' This was ridiculous. Surely this wasn't the full story. There must be more to it. I tried to think of a question I could ask without upsetting her. Of course there was one strong possibility for her distress.

We sat in silence, each with our own thoughts, before she said suddenly, 'There is another problem. He's been seeing someone else.'

'What?' Now that she'd said it, I felt my stomach churn over. Alan was the last person I'd have expected to be having an affair. Then again, how well did I really know him? For the most part our meetings with him had been at family events and with the children demanding our attention there wasn't much opportunity to chat.

Maura avoided looking at me. 'And it's with one of my best friends.'

'How do you know? Perhaps you've made a mistake.' But as I said this, I understood it wasn't likely Maura would have taken the step of leaving Alan without proof.

'No mistake. There were messages on his phone,' she said angrily.

'And why were you checking his phone?'

She looked embarrassed. 'I wasn't. Not really. It

was lying on the kitchen table when the call came through. I didn't answer it of course but then it went to voicemail. There was no way I could mistake what she said.' She began to speak in a voice that I presumed imitated the caller. '"Thanks for agreeing to meet up again on Friday. Lots to discuss. It's so hard keeping all this from Maura but it would be awful if she found out." I didn't listen to any more.'

'You did ask him what it was about?'

'Of course I did. But he was so evasive, so unwilling to explain. So when he said he'd take the children to his parents for a few days it seemed the ideal opportunity to have time away, time to think.'

While I understood how unhappy she was, this seemed like overreaction. Surely she should have stayed and tried to talk it over. Maura has always been the most sensible of my three children but not on this occasion.

'And,' Maura said, unprompted, 'there have been other signs. He's been buying trendy new clothes, for a start.'

As I began to say, 'There may be nothing in that, Maura. He may have thought it…' there was a banging at the front door.

Maura and I stared at each other as the thumping continued, louder this time.

'Hadn't you better answer that?' Maura said.

SEVEN

Dan Seliman, one of Simon's golfing buddies, stood on the doorstep, his hand lifted ready to knock again.

'What's the urgency?' I said, smiling.

Dan frowned, panting a little as though he'd been running. Beads of sweat trickled down his face. 'It's Simon... you'll have to come quickly. He's...he's had an accident.'

My heart gave a lurch and I put my hand to my mouth. 'Oh, no, what happened. Is he okay?'

Dan was one of the regulars at the Port Bannatyne golf course, always eager for someone to join him for a round of golf. Simon must have met up with him when he arrived at the course.

Shuffling his feet, Dan said, 'You know how hilly the course at Port Bannatyne is? How there are parts of it on a steep slope. It's one of the trickier courses on the island but because of its height it has great views over Kames Bay which makes it popular...'

'Of course I do,' I interrupted this description of the golf course. 'But what happened to Simon?'

Maura came up behind me. 'Something wrong?'

'It's Dad. He's had an accident.'

Maura took charge of the situation, pulling me gently aside to say to Dan, 'You'd better come in.'

Dan reached into his trouser pocket to take out a handkerchief and mop his brow. 'I don't want you to worry. I'm sure he'll be fine.'

'Worry?' By now I had visions of Simon being airlifted off the island in the emergency helicopter.

He'd be taken to the Queen Elizabeth hospital on the south side of Glasgow. What time was the next ferry? Why hadn't someone called me to go with him?

'I'll fetch my things,' I said. 'I'll pack a case. Go at once.'

Dan looked puzzled. 'Wait. Go where? Why would you need to pack a case?'

'To go to the Queen Elizabeth hospital of course. I'll take the next ferry over. There's one in half an hour,' I said, lifting my phone from the table to check the app.

'I'll come with you,' said Maura as Dan shook his head saying, 'No, no, you don't understand. He's not in hospital. He's at the clubhouse. One of the paramedics is attending to him. I said I'd come and let you know. I don't drive now. I had to give up my car after my last eye test. And Simon can't drive so he needs to be picked up.'

Suddenly overcome with relief but feeling like a deflated balloon, I sank onto the nearest chair.

'What happened?' asked Maura as I tried to catch my breath and stop my heart pounding like an express train.

Dan grimaced. 'He tripped on a tree branch in the undergrowth as he tried to retrieve his ball. It's his wrist. It might be broken.'

Mmm…as someone who prides himself on his golfing skills, Simon would have been furious about the way the accident had happened.

Maura gave a loud sigh of relief. 'So the game wasn't going to plan?'

Dan shook his head. 'He wasn't on form that was for sure. So unlike Simon to be caught out like that. You see, it's a par four at the fifth hole – three hundred and twenty yards. I teed off at the fifth with a driver – the best choice, you know. But for some reason Simon decided on a three iron. He wouldn't listen and then…'

'Stop!' I said, holding up my hand to interrupt him. 'I'll go and collect Simon now.' This wasn't the moment for a long description of their golfing skills. I had to find out what had happened.

Dan accepted the offer of a lift and he, Maura and I set off for the Port Bannatyne clubhouse. Despite Dan's attempts to make light of it, I dreaded what I might find. Simon's fall might not have been the simple accident Dan described. He might be seriously injured.

In the car park at the entrance to the clubhouse building I switched off the ignition and, jumping out of the car I rushed off, leaving Dan and Maura to follow.

Simon was sitting on one of the chairs in the dining room, looking sorry for himself, his right arm in a sling. The young woman paramedic beside him was packing up her bag.

'What have you been up to?' I said, trying to sound jocular rather than accusing.

'Crocked my right arm,' he said. 'I tripped on one of the branches lying in the undergrowth. Came down with a thud on top of my arm.'

The paramedic stood up and grinned. 'I wouldn't worry. It's a bad wrist strain rather than broken. A few days rest should see him right as rain.'

'We'd better get you home, Dad,' said Maura, helping him to his feet.

'There's nothing wrong with my legs,' Simon said grumpily, but he staggered a little as he stood up from his chair.

'You've had a bad fright,' Maura said, taking him

by the left arm.

Simon winced as he attempted to move forward but with Maura supporting him we managed over to the car and pulled back the passenger seat to ease him into it.

Dan came up behind us like a shadow. 'I told him he should use a driver. A three iron wasn't the right club but he wouldn't listen.' Perhaps he felt partly responsible for the accident but it wasn't his fault.

'We'll finish that round of golf as soon as you're able,' he said jovially. 'I'll keep the score cards,' he added, waving them in the air.

'I don't think so,' I replied more frostily than intended and Dan looked crestfallen.

Maura drove my car and I took Simon back to the cottage in his. Progress was slow; every bump in the road caused Simon to wince with pain.

'I think we should have that arm checked out,' I said. 'I don't want to disagree with the paramedic but your wrist may be broken rather than strained.'

'Don't fuss.' Simon said grumpily, but then he was in a lot of pain. 'The paramedic says I can call the doctor tomorrow if I'm worried. Meanwhile she's given me some painkillers which she says will help.'

Once settled in the large wingback chair beside the fireplace in the living room, he reached into his trouser pocket with his left hand to pull out a blister pack of pills. 'I'll take two now.'

Maura fetched a glass of water and watched as Simon gulped down the pills.

'It might be better to make up a bed downstairs for you. You'll have to be careful not to jolt your arm,' I said.

'I can try to make it upstairs,' Simon said but without enthusiasm.

‘Mum’s right. We’ll have to organise something here for you. The cottage stairs are steep and narrow. Besides, you might have to sleep sitting up for a couple of days. At the least until the pain eases off.’ She turned to give me a questioning look before saying to Simon, ‘Are you hungry? We’ll make you something to eat.’

Simon shook his head but I bustled off into the kitchen, glad of something practical to do.

I popped my head around the door and beckoned Maura in to join me. ‘What do you think?’ I whispered. ‘Is it more serious than he thinks?’

‘I’m sure he’ll be fine. If you’re worried the doctor will check him out and if he suspects any complication, that his wrist is broken, he’ll send him for an Xray to the hospital at Inverclyde. He won’t take any chances.’

Maura was right. If the paramedic had believed there was a problem she wouldn’t have been so reassuring.

Whether it was the shock of the accident wearing off or the effect of the pills but when Maura and I went back into the living room, bearing a tray with tea, sandwiches and an assortment of biscuits, Simon was sound asleep.

‘Don’t waken him, Mum. He’s better to get some sleep now. We haven’t had any lunch so let’s leave him and have ours in the kitchen.’

Neither of us felt hungry. In spite of Maura’s assurances I kept fretting that Simon’s injury might be more serious than we first thought. Maura did no more than pick at her food.

‘Thank goodness Dad is retired. There’s no complication about work,’ Maura said as she poured another cup of tea.

But as I lifted the cup to my lips a sudden thought came to me. ‘Oh, no. What’s going to happen about the boat? How’s he going to manage with his right arm in a sling? I’ll have to try to get in touch with Damien.’

‘What boat?’ Maura said, putting her cup down with a thump and spilling a little of the tea into the saucer.

Here was yet another problem.

EIGHT

Simon was understandably upset. He was annoyed about the accident at the golf course but wouldn't admit it was anything other than bad luck. 'Dan kept telling me I was using the wrong club – put me off my stroke. I don't know why I agreed to have a game with him. He's always been the same. Thinks he knows best.'

Ignoring this, 'If you do as you've been told you should recover quickly,' I said.

But if he was unhappy about the accident he was more worried about how being incapacitated by his strained wrist would create a problem with the delivery of the boat.

'I can't put Damien off,' he groaned. 'It's too late to get in touch. He'll be on his way to the Marina at Port Bannatyne. The last text said he'd set off. This is awful.'

I could only agree with him. I certainly couldn't offer a solution.

'Will there not be someone at the Marina who could help? Could do the …' Maura gestured vaguely, '…do the berthing or tying up or whatever it is you need.'

Simon made a face. 'I don't know anyone there. I'd every intention of going along to the Ardmeleish boatyard to chat to the owners, sort something out, but I didn't get around to it.'

'But surely you can't arrive in a Marina and berth your boat there without making prior arrangements?'

Maura made a face.

'Did it all online,' Simon mumbled. 'It seemed the easy way to do it.' Then defiantly, 'Everything is booked like that nowadays.'

'I suppose Maura and I could go to the Marina and be there when Damien arrives,' I said reluctantly.

Maura looked horrified. 'I know nothing about boats. I wouldn't be able to help.'

'I'm sure Damien will give us instructions.' I didn't relish the prospect either but I couldn't think of another solution in the short term.

'Wait a minute.' Maura scrabbled in her handbag to pull out the leaflet Brannan had given us. 'Perhaps Brannan would be able to help. I'm sure he knows about boats.'

'Really? Does he have a boat?' Another surprise.

'No,' she said, 'but he did have a part in a series called 'Those at Sea' or something like that in his acting days. I seem to remember it was a lot to do with boats.'

'But he's an actor. Surely that doesn't mean he knows anything about boats in real life.'

'Do you have a better suggestion, Mum? He can at least supply brute strength,' Maura said tartly. 'I think it's, if you'll forgive the pun, any port in a storm.'

She was right. Once the new boat was moored or berthed or whatever we could leave it until Simon had recovered. And part of me was looking forward to seeing this new acquisition of his. When Simon was fit again we could look forward to summer days sailing around the Kyles of Bute as he'd promised.

Simon frowned, looking less than happy at this suggestion. 'I'm not sure I want a stranger messing about with my boat,' he said.

'For goodness sake. You're hardly in a fit state to

do it and if, as you said, Damien is arriving tonight we have to make some arrangement…and quickly. Once it's berthed in the Marina you can leave it there until you feel able to cope. It'll be quite safe.'

Reluctantly he agreed, laboriously texting Damien with one finger of his left hand while Maura went into the kitchen to contact Brannan. I did notice she closed the door over.

'It's a stroke of luck the first circus performance isn't tonight,' I said. 'Brannan would have been too busy to help.'

'He hasn't agreed yet.' Simon was upset at the way things had turned out and I couldn't blame him. He'd been so looking forward to the arrival of his boat, to owning it.

'It's only a temporary problem. I know you're disappointed but once you've had a few days to recover you'll be able to deal with the boat. Tell me a bit about it,' I added to distract him.

This enquiry perked him up. 'I've only seen it on the internet but according to Damien it's a proper boat – a twelve V with full sailing rig but it has an engine as well. And it's big enough to have a cabin where we could sleep overnight if we decided to sail further afield.' His face glowed at the prospect. 'Who knows where we might travel once we've mastered sailing it.'

'And does it have a name?' I wasn't sure about his use of the word "we".

'Yes, it's called Hoppity the Third.'

'Really? That's not a great name. Can't you have a name that makes it more yours? That means something to you.'

Simon shook his head. 'No way. It's unlucky to change the name of a boat. It's Hoppity the Third and that's the way it'll have to stay. I wouldn't want to tempt fate further.'

Just then Maura came into the room, waving her mobile. 'Brannan says he's happy to help. He'll be along in a few minutes. He's in Rothesay at the moment.'

As travelling around the island is easy, partly because it's small and partly because traffic is light during the day, Brannan was as good as his word and arrived at the same time as another text came through for Simon.

'Happy to help,' he said as we thanked him for responding so quickly.

'That's Damien,' Simon said excitedly, waving his phone in the air. 'He's almost at the Marina. We'd better head down there now. Be in good time for his arrival.'

'Are you sure you should go? Take a couple of painkillers before we leave.'

'I may not be able to do much, but I can supervise,' Simon said sadly. 'It is my boat.'

Maura rolled her eyes but Brannan said, 'Of course. If it were my boat I'd like to check it for myself. I'm eager to see this boat of yours, Simon. What a great idea.'

He raised his eyebrows at Maura and she smiled, turning away to hide her blushes.

With some difficulty, trying to avoid bumping his right arm, Simon manoeuvred himself into the passenger seat of his car and I drove the short distance to the Marina at the far end of the village. Maura and Brannan elected to walk. A decision I wasn't entirely happy about.

'It'll be good to have some fresh air,' Maura said, but I didn't like the way Brannan steered her by the elbow as we left the cottage. This might be yet another complication in her problems with Alan. Again I wondered how well they had known each other in the past.

Preoccupied by the coincidence of Maura's meeting up with Brannan at a time when there were difficulties in her marriage, I almost knocked over an elderly woman crossing to the bus stop.

'Careful, Alison,' Simon said, grasping his right arm with his left hand and flinching as I braked in the nick of time.

The Marina was doing well, judging by the number of large boats in the bay and those laid up on the stretch of land beside the small portacabin which served as an office. The gigantic orange crane used to lift large boats in and out of the water stood immobile in the corner, its bulk brooding over even the largest yachts. Although the car parking bays were full I managed to squeeze into a space at the end of the line, leaving room for Simon to edge out carefully. He stood looking around for a minute before making his way over to the pontoon.

While we stood waiting for Brannan and Maura to arrive, Simon kept checking his phone for updates from Damien. This proved difficult as he was trying to do everything one-handed.

'Let me have it, Simon,' I said and he handed his phone over reluctantly to let me send a message to Damien as he dictated it.

'We should be able to see him soon,' he said over and over, scanning the bay, but there was nothing in sight that looked like the boat Simon had described to me.

Maura and Brannan came up beside us, laughing at something Brannan had said. We might need his help, but I was beginning to take a dislike to Brannan. Once we'd had his assistance with berthing the boat I'd try to make sure he had nothing more to do with Maura. Then I felt guilty. He was doing us a favour and I was probably seeing a problem where there wasn't one.

'We almost went into the boatyard on the other side of the road,' Brannan said, pointing across the road to the large shed with the name of the boatyard clearly visible.

'That's where they do repairs and store boats over the winter,' Simon said. 'It's a thriving business. Look how many boats there are beside the shed.'

'Mmm. We noticed the narrow garden along the wall outside the boatyard – the sign says it's the Midget Submarine Garden – what's that about?'

'During the Second World War the Kyles Hotel at Port Bannatyne was requisitioned, renamed HMS Varbel, and used as the headquarters for the submarine flotilla – the midget submarines. As you could guess, many of the sailors lost their lives. I suppose this is a way of honouring them. Though it was the beginning of the end for the Kyles of Bute Hydro Hotel. It was returned to civilian owners after the war – but it never recovered.

A new hotel was built on the site a few years ago, incorporating what was left of the old building.' Simon looked brighter as he recounted one of his favourite stories about the role of the island in the Second World War.

Brannan was suitably impressed. 'How brave those men must have been.' He shuddered. 'I'd hate to be trapped in any submarine, never mind a midget submarine.'

There was a noise in the distance and as one we

turned in the direction of the bay where the putt putt putt of an engine could be heard coming ever closer.

'Oh, I don't think it's your boat,' Maura said in a disappointed tone of voice, shading her eyes against the glare.

'No.' Simon said quickly. 'Much too small to be mine.' He moved restlessly. 'Don't worry. Damien will be along shortly.'

The boat approaching us was indeed too small-scale to be the one Simon had bought. But where was Damien with Simon's boat? He should be in sight at any moment.

The boat came closer and sailed over to one of the pontoons as we continued to scan the bay for any sign of Simon's purchase.

'Damien said he'd be here in a few minutes. Where can he be?' Simon sounded agitated and looked again at his phone. 'No further update from Damien,' he said. 'That's strange.'

'Don't be so impatient, Simon. Didn't you say sea times are never accurate? Perhaps he's been held up, delayed somewhere.'

'He's not likely to have been caught in a traffic jam out on the water,' Simon said with a nervous laugh.

Suddenly there was a shout of, 'Hello, there, Simon,' and we looked over to the pontoon where a swarthy man with a large black bushy beard, wearing a sailor's cap that was too large for him, was moving in to berth his boat. 'I could do with a bit of help,' the man said, holding out a rope.

Why was this stranger asking Simon for help? Was it someone he knew?

Realisation dawned as I saw the look on Simon's face. This must be the boat he'd bought, a guess confirmed by the name on the side 'Hoppity the

Third'.

Before I could stop myself I said, 'Is this yours? Surely not.'

As we hurried to the pontoon with Simon in front, instead of the yacht I'd imagined and my husband had promised, we found ourselves staring at a much smaller boat. On closer examination it did resemble the boat Simon had described to me, but besides the disappointment with its size, it was rather the worse for wear, the paint on the hull scratched and flaking, some of the letters of the name, Hoppity the Third, badly faded. Visions of summer days sailing around the Kyles, spending a night onboard, were quickly receding.

Then I thought, There must be some mistake?

Brannan ran over to help Damien tie the boat up and then Damien jumped down on to the pontoon. 'Nice little craft, isn't she? You'll have a lot of fun with her. This was a great choice, Simon.'

He noticed Simon's arm in a sling. 'At least you will when you feel better. What on earth did you do?'

Simon started to explain but I could see he was so dumbfounded he could scarcely speak. Finally he croaked. 'Are you sure this is the right boat? It doesn't look like the pictures.'

Damien appeared puzzled by this comment. 'Of course. She's a lovely little twelve-footer. Beautifully built. Easy to sail if you don't want to use the engine. Everything you need is there.'

Simon said, 'It's not as big as I thought – the description said twelve V, twelve metres.'

Damien looked puzzled. 'No. The reference to twelve V is the voltage.'

This wasn't going well. There was something wrong. Simon must have made a mistake. Then I remembered – he'd bought the boat from photographs without seeing it. Surely he hadn't made a miscalculation about the size? I didn't dare look at him but instead continued to stare at the boat as Damien, apparently unaware of Simon's reaction, continued to explain how everything worked.

This was a disaster, but there was nothing we could do. Simon could hardly ask Damien to take the boat back. Perhaps it would turn out okay. Perhaps.

I didn't dare turn around. Behind us I could sense Brannan and Maura trying not to laugh.

NINE

'Certainly not. It's a ridiculous suggestion.' My mind was made up despite Maura's pleas.

We were sitting in the kitchen having a late breakfast and I was looking forward to a leisurely day. After much discussion (once Damien had departed in a taxi to Rothesay to catch the ferry back to the mainland) we agreed that somehow Simon had made a mistake about the size of the boat he'd bought.

'I was sure it was much bigger,' he kept saying. As soon as the boat was securely berthed, we returned to the cottage and Simon's first action was to look for the information he'd run off from the internet.

He admitted, 'When I think about it, it was difficult to judge the size in the photos Damien showed me because there was nothing in the background to measure it against.'

And when we reread the details we agreed the boat was smaller than he'd thought. The print was blurred, the particulars not quite clear. Simon admitted he might have confused something in the description but when I looked at the page again, an idea about what had happened struck me. He hadn't replaced the ink cartridge in the printer.

And now this request from Maura was the last thing I'd expected. She sounded determined as she repeated her request. 'Brannan wouldn't have asked had he not been desperate. And remember how he helped us with the boat…and at short notice. Surely it wouldn't be a lot to ask and it is only for one night.' She gave me that pleading look that had worked so well when she was a child. 'They are short-staffed. And everything is topsy-turvy with Jonas not being there. Brannan says the latest word is he won't survive. It's been too massive a stroke.'

If anyone had the correct information about Jonas, it must surely be Brannan. The rumours about a murder were exactly that – rumours. 'What about his son?' I asked.

'Nicolas Gastrell is supposed to be on his way over to the island to take charge but no one knows when he'll arrive. It's not easy for him taking over at short notice: Brannan says there's a finance deal to be finalised before Nicolas comes to Bute.'

'Ah, so Brannan has discussed the problem with you? Jonas Gastrell's son has agreed to take over?'

She frowned. 'I guess so. That's what Brannan said as we chatted last night while we were waiting for Dad's boat to arrive. Or that's what he hopes. Else there's no idea about what might happen.' She paused. 'Though there's a worry it might only be on a temporary basis while Nicolas decides what to do with the circus…especially if Jonas does die. There's a feeling Nicolas isn't as interested in maintaining the family business as Brannan would like. Nicolas is in charge of the company finances but he doesn't have anything to do with the day-to-day running of the circus.'

'I thought Nicolas had a top job with a finance company?'

'He did, but he left that a few years ago and Jonas put him in charge of the circus finances. Meantime the show must go on. Especially as it has cost so much to come to the island and to set up. The tickets have sold well – a full house for most nights of the run,' Maura said.

'There must be someone employed at the circus who could assist.' This discussion wasn't going the way I wanted.

Maura shook her head. 'Everyone is fully stretched. Brannan has assured me there are two new recruits coming over to the island. It will only be for one night.'

Simon came into the kitchen. He'd fretted so much about his injury we'd made an appointment at the surgery. The doctor had confirmed he had a strained wrist and I wondered if disappointment about the boat had anything to do with his mood. He hadn't mentioned Hoppity the Third again. The best solution might be to resell it but I'd a feeling he wouldn't be receptive to that suggestion.

'What's the problem?' he said. 'I heard you arguing.'

'Not arguing.' Maura smiled. 'I'm trying to persuade Mum to help out at the circus tonight. Brannan has been let down.'

Simon threw back his head and laughed heartily, then he said, 'I think your mum is a bit old to be doing acrobatics.'

'It's only selling programmes. Kanzi's is short of staff for the opening night. The staff they recruited on the island have both gone down with a virus and the agency they've signed up with can't get replacements over until the day after tomorrow.'

'Doesn't sound too difficult. Selling programmes, I mean. And Brannan did give us a lot of help yesterday to get the boat berthed.' Simon looked over at me as he negotiated sitting in the chair opposite. 'Doesn't seem much to ask.'

‘Yes, yes, Maura has already used that line,’ I replied, wondering if I should suggest that, as it was Simon’s boat Brannan had helped berth, it be more appropriate if Simon was the one helping out. But of course he couldn’t because of his accident.

Maura pulled her phone from her pocket. ‘I’ll have to let Brannan know our decision now. He’s waiting for a reply. I’ll go along to help even if you won’t.’

Her attempts to make me feel guilty worked and beginning to relent, knowing we couldn’t have managed the boat without Brannan’s help, I said, ‘Are you certain it’s only for tonight? I’ve been caught out before – becoming involved for a short time and then finding I was trapped doing something I didn’t want to.’

Maura shook her head. ‘I wouldn’t want to do this longer than one night either. I’m sure Brannan has organised replacements.’

I tried one last throw of the dice. ‘I don’t think selling is my strong point. I’m not good at persuading people to buy.’ Memories of school raffles where I had to sell tickets surfaced. On many of those occasions I’d bought all the tickets myself. Not that I’d ever won.

‘Nonsense. These are glossy souvenir programmes. Brannan assures me they sell well… practically walk off on their own. And it would make me feel we’d repaid Brannan. It’s not as though you’re busy, is it? You don’t have any work outstanding?’ She said this as though I should be glad of something to fill my time.

But I had to admit she was correct. A leisurely life wasn’t proving to be the wonderful option we’d imagined. And now Simon’s accident presented another problem.

With no reasonable answer to her arguments, I agreed, 'On condition I don't do it more than once. It's not something I'll enjoy.'

'Terrific,' Maura said. 'I'll let Brannan know …and you'll be able to see the circus for free.'

This was an incentive of sorts. Circuses had changed so much in recent years it would be interesting to see a modern show.

The plan was that we go to the circus that afternoon to have an introduction to our 'duties'. This sounded much too formal to me when all we were doing was selling programmes but I reminded myself we were only committing to one night.

We had an early lunch and, leaving Simon sitting in the garden at the back of the cottage, we set off for The Meadows. I'd a feeling he was glad of time on his own.

'At least Dad won't be bored,' Maura said. 'But do you think he'll manage? That wrist strain must be troublesome – it so restricts his movements.'

'Yes, I don't know what else we could have organised for him,' I replied, thinking of Simon comfortably settled with the radio, a pot of coffee, a plate of biscuits, the newspaper and two books. And his phone beside him in case of emergencies. 'And it's not as if we're going to be long at the circus. Selling programmes can't be difficult. It won't take a lot in the way of instruction.'

Maura didn't reply. She seemed much more buoyant and I hoped her change of mood was nothing to do with meeting up again with Brannan. I'd tried to broach the subject of Alan a couple of times but she would say little except that she wanted to enjoy a few days away. Several times she used her mobile within earshot but from the snippets I couldn't help but overhear she was speaking to the children rather than to Alan. Simon was right. I couldn't interfere but keeping quiet was proving a challenge.

The hum of the huge generator attached to one of the pantechnicons grew louder and louder as we drove up the High Street and came closer to where the circus had set up in the King George V playing fields, known locally as The Meadows. Many major events on the island, including the Highland Games and the Agricultural Show in late summer, took place here and thinking about the Highland Games reminded me of another occasion when I became involved in a difficult situation. Stop it, I said to myself. You're only helping out for one night. And it would be an opportunity to see the circus at close quarters. I could feel the excitement mounting despite my reservations about my capabilities as a programme seller.

I swung into the car park at the long low building that is the Rothesay Leisure Centre and reversed into a bay at the far end.

'Gosh,' Maura said, as we came out of the car to take the short-cut towards where the circus was situated, 'This children's playpark is well-used.' The play area behind the Leisure Centre was busy – the jungle ropes and slide the main attractions as the children rushed about, whooping and yelling. There was a sound of crying as one youngster attempted to oust another from the slide – a quarrel quickly settled as two adults ran forward.

This area of The Meadows beside the Leisure Centre was set up for rugby and football and we went through the gap in the low dry-stone wall, carefully avoiding the overhanging branches of a solitary tree, forlorn looking despite the abundance of leaves. At one time there were probably many trees in these fields and this was the only survivor.

A short distance from the deserted Grandstand, the centre of the field was taken up by an enormous tent-like structure in shades of pink and purple. A large triangular flag flew from the top, emblazoned with the words KANZI'S CIRCUS in bold black letters. Several large pantechnicons took up much of the remaining space and tangles of cables from the generators crisscrossed the field, some leading directly to the Big Top, others to a row of caravans on the far side.

'Mind your feet,' Maura said, stepping carefully over the cables. 'This could be dangerous. We don't want another family accident.'

'It's bigger than I imagined,' I said as we came towards the main entrance.

There were one or two muttered comments from the queue for advance tickets snaking around the side of a kiosk at some distance from the Big Top and I tried unsuccessfully to indicate we weren't trying to sneak in ahead of everyone else. The circus was on the island for one week and, judging by the size of the queue, demand would be high.

'Guess its size is why it's called a Big Top,' Maura said with a laugh. 'Come on. Let's find Brannan. He said he'd be in the ring preparing for the grand opening tonight.'

As we came closer we could see how tightly the tent was anchored to the ground by numerous guy ropes snaking out across the field.

'It must take some effort to secure a structure of this size.'

'Yes, I expect that's why they do at least a week at a time in each location. It would be too much work to set up and take down for a couple of days of performances. And I suppose they need to add in extra days either side to set up and to dismantle it. Brannan said the week on Bute is a preview really and the next venues are much bigger. The circus will be performing for a minimum of two weeks in each place.'

'You know a lot about it, Maura.'

She smiled. 'Brannan is very enthusiastic.'

We tramped across the field and reached the row of caravans parked on the far side of the Big Top. Each displayed the name of Kanzi's Circus on the side but there was one immediately beside the Big Top which appeared to be a series of mini caravans joined together.

'Do you think those are where the performers live? They look rather small.'

'You can ask Brannan,' Maura said. 'Here he comes now.'

Brannan came out of the Big Top, striding across to meet us, resplendent in his Ringmaster's outfit of bright red topcoat and tails, heavily adorned with gold braid. His crisp white shirt emphasised his tan and I wondered idly if it was real or the result of sessions on a sunbed.

He shook me warmly by the hand. 'Thank you so much for helping out. The new members of staff should be here tomorrow but this is our big night. Everything depends on the opening. We've a full house but we need people to tell their friends how good it is.'

'Problems for the rest of the tour then?' Maura frowned.

'Not quite. Most nights are okay but midweek can be a problem.' He began to move away. 'That's a concern for later. Follow me.'

He strode briskly towards the Big Top and we followed behind him, trying to keep up.

'Are the caravans for the performers? Some of them appear to be rather compact.'

Brannan nodded, waving his hand in a direction beyond the Big Top. 'The individual caravans behind the circus tent are where the performers live. Touring as we do you need decent living quarters. Some of the caravans are quite palatial. That set of caravans you pointed out is for administration and storage – it includes an office, a canteen, together with a few smaller caravans for temporary acts. The site is like a small village really.'

By this time we'd reached the entrance to the Big Top and he pulled aside the canvas flap that was the entrance.

At first I was dazzled as we came into the brightness of the arena from outside. The performance area was huge and illuminated by an array of coloured lights – purple, pink, and blue, swirling in time to the loud music coming from behind a gaudily painted backdrop displaying 'Welcome to Kanzi's Circus' in gigantic letters. Scaffolding had been set up around the sides and tiny strategically positioned lights moved in sequence to pick up the glitter on the floor of the arena.

Brannan grinned. 'We're doing a last run-through. You've missed Timor the trick cyclist but Fabio and Melody Blue will be on soon with their trapeze act. You'll enjoy that, though they won't be performing all the tricks they'll do tonight. I'll take you backstage where we keep the programmes once the clowns come on. Sit wherever you like but you'll have a good view from here.'

He motioned us to seats in the front row of the tiers

of seats around the ring. 'Excuse me a minute. I have to cue them in.' Brannan moved over to the arena and grabbing a microphone, announced, 'Ladies and Gentlemen prepare to be amazed by our next act – Fabio and Melody Blue – The Flying Volantes. Direct from their success in France, where they astounded audiences with their daring act.'

He gestured towards the back of the arena and to a fanfare of loud music The Flying Volantes came bounding out and into the centre of the ring – she dressed in a sparkly blue leotard, her head adorned with a close-fitting sequined cap and he in a tight blue jacket and trousers also glittering with sequins.

With amazing agility, they took hold of the trapeze which descended suddenly from the centre of the Big Top and began to clamber up, using the scaffolding at the side of the ring before catching the swinging trapeze.

Several times I held my breath as they performed, working together and singly on the trapeze.

Beside me, Maura whispered, 'You can see why they are so successful. How on earth do they do that?'

Just when I thought it couldn't become any more dangerous the woman slipped down to hold on to the man's hands as he secured his feet on the bar. And then as the trapeze began to swing around the ring he let go of one of her hands in a sudden movement as they spun faster and faster, further, and further until they were spinning around the outer edge of the arena. His hand began to slip down her arm and for a moment I thought he wasn't going to catch her in time but then he made a sudden movement and grabbed her.

I was so involved I could scarcely breathe and I heard Maura give a loud gasp.

Brannan came up beside me. 'Quite an act, aren't they?' he whispered. 'We've been lucky to engage them for the entire season. And wait till you see the finale tonight.'

'It looks incredibly dangerous,' I said.

'They're experts.' He shrugged. 'Don't worry. It's well-rehearsed.'

'And there's no safety net,' Maura said. 'That makes it more dangerous.'

Brannan smiled. 'Makes it more exciting that way.'

'That last move looked particularly difficult – the way he almost let go of her as they moved about on the trapeze.'

'Mmm – it's a particularly difficult move. But tonight they'll be performing something even more dangerous – called the Dead Drop.' This seemed to give him pause for a moment before he said, as though speaking to himself, 'It'll be fine.' Then he added briskly, 'As you'll see. Now come along and I'll show you where the programmes are and explain what you have to do.'

As we followed Brannan over to the far side of the arena, I looked back at The Flying Volantes. Melody Blue had left but Fabio was standing in the centre of the arena as the trapeze slowly made its way back up to the top of the arena.

As I watched one of the clowns came out and went up to stand in front of Fabio. Even from a distance I could see this clown was angry, shaking his fist and pointing to the rapidly disappearing trapeze. Fabio was attempting to calm him but with little success and the clown stomped off towards the exit leaving Fabio standing looking after him. Then Fabio seemed to recollect himself and hurried into the back of the arena.

None of my business of course but I couldn't help but be curious about this argument.

As Brannan noticed me staring at Fabio and the clown he shook his head. 'Pay no attention. That's Joffo, one of the three clowns we have here. The most quarrelsome one, but popular with audiences. More's the pity.'

There was no time to comment as Brannan said, 'This is where the programmes are kept for each performance.' He pointed to a small booth at the entrance to the Big Top. 'We do have more stock in the cupboard at the back of the arena – I'll show you later. And there are additional boxes in one of the trailers where we store the equipment. As you can see they are souvenir programmes and cost a lot to produce so we have to account for each one.' He said this in a stern tone of voice.

'They are well-produced,' said Maura, flicking through one of the glossy brochures.

And the programmes with their publicity photographs of the performers were indeed special, though I wondered how many people would buy them when they saw the price.

'Now,' said Brannan, 'Before the performance begins you can collect a set of programmes from the booth. We anticipate seventy per cent sales and given the capacity of the Big Top, that would be an awful lot of programmes. That's why they're stored in the booth. When you look as if you might run out, just collect some more. Each programme costs £8 – it's easier with a round number and you'll have a float of £1 and £2 coins. Any questions?'

'What if people want to pay by card? As is more likely now.'

'Direct them to Connie in the kiosk. There's a card

machine there.' He pointed to a glass kiosk at the entrance where light sabres and clown hats were piled up in every corner.

'That all seems perfectly straightforward,' Maura said, quickening her pace to keep up with Brannan who was marching towards the entrance.

'Sure that's clear?' he said as he escorted us out. 'Any problems, ask Connie. She's been with us a long time. She'll help you.'

'Why doesn't she sell the programmes?' I said.

'Creates too much of a logjam. As you can see there are other items for sale in the kiosk – light sticks and fancy clown hats for the children – so it's better to make as many cash sales as we can.'

We said goodbye, promising to be back at the Big Top by six o'clock in good time before the doors opened at seven, though the performance didn't start until seven thirty.

I couldn't resist asking. 'Is there any more word on Jonas Gastrell? Is he likely to recover? The stroke is said to be serious.'

Brannan stopped so suddenly Maura and I almost collided with him.

'Why do you ask that?' he said, sounding displeased.

Even so, I couldn't resist asking, 'How are you managing without him?'

It was as though a curtain had come down.

'He's more seriously ill than the news suggests and he might not survive,' I went on.

Brannan pursed his lips. 'Where did you hear that?'

Maura glared at me. Oh, dear, was what Brannan told her supposed to be confidential?

Brannan said brusquely, 'There are too many rumours on this island.'

Attempting to make amends for my earlier blunder, I said, 'Good news that the circus will continue.'

Brannan hesitated before replying. 'I've had word his son Nicolas is taking over the running of the company meantime. He manages the circus account and his father's business affairs. But he hasn't arrived on the island yet.'

He strode off, calling over his shoulder, 'I'll see you at seven.'

'What makes people want to earn their living that way?' I said to Maura as we made our way back to the car.

She looked thoughtful. 'The adrenaline, I guess. The thrill of the performance, the sound of applause. The same as any performer.'

'Yes, but these acts are incredibly dangerous.' I flicked through the programme Brannan had given us for Simon to look at. 'Fire eaters, jugglers, high wire acts, The Flying Volantes…'

'You heard what Brannan said. It's well-rehearsed. It wouldn't be allowed otherwise.' She laughed. 'Don't worry. Our job is to sell the programmes.'

I started up the engine. We'd have an early dinner before going back to The Meadows. I was looking forward now to seeing the full performance. And we were doing Brannan a return favour. The only one. After that we'd have repaid his help with the boat.

Even so I couldn't get the spat I'd witnessed between Joffo and Fabio of The Flying Volantes out of my mind. The act had all looked perfectly polished to me but then I knew little about it. It must be difficult living life on the edge no matter how easy they made it appear.

And Brannan's response to my question about Jonas had been interesting. Or rather his lack of response. If he had taken over as manager meantime possibly he was concerned about what would happen when Nicolas arrived. Concerned he might be replaced.

Or was it possible the story of Jonas's stroke was a smokescreen and he had indeed been murdered? Nonsense, I told myself. And certainly not my concern.

Then, as Maura said, 'I'm looking forward to this evening, though I wouldn't want to do it as a permanent job – sell programmes, I mean,' my mind drifted to other matters. I'd no idea if she'd been in contact with Alan or if she'd made any plans to return home. There had been a couple of calls on her mobile which she hadn't answered and I suspected these had been from her husband. What's more, it seemed to me she was settling in rather too well at the cottage, though it was evident from our conversations that she was missing the children. And I didn't want her becoming involved with Brannan just because her relationship with Alan was going through a sticky patch.

I had to find a way of asking Maura what she intended to do next. It wasn't going to be easy.

But right now we had to have dinner with Simon before returning promptly to the circus.

TEN

It had been a difficult week. Brannan had been apologetic. 'The agency has let me down. They can't find replacements for the programme sellers. Could you possibly continue while I sort something out?'

But despite Brannan's pleading Maura had declined to continue after the first night and I was left on my own. It had proved hard to resist Brannan's sad face when Maura said, 'We agreed one night only, Brannan. I can't do more than that.'

She refused to change her mind or to offer him an explanation.

I had my suspicions, confirmed when she said later, 'I've spoken to Alan. I've told him I want some time on my own.'

'Oh, dear, how did he react?'

She bit her lip. 'He's puzzled. He can't understand what's wrong.'

'Maura, I know this is difficult but don't you think you have to discuss the situation sensibly. You've always been so practical.'

'Yes, but I never guessed this would happen to me.'

What could I do but offer my support. And I'd the feeling she didn't want to commit to helping Brannan when she might decide to return home at short notice.

On the other hand, I was unable to think of a good excuse to refuse him and I agreed to carry on meantime. The task had proved to be as easy as Brannan had suggested. So many people bought the souvenir programmes he had to order another batch.

There had been a full house at every performance and surprisingly I found myself enjoying seeing the exciting acts that made up the show.

'Brilliant. You're doing a great job of selling these, Alison,' Brannan said gleefully, rubbing his hands as he came up beside me at the interval on the second night.

In vain did I protest the programmes would have been selling well no matter who was in charge. Despite my doubts the price didn't affect sales in the least.

I spent time before each performance wandering around, organising the programmes, liaising with a reluctant Connie. 'Why can't people just use cash?' she said almost every time I directed a customer to her kiosk.

Using a card meant a lot less work for me but I wasn't going to say so. I smiled brightly as I handed out the programmes and directed most of the audience to Connie's kiosk.

And the news about Simon's wrist was good. Little by little he was making progress and he'd been given exercises to improve his dexterity. But now there was a different problem. As he couldn't go to the golf course or sail his boat, he was content to read and watch daytime television. And study the maps he'd bought which were taking over more and more of the limited space in the house.

'Look at this, Alison. If we set off early we could sail from here to Tighnabruaich in a day,' he said as he spread the map out on the kitchen table.

I nodded, saying, 'Sounds good but you will clear this away before dinner time, I hope.'

He didn't reply, too engrossed in tracing a route on the map with a fine tip red pen.

On the second last night of the circus stopover on Bute there was to be a special performance for the passengers of the cruise ship, The Niobe, docked in the bay and Maura had finally been persuaded to help sell the programmes. Perhaps she'd regretted her earlier decision, listening to my stories of how enjoyable it had been being part of the circus, even in a marginal way.

'You could come with us, Simon. Your wrist is much better. I'm sure you'd enjoy this evening.' I frowned. 'Wouldn't you like to see the circus? There might not be another opportunity once they leave Bute.'

Simon was sitting in the chair by the window in the living room, turning over the pages of his book, Weather Forecasting for Sailors, with his good hand. He'd already purchased a ship's log book which seemed somewhat ambitious for the size of boat he owned.

'Don't think I could manage,' he said, raising his arm and grimacing. 'This is still painful at times. Besides, didn't you say this performance was a sell out? There won't be any tickets left.'

'I'm sure they'd be able to fit you in. Better than sitting here on your own.' Maura also attempted to encourage him but she'd no more luck persuading him as he said, 'It would be too much fuss. You go and enjoy yourselves.'

'We'll be working,' I said, disappointed at his response. And I had to confess to a sneaking worry he might spend the evening on the internet ordering more equipment for the boat. So far, in addition to the many maps, he'd bought sailing jackets and trousers for both of us, lifejackets, an elaborate compass, a barometer, heavy duty cutlery and yet more books on sailing.

'We'd better go.' Maura lifted her bag from the hall table. 'We want to be there in good time.' She'd been surprised to learn that in recent years large cruise ships had started to call in at the island and tonight's show was exclusively for the passengers of The Niobe.

With a quick farewell to Simon we hurried to the car. The evening had turned cool, the offshore breeze making me shiver. 'I should've brought a coat,' I said but Maura shrugged. 'It'll be warm inside the Big Top.'

The traffic in the High Street was busy, much busier than usual, even allowing for the circus audience.

'It's going to take ages to get to The Meadows,' Maura said as we came to a halt behind a line of cars a little way past the Police Station.

'We'll manage to squeeze in somewhere,' I said.

Maura looked doubtful. 'Perhaps we should leave the car in Stuart Street, outside the Bute Museum? It's not far to walk. There's going to be a huge traffic jam after the show as the coaches load up the passengers and try to get away quickly. We don't want to be caught up in that.'

I shook my head. 'I don't think it matters. We'll be among the last people out. Brannan says we should wait until everyone in the audience has left the Big Top.'

But later I was pleased I'd agreed to Maura's suggestion about avoiding the traffic because by the time we left the car and walked up to The Meadows the coaches were disgorging their passengers and the traffic had ground to a halt. I should've realised the size of the cruise ship would be an indication of the number of people in the audience.

As we came closer to the entrance, there was a strong smell of burning sugar, wafting over to us from a large van selling candyfloss and toffee apples. We stopped for a moment to watch as the vendor swiftly twirled the fluffy candyfloss confection around and around on a stick before placing it with a flourish in a specially designed holder.

'Not many takers tonight,' said Maura as we passed a few people clustered around the serving hatch.

'Yes but it's been popular with the children who made up most of the audience at previous performances.'

'Would you like some?' Maura said with a grin, gesturing towards the van. 'My treat.'

'You are joking.' The very thought set my teeth on edge.

Brannan came running over. 'Great. You made it. There's something on at the Rothesay Academy tonight – that's why the High Road is so congested. Come and collect your bundle of programmes. I brought them out for you but you know where they are if you need more.' He handed us each a set of the brightly coloured programmes where a little strip of paper across the introductory page about Jonas Gastrell made reference to the owner being "incapacitated" and telling how he'd successfully built up the circus in difficult times. Rumours about what had happened to him continued to circulate on the island but there had been no further public information about his condition.

'A reminder that if you have any problems, Gloria...' who tonight had bright pink hair and was attired in a highly patterned outfit of trousers and a loose top... 'will be in her kiosk at the entrance as usual. I'll be in the arena for most of the show so I can't help.'

'I've managed perfectly well so far, thanks,' I said but by this time Brannan had disappeared into the back area of the circus ring.

Gloria smiled at us before turning back to the small line of people purchasing light sticks and clown hats. Probably for their children or even grandchildren judging by the age of those in the queue. Tonight she, like the candy floss seller, wouldn't be as busy as usual and it was important we sold lots of programmes.

Maura and I made our way to our assigned positions on either side of the entrance. Sales were slow as the cruise ship passengers trickled in, chatting and laughing, but as we came near time for the performance to start business began to pick up. Most people wanted to pay by card and we directed them to Gloria who became more and more harassed as the queue for programmes showed no signs of decreasing.

The minutes ticked down to the time for the performance to begin and the volume of noise increased until it was almost deafening as the audience became increasingly restless.

'I wouldn't have thought there would be this level of excitement given it's adults only tonight,' I murmured. Here and there I spied a light stick being waved around. 'An opportunity to relive memories of childhood,' Maura said, nodding in the direction of an elderly gentleman wearing a clown hat.

At last it was time to close the entrance flap, letting the coach drivers sidle in to take their seats and, with a fanfare of trumpets, the show began and the purple, pink and blue spotlights sprang into life, sweeping back and forth, illuminating the centre of the ring.

Maura and I positioned ourselves near the first row of tiered seats. There were two rows of ringside seats but 'We don't want to be too close to the arena when the clowns start that part of their act where they throw water everywhere,' I said to her when she questioned my choice. And there was the possibility someone might decide at the last minute to buy a programme.

By now the excitement in the Big Top had almost reached fever pitch. This promised to be another night of spectacular entertainment.

Brannan strode into the middle of the ring. In addition to the outfit of tails and top hat he was carrying a somewhat fiercesome-looking whip, which he cracked with great gusto as he welcomed everyone. 'Ladies and gentlemen, welcome to this performance of Kanzi's circus on the beautiful Isle of Bute. We're pleased to have this special evening for the passengers on the cruise ship, The Niobe. We hope you'll enjoy our show as part of your visit.'

A cheer went up from the audience and he acknowledged this approval with a bow.

He raised his voice as the music began. 'Prepare to be amazed as you watch The Flying Volantes, El Gran Fuego the Fire Eater, the Sixtus family troupe of acrobats, Salome the Tightrope walker, Timor the trick cyclist and of course everyone's favourites – the clowns, Joffo, Boffo and Stoffo. Sit back and enjoy the show.'

A burst of loud clapping followed his announcement as I whispered to Maura, 'The performances seem to get better every time. Tonight should be special.'

Right on cue the three clowns, Joffo, Boffo and Stoffo came tumbling out from the back of the arena, the spotlights concentrated on their garish costumes as they came up behind Brannan, imitating him, pulling at his coat tails and making mock of his attempts to control them.

The audience dutifully responded with thunderous applause accompanied by gales of laughter.

'What are you up to?' Brannan stood aside, cracked his whip, and then began unsuccessfully to chase the clowns as they bounced about the ring, pushing each other over, tumbling and jumping up on the ringside platform. Their comic timing couldn't be faulted and as they ran out of the ring to leave the way clear for the first act, another burst of applause followed them.

'Not easy being a clown,' I said.

Maura grinned. 'Do you know that every clown has a face which is exclusively registered to him or to her and there is an egg with that face for every one of them stored in the British Museum? It must be difficult coming up with an original face.'

Many of the acts were standard circus entertainment, each one interspersed with an appearance by the clowns, involving lots of slapstick and much throwing of water, including the use of a giant-sized water pistol. I was glad we'd opted to stay back as several of those in the front ringside seats were liberally doused with water.

'All part of the fun,' said Maura.

Then once again Brannan chased the clowns off into the back of the ring to announce, 'Give a big welcome to our last act of this first part of the show – the astonishing Sixtus family.'

This troupe of acrobats of varying ages came running into the arena and began tumbling and climbing with amazing agility, balancing large, inflated balls on their shoulders, working in twos and then threes, culminating in a finale where they climbed quickly onto each other's shoulders till the smallest stood upright at the top of a human pyramid some six people high.

'He looks too young to be doing that,' I whispered to Maura. 'No more than a child.'

'Looks can be deceptive,' she shrugged. 'It's highly regulated now. Think about the clowns. Being small, they could easily be mistaken for children but they're adults.'

With a final flourish the Sixtus family troupe jumped down one by one to acknowledge the applause and ran off to shouts of approval, leaving the arena clear for the interval.

The arena lights dimmed, the house lights came up and there was a great rush for the ice cream vendors positioned at the side of each tier of seats. Thank goodness I hadn't been asked to do that. It looked much too frantic, though the ice creams were tempting. It had become stiflingly hot inside the tent.

About to say to Maura, 'I'm going outside for some fresh air,' I was detained by the arrival of several members of the audience now eager to buy a programme as a souvenir of the evening. By the time I'd sold a programme to the last person in the queue it was too late to escape before the second half of the performance began.

The music started up again as the clowns returned with a highly skilled juggling act before Brannan strode back into the ring.

'And now,' he announced, 'prepare to be entertained by one of the most daredevil acts you have ever see. Exclusively to Kanzi's Circus, please welcome Melody Blue and Fabio – The Flying Volantes.'

Slowly, inch by inch, 'To build the excitement,'

muttered Maura, a trapeze was lowered from the central point of the Big Top to reveal The Flying Volantes sitting sedately on the bar. The trapeze began to move leisurely at first as Fabio and Melody Blue performed a series of acrobatics. Then the music grew louder, the lights flashed in rapid sequence and the trapeze with the two performers went faster and faster – whizzing around, as they were balancing up and down, one on the trapeze, the other holding on with one arm, then Melody Blue dropped down till she was holding on only by one foot. Heads swivelled upwards, willing the duo to keep moving, urging them to greater stunts. I'd seen this before but each time was as thrilling as the first.

Suddenly there was a movement which made everyone gasp. Fabio pulled Melody Blue up then she slid down holding his arm until she was only clinging on by her fingertips. You could sense the fear in the audience as they waited for what would come next.

'This is even better than the first night,' whispered Maura. 'Have they changed their routine?'

'No, but I think they're more practised than they were when you saw them. Each night there's a subtle difference – the acts become slicker.'

As the music grew louder and louder, the strobe lights flickered faster and faster to match the pace of The Flying Volantes, adding to the tense atmosphere. What could be more daring than this? I shivered despite the heat in the Big Top.

'Surely this must be the most dangerous part of their act? I don't remember this,' Maura said.

'Me neither. Maybe they've added this to please an adult audience?'

There was a hiss of fear and although I knew it had been well-rehearsed, I'm sure I wasn't alone in feeling my heart racing. 'How can anyone do that?' Maura murmured.

'Lots of practice I guess…and nerves of steel. I suspect it's something they've added in for the next venues on the tour?'

But the show wasn't over yet. Another trapeze was lowered alongside the first one and with one deft movement Melody Blue jumped across to sit on it. The trapezes began to move again, swinging back and forth, faster and faster till they reached a dizzying speed.

There was not a sound to be heard as the light sticks a few people had been waving enthusiastically were stilled.

'She must be going to jump over to be caught by him,' I said, but Maura didn't reply, too intent on gazing with everyone else at this dangerous trick.

I was right. He swung down from his trapeze, latched his feet over the bar and pulled out a short piece of chain. Even from this distance I could see him give the signal, see her nod in reply and then leap off the fast-moving trapeze to catch the chain he was grasping tightly.

This trick was much more dangerous than anything I'd seen on any of the other nights. This must be the Dead Drop routine Brannan had mentioned

There was a collective gasp from the audience as she caught it, then a burst of rapturous applause and cheering as the duo slowly reduced their speed.

But the elation was short-lived. There was a creak, followed by a sudden snapping sound as the chain broke. There was a moment as Melody Blue appeared suspended in space then, with a blood curdling scream, she fell to earth to lie completely motionless in the arena as chaos erupted.

ELEVEN

'It was so sudden,' I said with a shiver. 'The act seemed to be going well. They'd added in an extra routine, something they hadn't attempted before.'

Maura and I were back at the cottage, trying to work through the horror of seeing Melody Blue plunging to the ground. We were both still shaken by witnessing the event and I kept going over and over what had happened, trying to describe to Simon the horror of what we'd seen.

'Might have been better if they'd had a safety net,' Simon said. 'I can't understand why they would perform a trick like that without one. Talk about risky.'

'It makes it more exciting, that's why. The circus depends on the thrill of acts like The Flying Volantes to bring people in.'

Maura cradled her glass of wine as we sat together in the living room. It was late, but none of us had the inclination to go to bed any time soon. As soon as I closed my eyes I'd be haunted by that picture of Melody Blue hurtling to the ground, hear again her blood-curdling scream. But as the clock ticked past midnight I finally had to admit defeat

'I'm going to bed,' I announced. 'There's nothing to be gained by going over and over the same story.'

'Yes, better try to get some sleep,' Simon said. 'I can't imagine how awful it was for you and for Maura to witness the accident.'

But, as I'd suspected, once in bed I couldn't sleep

and kept thinking about the night's events, trying to work out how such a terrible accident might have happened.

Brannan had taken charge so efficiently, quickly realising something was seriously wrong and running out to cover Melody Blue with a large rug. The Big Top arena had no curtains to screen her off from the audience but several members of the Sixtus troupe came rushing out from the back area to pull forward the metal structures at the side of the stage in an attempt to give her privacy.

'Shut off that music. Cancel the lights!' Brannan yelled to the unseen technician located somewhere in the back area of the arena. Suddenly the colourful lights dimmed, leaving only the emergency lighting at the sides of the rows of seats before the house lights came on.

After shouts and shrieks of alarm as the audience realised what had happened, there was a deathly hush, broken only by the occasional whisper.

I heard someone close beside me say, 'Is this part of the act?' and her neighbour reply, 'I don't think so,' but he sounded doubtful.

Brannan ran back to the microphone. 'Ladies and gentlemen, there has been an unfortunate accident and the rest of this evening's performance will be cancelled. The stewards will guide you out. Please leave quickly and quietly.'

Then ever the showman he added, 'Your tickets will be valid for another performance as soon as we are able to resume.' I was amazed at how coolly he handled the situation but possibly the horror of what had happened hadn't kicked in and he was reacting spontaneously. Not that any of this audience would be able to return – this performance had been organised as a good way of ending the visit of the cruise ship to Bute. Tomorrow The Niobe would depart for the next destination. If the police allowed the vessel to depart, given everyone in the audience was a witness to the event.

The sudden silence that had followed the cries of alarm was replaced by low whispers among the audience as they filed out slowly, craning to see what was going on in the arena as the stewards ushered them to the emergency exits.

Once outside, many of them appeared reluctant to leave. Little knots of people lingered around the entrance to the Big Top, conversing quietly before the coach drivers began shepherding them towards the waiting buses for the return journey to Rothesay Harbour where the boats were waiting to take them out to the cruise ship. A few were reluctant to leave but at last they were safely on board and Maura and I stood watching as they drove off towards the harbour.

'What an awful way to finish a trip to Bute,' she said.

'Let's go back in. See if we can help,' I replied.

In silence we returned to the Big Top. The trapeze that had caused the accident still hung over the arena, a grim reminder of the awful events earlier.

We stood gazing around, at a loss what to do next. After a few minutes Brannan came scurrying towards us, his tailcoat unbuttoned, his face ashen under his tan, leaving Fabio to stand guard over Melody Blue as they waited for the ambulance to arrive. Someone was bending over her – the First Aider I guessed – but she was so still I feared the worst.

'Is there anything we can do?' I said to Brannan. Having so quickly assumed command of the situation earlier he now looked shell-shocked, his carefully gelled hair now rumpled as he kept fiddling with it.

'How can this have happened?' he said. 'Everything is checked and double checked. You've seen all the previous performances, Alison. The tricks went with clockwork precision.' He sat down with a thump on the low barrier around the arena and put his head in his hands. 'This is a disaster. How will we ever recover?'

'The last part of the act was new though? I don't recall seeing them do that in any of the previous performances.'

'What? Oh, yes, but they did rehearse this afternoon while I was discussing some last-minute changes to the clowns' act. We had to make a few adaptations because we had an entirely adult audience. And this was one of the tricks they wanted to add for the performances in Glasgow. It looked fine. We are careful, take every precaution.'

He said this as though he might be accused of negligence.

Looking back at the prone figure of Melody Blue he said, 'This will be awful for the circus. Just awful.'

I'd be more concerned about Melody Blue, I thought, but his reaction could be because he was in shock.

Further discussion was interrupted by the sound of the ambulance arriving. Brannan recovered sufficiently to speak to the paramedics though they avoided giving an answer as he kept saying, 'She will be all right, won't she?'

There was a murmur of conversation and a flurry of activity and at last Melody Blue was taken off in the ambulance, accompanied by Fabio who kept saying, 'It wasn't my fault, it wasn't my fault,' as he kept wringing his hands.

We stood beside Brannan to watch the ambulance drive slowly down the High Street, siren wailing. All we could do now was wait…and hope she would recover. Sadly the outlook was grim. It seemed impossible she could have survived that fall.

A few minutes later another siren heralded the arrival of the police. Brannan rushed forward to meet them and a terrible thought crossed my mind. If Melody Blue died the police were going to have a very difficult task with so many people to interview. Not only the members of the circus but everyone in the audience who had witnessed the fall. How would the police manage that?

In silence, Brannan, Maura, and I trudged back to the Big Top to join some of the other performers who were huddled together in the top tier of seats, speaking in whispers.

The police sergeant, someone I didn't recognise, came into the Big Top.

'Who's in charge here?' he asked and expressed disapproval that Brannan had let the audience return to the cruise ship. 'You should have kept them here until we arrived,' the sergeant said but he grudgingly accepted Brannan's explanation that he'd been so upset by what had happened he wasn't thinking straight.

'I suppose so,' the sergeant said. 'I'll send a couple of officers down to the cruise ship immediately. Don't allow anyone else to leave.'

As this included Maura and me, I had to call Simon to tell him about the accident, refusing his offer to call a taxi and come along to the circus.

'There's nothing you can do to help,' I said. 'I daresay we won't be too long.'

Although this was said more in hope than

expectation we were eventually released after giving a brief statement and told in no uncertain terms that we'd be called again.

I tossed and turned, going over and over the events of the evening until eventually, around dawn, I must have drifted off and wakened to the noise of the radio downstairs.

Groggy from lack of sleep, I pulled on my dressing gown and went down into the kitchen where a welcome pot of fresh coffee sat on the stove.

'You didn't sleep well?' Simon said sympathetically as he stood up and went to fill a mug for me.

'No, I kept re-living what happened, kept seeing Melody Blue plunge to the ground,' I said, taking a large gulp of coffee then wincing as I realised how hot it was.

Simon leaned against the worktop and listened without making comment as I went over the story of the accident yet again. 'And now I'm worried about the interview with the police. I seem to have had so many encounters with the police on the island in recent years.'

In his usual reasonable way he said, 'But some of the audience would have had a better view than others. There will be lots of people to interview besides you and Maura.'

'I suppose so.'

'The police will have a strategy for dealing with such large numbers. It's not your concern. Try not to worry about it.' He stopped and came over to put his arm around my shoulders. 'All you and Maura can do is tell the police what you saw.'

'I suppose so. We had an excellent view of The Flying Volantes. And I was there every night.'

Maura appeared at the kitchen door, yawning, and meandered over to lift the coffee pot. She echoed my thoughts as she said, 'I heard you talking to Dad. There's nothing to be gained by going over and over the accident, Mum. We'll tell the police anything else we remember when we go to the police station later to sign our statements.'

Maura lifted a mug from the cupboard and started to pour a coffee, looking in surprise as only a trickle came out.

'Sit down and I'll make another pot,' said Simon.

'I'll do it,' Maura said.

'My wrist is much better,' Simon said. 'I managed to make the last pot without a problem.'

Maura ignored this and began to empty the coffee dregs into the recycling bin, saying, 'Fortunately we don't have to be there too early. I suspect the police will go to the Cruise ship first and take statements from the passengers who were at the performance last night. We're due at noon.'

A few minutes later Maura lifted her mug of coffee, 'I'm going back to bed,' she said, leaving Simon and me on our own. I shook my head at his offer of a second cup. 'I'm jittery enough. I don't think I need more caffeine. Goodness knows what will happen to the circus now.'

'Yes, what a blow,' Simon said. 'I suppose that will be the end of the circus performances. There will be all sorts of Health and Safety implications. And the police are involved. They won't let the last performance tonight go ahead I'm sure.'

'It's disastrous,' I said. 'Not only because of the money they'll lose if the circus is shut down but think of the performers. They were booked for the season and now they have no work unless this can be sorted out quickly. They are supposed to be going to Glasgow next but from what the police sergeant said they may have to stay on Bute a few days longer. Poor Brannan. First he's had to deal with the illness of the owner and now this. Thank goodness the owner's son, Nicolas Gastrell, is coming to take over. He was on his way to Bute before this happened. It'll be up to him to make the decisions.' I frowned.

'Lucky that Jonas has a son ready to take over. What does he have to do with the circus?'

'I've been told he handles the circus finances.'

'Surely the performers will have contracts. And there must be insurance.'

'No idea.' I stretched, my lack of sleep catching up with me. 'Maura's right. There's no point in going over and over the accident. Sorry as I am about what had happened, there's nothing I can do.'

But as I went upstairs to dress I couldn't help seeing again those final moments, watching as the chain snapped and Melody Blue came hurtling to the ground, hearing again that dreadful scream.

A picture flashed into my mind. Something to do with the couple of minutes before the fatal fall. What was it? I tried to imagine the scene but I couldn't grasp whatever was nagging at me. It was there but just out of reach. Perhaps if I tried not to think about it, turned my mind to something else, that would help. But unfortunately the something else that popped up was Maura's situation and I started fretting about that, so that was no better. Either this rift with Alan was genuinely serious or she was making a fuss about something trivial. Was it likely her suspicions were correct? That Alan was having an affair?

Meanwhile Maura and I had to go to the police station.

TWELVE

When I came back downstairs having showered and dressed, it was to find Simon and Maura sitting in the kitchen with Brannan.

Before I'd time to think I said, 'What are you doing here?' Then I added hastily, aware how rude that sounded, 'Not that you're not welcome but I thought you'd be busy helping the police.'

Simon jumped in before I could make another blunder. 'Brannan has brought bad news. Melody Blue is dead.'

'Oh, no, how terrible.' Privately I thought, How did he think anyone could anyone survive that fall?

Maura bit her lip. 'A shock for everyone.'

Brannan shook his head, staring fixedly at the coffee cup in front of him.

'Have you any idea what happened? Mum says everything seemed fine during the previous nights' performances,' Maura said.

Brannan didn't reply directly but, making a face said, 'I'm looking for some help, if I'm being honest. That's why I'm here. From someone who doesn't have direct contact with the circus. Who's not one of the performers or the other employees.'

'But surely in the light of what has happened to Melody Blue the circus will have to close, abandon plans for the tour?'

'Health and Safety inspectors came early this morning and have started an examination of every piece of equipment. I can't understand it. We make sure everything is double checked. And you were there every night this week, Alison.' He looked close to tears. 'It's going to be a few days before they report but I'm hoping we'll be able to salvage the rest of the tour. We're lined up for Glasgow during the second half of the Glasgow Fair fortnight and then we're travelling to Perth, Dundee, and Aberdeen.'

'All major cities,' I said.

He grimaced. 'That's why we chose this week to come to Bute. Gave us a chance to try out some of the routines in a small venue before we hit the big cities.'

This sounded optimistic to me. With such an accident occurring at the beginning of a long tour surely the Health and Safety Inspectors would declare this year's performances at an end? That's if the police didn't make the decision first. However as Brannan was looking so despondent I didn't want to add to his troubles. 'Let's hope that's the case, Brannan. That the investigations are completed quickly and you can leave soon for Glasgow.'

Simon mumbled something I didn't quite catch and Brannan frowned.

'What's that?' I said, leaning forward. Simon shook his head.

There was a silence and then Maura, who had been sitting quietly, said, 'Brannan has concerns that what happened wasn't an accident. Someone deliberately tampered with the holding chain for Melody Blue.'

'Surely not.' This seemed far-fetched. 'It's such a dangerous act it must have been an accident – the chain wasn't properly checked. Things can get overlooked.' Simon gave me a look which quite clearly said, Why are you interfering?

Brannan shook his head. 'Each act is responsible for checking their own equipment in the first instance but we also have a team of technical people – well three – who double-check everything. We can't afford to take risks. I've questioned them individually and each of them is certain that everything was in order when tested. Something must have happened between that test and the performance last night.'

His explanation made sense but there was a lingering doubt. 'Who would want to sabotage The Flying Volantes? It seems a strange thing to do.' Then I thought …unless someone had a grudge against them? Aloud I said, 'Do you know of anyone who might want to cause them trouble?'

'Or have a grudge against Kanzi's circus. Now that Jonas Gastrell is out of action,' Maura interrupted. This suggestion was only making matters worse and Brannan looked even more miserable.

'But that was a stroke, surely.' Simon said, trying to inject a note of common sense into the conversation. 'You said yourself, Brannan, that he had well-documented health problems.'

'That's true. They're still doing tests. The latest report is that he's not likely to be out of hospital any time soon. He's lost the power of speech. It's possible he'll never be well enough to run the circus again.' Brannan's reply was almost a whisper.

I'd heard the rumours about Jonas of course, some of them suggesting he was dead but the circus didn't want to release this news in case it affected takings. At least the idea he had been murdered seemed to have been discounted. But until there was reliable information about his condition, speculation would continue.

There was silence in the room as we considered Brannan's suspicions about Melody Blue. Was it possible Brannan was right? If so, this was horrific.

An accident was bad enough, but deliberate sabotage of the equipment was worse. There was some undercurrent, some problem Brannan might not be aware of. Someone wanted to cause difficulties for the circus.

'The police will be on the case,' Simon said at last. 'You should leave it to them. This kind of thing is no business for an amateur.' He looked over at me as he spoke.

Brannan looked surprised. 'Of course they will. But how long will that take? If Health and Safety decide the equipment was tampered with we can't wait for the police to find the culprit. We have to be able to re-open as soon as possible. That way we can probably manage to save our next venue – and make some money. It's an expensive business running an organisation like a circus. And the advance ticket sales for Glasgow have been excellent.' He looked gloomy.

'Surely that's a decision for Nicolas Gastrell? As soon as he arrives it will be out of your hands.'

Brannan must have noticed the frown on Maura's face as he said, 'You're right. And I know that sounds heartless but it's not only about making money. It's about keeping the acts in employment. If we have no money coming in we can't afford to pay them.'

'So what do you intend to do? Is it not best to wait for the new owner to arrive? You might be wrong. He may be prepared to keep the circus going. From what you've said it's been in the family for many years.'

Brannan avoided my gaze as he said, 'Until he does he asked me to continue to take charge. I spoke to him last night to tell him about Melody Blue.' He didn't elaborate on the conversation.

When no one else ventured an opinion he said, 'I've

had an idea. I thought if you and Maura could continue as programme sellers, you might be able to pick up some information. No one would suspect you of being spies. Or rather,' he went on hurriedly, 'not spies exactly. But you could be around, listen to what's being said. I'm sure Melody Blue's death will be the only topic of conversation backstage.'

Maura looked aghast. 'No way. Mum and I did that spell of selling programmes as a favour.'

'Wait a minute,' I said. 'If the circus isn't running tomorrow night surely there'll be no need for programme sellers?' Brannan's request was odd.

'Ah, but I thought you could be part of the team. Continue to be in charge of the programmes – sort of linger around.' He sounded vague as though he hadn't thought through this suggestion. 'There will have to be continuing rehearsals for one thing – these performers have to keep themselves fit. No one knows how you were recruited. As far as they know you were enlisted locally – which is true after a fashion.'

Simon spoke up. 'I don't think Alison wants to be involved in this.' He looked over at me. 'She's been associated with too many strange events on the island in the past. We're here for a quiet life. So no, she won't do it.'

The wrong thing to say. I bristled at the idea that Simon might think he could speak for me. 'I might be able to help as long as it's for a short time,' I said, glaring at him.

'Count me out.' Maura held up her hands. 'I'm not sure what I'll be doing over the next few days.'

Ah, so there might be progress in her quarrel with Alan. She wanted to leave herself clear of any commitments.

‘I’ll come over tonight,’ I said as Simon shook his head.

‘I’m so grateful,’ Brannan said, getting to his feet. ‘Any snippets of information you can pick up will help. If we can find out what really happened it will be all to the good. We have to get this show back on the road as soon as possible. You do understand that, don’t you, Alison?’

As Brannan stood up to leave, I was already beginning to regret my hasty decision. Simon was right. Too often in the past I’d become involved where I shouldn’t. But then again what danger could befall a lowly programme seller? And it was more than likely Melody Blue’s accident was exactly that – an accident. For some reason the chain had broken – it may well have been weak and the addition of that final trick to the act made it snap.

What’s more, Simon might be glad to have Brannan on his side. Although he’d made progress with his strained wrist we might have to call on Brannan once more to help with the boat, lying unused in the Port Bannatyne Marina.

THIRTEEN

Although Brannan had given me a tour to help me understand the layout of the Big Top and I'd had several nights selling programmes, I couldn't but help feel apprehensive as I drove from the cottage. My cover, now that the final show had been cancelled, was that I'd been put in charge of the programmes and would have to keep track of the stock while we waited for the circus to resume its tour. This didn't seem like much of a cover story to me. Even so, Brannan insisted keeping a note of the numbers was an important job. 'We move around so much and things can get lost. These programmes are an important source of revenue so we don't want any mishaps.'

Simon's last words rang in my ears. 'Remember you're supposed to be looking after the programmes. That's all. Do the minimum. Don't get into trouble.'

I'd no intention of doing more than was strictly necessary. Whatever might happen to Jonas Gastrell the impact on the circus was a problem for Brannan. And as for the trapeze artiste, Melody Blue, the latest news was disturbing.

'The chain held out until the last minute,' Brannan had said. 'If only The Volantes hadn't put that last trick into their act.'

But even if the circus was cleared by Health and Safety this still left The Flying Volantes in difficulties. Without Melody Blue, Fabio wouldn't be able to continue unless he decided on a solo performance. Or so I thought until I arrived at the circus that evening, leaving an unhappy Simon to grumble to Maura about my foolishness in agreeing to help.

I walked across the field, past the performers' caravans, deep in thought about Melody Blue. A sudden movement over by the performers' caravans caught my eye. It was a young fair-haired woman, someone I didn't recognise as one of the circus performers or staff. As I stood watching, she went up to Joffo's caravan and without knocking she opened the door and went in. So Joffo wasn't the grumpy persona he presented to the rest of us. And if he was having a relationship with someone on the island he wouldn't be able to keep it a secret for long.

Chuckling about this discovery I went into the Big Top and to my surprise Fabio was up on the trapeze, seemingly instructing a young woman in the moves of the act. How had they found a replacement for Melody Blue so quickly? And for such a dangerous act?

Engrossed in watching them, as they began their first spin around the ring, I didn't hear Brannan come up beside me. 'Yes, it's amazing, isn't it. Luckily Chiara was able to step up. Once we get the go-ahead from Health and Safety she'll be able to perform with Fabio and The Flying Volantes act will be saved for the next part of the tour.' He rubbed his hands together, looking much more cheerful now there was a possibility the tour would go ahead.

Then he looked gloomy again, saying in a flat monotone voice, 'The police have asked us to remain on the island for the next few days. I'll have to reorganise the Glasgow part of the tour.'

I glanced up at Fabio and his new partner Chiara.

'Isn't it rather a difficult act to be learning the moves at such short notice? I'd have thought this a dangerous gamble, given what had happened before.'

Brannan gave the ghost of a smile. 'That was another bit of luck. You may not have noticed with the change of costume but Chiara is a member of The Sixtus Troupe. They're a talented group of acrobats from Italy. It turns out Chiara has done trapeze work before. She was a trapeze artiste when she worked with one of the Italian troupes in Europe. Many of the people who choose a circus life have a variety of skills. They're all acrobats in the end. That's one of the interesting things about these circus folk. Of course Fabio may have to cut out some of the more difficult parts of the act. Rehearsals can't bring Chiara quite up to the level of Melody Blue.' He didn't mention which part of the act they would cut but I had a good idea.

'Ah, that's why she was able to step in so quickly?' I tried to disguise a note of surprise as I said, 'I suppose without Chiara The Sixtus Troupe will be a Quintet?'

Brannan stared at me as though he didn't understand my attempt at a joke. He might be a pleasant young man, but he lacked a sense of humour. 'No, we'll rearrange the programme so that she can perform in both. The Flying Volantes will now come on in the first half and the Sixtus Troupe will come on last in the second half. We'll cut her part so that she does the minimum. Not ideal as it means Salome, the tightrope walker, has to perform earlier, but I'm sure it'll work okay. We'll cut the trapeze act by a few minutes, leave out some of the most daring parts. The new audience won't realise and it will let us keep this act in the show. And when we reach Glasgow there will be a couple of days in hand before the first performance there. Hopefully we'll manage to catch the tail end of the Glasgow Fair but I've a bit of juggling to do with the advance tickets.'

'Great.' I didn't want involved in the complexities of the circus performances. A thought occurred to me. 'Will you have to change the souvenir programme? It gives the order the acts appear in.'

Brannan dismissed the problem with a wave of his hand. 'I'll say a word about that at the beginning. There's plenty else in the programmes – lots of glossy photos of the performers and snippets of information about them and about Kanzi's circus. That's why it's designed as a souvenir programme. Might even be worth a bit in years to come – you know, on that television programme where people bring along their old items in the hope of making a fortune.'

'Oh, the Antiques Road Show?' Somehow I doubted it. Surely Brannan wasn't seeing the accident as a way of increasing numbers to the circus. He was a shrewd businessman, that was for sure, but this was a step too far.

We were saved from further discussion by the appearance of one of the clowns.

'Hello, Joffo,' Brannan said.

Joffo bowed low. This was the first time I'd seen him close up. He was in full costume: a purple and green checked suit several sizes too big for him and long pointed shoes. Although he was a little taller than I am, it was obvious his feet inside the shoes were tiny which gave him a curiously lopsided appearance. His face was fully made-up and, remembering Maura's story about every clown having a different face, I looked closely at him. Over the white paint covering his face, his bushy black eyebrows and extended eyes and mouth, a slash of bright red, gave him a somewhat sinister air, a feeling added to by his frizzy green wig. I remembered his encounter with Fabio, how angry he'd been. None of my business. Nor was the woman I'd seen entering his caravan.

Joffo turned to Brannan. 'Any more word about Melody Blue's accident?' He spoke in a high-pitched voice I suspected of being no more than an affectation, part of his act.

Brannan said, 'Not since the terrible news last night. The police will want to conduct a full investigation. This is more than a matter for Health and Safety. It very much looks as if the chain was tampered with.'

Joffo said nothing, but I couldn't help but comment. 'It's dreadful. If it was deliberate, you mean this is a murder enquiry?'

Brannan nodded, his face grim. But ever mindful of the need for the circus to continue, he said, 'We're lucky Chiara was able to step in at short notice. That will save a major headache for the remaining venues.'

Brannan avoided eye contact as he said this, leaving me wondering if he knew more about Melody Blue's death than he was saying.

It was difficult to gauge Joffo's expression under so much makeup but I caught some of what he muttered to Brannan. 'She was always a troublemaker, never happy unless she was the centre of attention. As for Chiara, she's shown no loyalty whatever.'

'Oh, come now,' Brannan said. 'Let's not make too much of it. It's good for the circus that she could take Melody Blue's place so easily. Just because you and she aren't the best of friends.' Not forgetting his squabble with Fabio, I thought.

To reinforce this, he added, 'Fabio and Chiara

appear to be getting on well – the act seems to be coming together nicely.'

'A bit too well,' sneered Joffo. 'I don't know why you had to use Chiara as a replacement.'

'We had to find a substitute for Melody Blue at short notice and Chiara was the obvious choice.'

'There are others in the circus every bit as able to take on that role.' Evidently Joffo wasn't a fan of Chiara.

I looked over. Fabio and Chiara had come down from the trapeze and were standing in the centre of the ring. Fabio had his arm around her shoulder and was leaning into her.

'Yes, they're getting on very well indeed,' Joffo said. He sniggered.

'Oh, I'm sure he's only trying to put her at her ease. Their act is one based on trust – you must have complete confidence in your partner.' Brannan was trying to make light of the situation but I could see what Joffo meant. Fabio and Chiara were looking very cosy indeed, the way he had his arm around her waist and was whispering to her as she kept running her fingers through his hair.

I had a terrible thought. Surely Fabio didn't have anything to do with the accident. Then again, he'd replaced Melody Blue with Chiara very quickly. But even had he wanted to switch Melody Blue for Chiara the idea he would do so by murdering his partner was too far-fetched. Or was it?

'I'll report back to the others,' said Joffo, sidling away, saying, 'Poor Melody Blue. To be forgotten so easily.'

Brannan shook his head. 'Ignore what you just heard, Alison. Joffo's also a bit of an agitator.'

'I always thought clowns were such jolly people,' I

said.

Brannan stared at me as if I'd said something odd. 'Whatever gave you that idea? Clowns can be among the saddest people in the circus. There's something about hiding behind all that make up, that happy persona.' He sighed. 'But pay no attention to Joffo. The other two, Boffo and Stoffo aren't quite as melancholy. Let's go to the back area from where the performers access the ring. The important thing is for you to keep an eye on the rest of the regulars, the permanent acts who travel around with us all the time. That's where you're most likely to find out information.'

'Oh, how many acts are permanent with Kanzi's?'

'We have a core of performers – the clowns, The Flying Volantes, the Sixtus Troupe, El Gran Fuego, Salome the tightrope walker, Antana the juggler and Timor, the trick cyclist. They are the most skilled, the ones people really want to see. But we need to have as much variety as possible and find this works best. People are always looking for something new and we have loyal supporters who come every year – often more than once. The temporary acts are often youngsters starting out. Working with a circus like Kanzi's gives them great experience.'

That did make sense. But it also meant it was unlikely that any of the temporary acts would have been responsible for sabotaging the trapeze chain, if indeed it had been deliberate. They would have nothing to gain. Then again, if one of the permanent acts was out of commission perhaps there would be an opening for one of the temporary acts. Brannan must believe one of the regulars had a motive.

My suspicions were quickly confirmed by Brannan's next words. 'I can't understand why this happened. It benefits no one.'

This certainly cut the number of suspects. And there were other possibilities. Simpler explanations. It could be down to the carelessness of one of the technicians. Or the chain had a weak link that was difficult to spot. Not that I'd any intention of spending time on this or so I told myself. I'd enough problems with Maura and her domestic situation, I thought as I followed Brannan towards the back area of the Big Top.

Here there were a number of makeshift dressing rooms crammed together, each furnished with a couple of small tables with lighted mirrors above. Racks of gaudy costumes took up most of the remaining floor space.

'It's a tight squeeze,' I said gazing around at the hastily constructed partitions. Behind the glitz seen by the audience, life backstage was far from glamorous.

'Oh, this is only for any quick-fire changes that might be necessary during the show. The permanent performers who have caravans behind the Big Top put on their costumes there and this is used when they need to change quickly. The gorgeous outfits are an important part of the show.'

'Ah, I noticed those caravans on the way in.'

Brannan laughed. 'The major performers like El Gran Fuego have more spacious accommodation at the far end of The Meadows. The temporary acts that we recruit on a tour to tour basis have to share.' Brannan said this as though he didn't approve of some of the performers having better accommodation than others but I suspected it came down to a question of money.

The permanent performers' caravans he was describing sounded as if they were luxurious but I couldn't imagine spending my life in somewhere so cramped. The cottage sometimes felt claustrophobic, especially now Maura was living with us.

'It seems quiet,' I said, gazing around.

'Not all the performers are rehearsing. Some are taking advantage of a break in the routine to go on the West Coast tour bus – the one that travels around places of interest on the island,' Brannan explained. 'They'll be back later to go through their routines. They'll continue to rehearse no matter how long we have to stay on the island. You can't afford to have too long a break – remember these performers are athletes. You quickly lose your skills, lose your suppleness, if you don't practise.' He seemed to be terrified this might happen.

'Come with me,' Brannan said and we walked in and out of these makeshift rooms at the back of the arena where we found some of the acts sitting around chatting: Salome the incredibly agile young Asian girl who worked the tightrope, El Gran Fuego the fire-eater and Antana whose speciality was juggling with what seemed like a dozen balls at the same time. Everyone was pleasant enough but there was a general subdued air as we came in.

'We've just heard from Joffo,' Salome said, fidgeting with her long chiffon scarf. 'Let's hope nothing else happens.'

Antana looked close to tears as Brannan said, 'Everyone is upset, but we have to be positive. This circus has a bright future.'

'We hope,' Salome said. 'No one feels like practising.'

This contradicted what Brannan had said but before he could reply Stoffo and Boffo came sauntering in with Joffo came trailing behind them.

‘Alison has come to help us with the programme selling,’ Brannan said as I smiled.

‘Not much chance of selling many programmes if we can’t open,’ Joffo said. He was most certainly a surly character.

‘That’s right,’ Boffo nodded and Stoffo echoed, ‘Not much chance.’

Up close I could see what Maura meant about every clown having a unique face. Boffo’s mouth was more upturned, his face a mask of white and he wore a traditional clown’s pointed hat with wisps of blue hair sticking out, while Stoffo had no eyebrows at all. Or if he did, they were covered by greasepaint and his mouth was purple rather than red, matched by a long purple wig. Boffo’s suit was a loud yellow check, while Stoffo had opted for striped trousers in blue and red and a top made of purple spotted material. Designed to make sure they would stand out in the spotlights in the arena.

Brannan frowned. ‘We have to keep our spirits up. We’ll be open again soon. We must continue, be ready to perform for the public.’

As no one appeared convinced by this attempt to boost their spirits, he hurried on, ‘We’ll need people to sell the programmes when we reach Glasgow of course but as Alison is local I thought it would be a good idea for her to train a couple of the young admin staff. That way we’ll be ready for our next stop on the tour.’

‘Not much in training people to sell programmes, surely? Take the money, hand over the programme.’

At this curt remark by Joffo I was beginning to understand what Brannan had meant by the clowns not being quite as jolly as they appeared to the public.

‘Whatever.’ Brannan dismissed this comment with

a wave of his hand. 'That's what I've decided and that's what we'll do.'

Brannan turned to me. 'The temporary members of the troupe will be back later. We hope to sell as many souvenir programmes as possible once we hit the road again so I'll introduce you to a couple of our junior staff who are general helpers. Isn't that what you want?' He addressed this question to Joffo. 'The more publicity the better?'

Exactly as I thought. It was difficult to tell what Joffo was thinking but he said, 'I've things to do,' and made a hasty exit with Boffo and Stoffo trotting behind him, trying to keep up as he strode away.

'Ignore that...' But Brannan didn't finish his sentence as the flap of the backstage tent was pushed aside and Fabio and Chiara came in laughing.

They stopped abruptly as they saw the little crowd of us gathered together.

'Something else happened? Not more bad news I hope?' Chiara sounded alarmed.

'No, no,' Brannan said and proceeded to introduce me again and go through the story of my role as a programme seller and why I was there even though the circus hadn't been given permission to re-open.

Fabio said nothing but stood with his hand on Chiara's shoulder. Her face was sullen. Up close she was older than she appeared in the ring but her sparkly costume and elaborate hairstyle gave her an aura of glamour.

'A ridiculous waste of money,' she said. 'Employing someone to do a non-existent job.'

Patiently Brannan explained the situation but he faltered slightly as he came to the bit about training.

'I suppose you're in charge.' Still no hint of a smile. 'Come, Fabio,' she said and grabbed his elbow to pull him away.

With an apologetic shrug, Fabio allowed himself to be led off.

'Temperamental artistes, eh?' Brannan attempted to make light of the situation but he was clearly upset at this lack of co-operation.

I wasn't so sure. The response to Brannan's suggestion that I be employed as a helper hadn't been exactly warm. First Joffo and now Chiara. How on earth was I to make headway with finding out what Brannan wanted if the performers were so hostile? Once again I regretted my willingness to agree. But I was trapped now. What's more, Joffo was right. Training programme sellers would take no time at all.

There was one possibility that cheered me. If I did this favour for Brannan Simon could call on him to help with his boat. I'd a feeling that launching the boat wasn't as easy as Simon imagined. Even when fully recovered there was a strong possibility he'd need assistance.

FOURTEEN

Feeling unhappy about the task I'd taken on and wishing I'd listened to Simon's advice about not becoming involved, I was up later than usual the next morning and went to sit outdoors with my coffee.

The High Road behind the garden was quiet and I sat enjoying the summer sunshine, mulling over my options. I could take the sensible way out and tell Brannan this was too difficult an assignment for me. That it was best left to the police now that it had been confirmed that Melody Blue had been murdered. Or I could apply myself diligently and use my investigative skills to find out the truth, attempt to discover if one of the other circus performers had anything to do with her death.

I'd solved mysteries on the island in the past but only with help, I had to acknowledge, trying to put aside memories of the times I'd been rescued from dangerous situations. And with no other work planned, there was nothing to distract me. And if we didn't have Brannan's assistance I wasn't sure Simon's boat would ever set sail. Even if his wrist healed quickly, Simon's lack of experience might prove a difficulty in launching the boat, never mind sailing it.

Despite my doubts I knew what my decision would be. I lacked the courage to say no, to let Brannan down and I didn't want the reputation of backing out of something I'd agreed to. That left only one choice, much as it pained me – to try to establish the truth about Melody Blue's death.

Would it be worthwhile asking Simon for advice, have a fresh perspective on the problem? Although he hadn't been in favour of my agreeing to do as Brannan asked, I knew this was no more than concern for my safety. He'd be willing to support me as he had so often in the past. Whether I would take his advice was a different matter, however, and sighing deeply, I went indoors.

Simon was in the living room, watching a cookery programme on television. This struck me as a strange choice.

'Thinking of taking over the cooking now that you're retired?' One could always hope.

'I'd love to,' he said, 'but not much chance at the moment,' and then, raising his arm. 'I can still only comfortably use one hand. But this chef has some great ideas and the recipes look easy to make.'

'Is Maura still in bed?' I hastened to change the subject before he tried to persuade me to try out any of these new recipes, which would involve a trip to the Co-op for ingredients.

'No. She went for a walk around Kames Bay to take advantage of the good weather. Or so she said. She'll have her phone with her so perhaps she wants to speak to Alan without being overheard. It's difficult to have privacy in this small cottage.'

'Well, let's hope she does contact Alan and that they sort out whatever's the problem. I hate to see her like this. Goodness knows what's going on with the pair of them.'

Simon frowned. 'Don't interfere. It's for them to discuss. If she wants our help she'll ask for it.'

'That's all very well but she can't delay much longer. And what about the children? What's to happen to them?'

'Don't exaggerate, Alison. It's only been a few days. Give her a chance to think things through. And the children will be having a great time with their other grandparents. They'll be spoiled rotten.'

It wasn't like Simon to be so accommodating. Had Maura been confiding in him despite his warning that we shouldn't interfere?

Our conversation was cut short as we heard the front door open and Maura came in, clutching her phone.

'Good walk?' I said, busying myself with tidying the newspapers lying in a heap on the floor, as a way of avoiding her gaze.

She looked upset. 'I tried to call Alan but it went straight to voicemail. That's the second time I've tried him today.' She sounded cross. 'I've left a message, told him to get back to me as soon as possible.'

This was a turnaround. That she who had ignored his calls should now be complaining because Alan wasn't responding to her. On the other hand, this might be a hopeful sign that she was willing to give their relationship another chance.

'He may be out of range or his phone may be switched off if he's in a meeting. Be reasonable, Maura. I'm sure he'll call you back soon.'

'Out of range in Kent? I don't think so. It might happen on Bute but I don't think it's likely where we live. He always has the latest version of his phone. It's essential for his job. There's some reason he's not replying to me.'

Her eyes brimmed with tears and I went over to put my arm around her shoulders.

'I'm sure it'll be fine. He's certain to call you back

later.'

She shook my arm off, saying, 'I'm taking my book and going out to sit on the far side of the bay for a while. And hope if he calls the Wi-Fi on the island will work.'

She trudged off upstairs leaving Simon and me looking at each other.

'Might be a good sign,' Simon said before I could comment. 'It looks as if she's missing Alan more than she thought. It might be he's deliberately not answering to bring her to her senses.'

'She's certainly missing the children,' I replied. 'But it was her decision to leave Alan and come here.'

'Don't fret so. It will sort itself out.' Then he said, 'Is it too early to be thinking about lunch. Watching that cookery programme has made me hungry.'

'It's only eleven o'clock – a cup of tea might be more appropriate.' And hopefully by dinner time he'd have forgotten about the delights of the cookery programme and be happy with whatever I could muster.

'Sounds good. Is there any of that fruit cake left?'

'I'll check.'

I went into the kitchen to make the tea as Simon turned back to the television and switched channels to a sports programme.

Just then Maura came downstairs. 'I'll grab a bottle of water to take with me,' she said. 'It's too nice a morning to waste indoors. I'll be back later.'

She left quickly, banging the door behind her.

I hadn't given a thought to dinner and I'd have to investigate the freezer in the hope there was something I could pull out that wouldn't take too long to cook. Simon might be fascinated by the possibilities highlighted by the cookery programme he'd just watched but I didn't want to spend longer than necessary in the kitchen.

Tea made and the last of the fruit cake added to the tray (I'd have to remember to put that on my shopping list) I was about to go back through to the living room when the doorbell rang, followed by a loud knocking on the front door.

I put the tray down on the table in the hallway, calling out to Simon, 'I'll answer it.'

Not that he showed the slightest inclination to move. Since his accident he'd been spending far too much time sitting in front of the television.

More knocking. 'I'm coming, I'm coming,' I said crossly, hurrying down the hall. Who could it be this time?

I don't know who or what I'd expected to find, but this wasn't it. I pulled open the door to see Alan standing on the doorstep. I took a step back in surprise. 'Good gracious,' I said. 'Alan.'

'I've come to see Maura,' he said. The expression on his face was grim.

FIFTEEN

Once we'd recovered from the shock of seeing Alan so unexpectedly the next problem was what to tell him about Maura.

'Come in, come in,' I said. 'Maura's gone for a walk around the bay. She won't be long. Unless she's met someone and got chatting. Oh, she's taken her book with her so…' I chattered on as he followed me into the living room.

A shake of the head from Simon silenced my ramblings during which Alan hadn't said another word.

'Hello, Alan,' Simon said. 'What brings you here?' Then silence as he realised this wasn't an appropriate welcome for his son-in-law in the circumstances.

Refusing the offer to sit down, Alan said, 'Where did Maura say she was going? I have to find her.' He sounded upset.

'She won't be far. She left not long ago,' Simon said. 'Alison can give you a lift. And…'

I interrupted him. 'Why don't you wait here till she comes back, Alan. You must be tired after the journey. Would you like some tea? It's no problem to fetch another cup.'

Alan made a face. 'I think I'd be better trying to find Maura. I'm sure I'll catch up with her,' he said and turning on his heel, he left, pulling the front door closed behind him. 'And please don't phone her to say I'm on my way,' were his final words.

'Why did you tell him where Maura was?' Now I

was cross with Simon.

'What was the point of not telling him? He knows she's living with us,' he growled. 'Anyway, much better that they meet up away from us.'

That might be true but I'd visions of an almighty row taking place in public much to the interest of any onlookers. Why had Alan not told Maura he was coming? Was he afraid she'd refuse to see him? This was becoming worse and worse.

We drank our tea in silence staring at the television, though I didn't register anything that was happening on screen.

The minutes ticked past until I could stand it no longer. 'I'm going into town,' I said.

'Don't try to look for Maura and Alan,' Simon warned. 'They're best left on their own.'

'I've no intention of doing that. I'm going to call in at the circus, begin talking to some of the circus people about what happened to Melody Blue.'

Simon looked as if he didn't believe me, but I'd no intention of seeking out my daughter and her husband. And this was a good opportunity to go back to the circus to do as Brannan had asked.

'And I'll have a word with Brannan about helping with your boat. Your wrist seems much better and it would be a good idea to have him on hand if you manage to go along to the Marina in the next couple of days.'

This brought a smile to Simon's face. 'Yes, that's a good idea. I can make a list of anything else we might need for sailing her.'

And before he could raise further objections, I lifted my jacket and my bag, checking I had a notebook, and hurried off.

To be honest, I'd no idea where to begin. I

understood Brannan's need to find out the truth about Melody Blue's death. The suspicion that the chain had been deliberately tampered with was awful. Though I was still finding it hard to believe anyone I'd met at the circus was responsible. And what might be the motive? Once again I considered how quickly Chiara had taken Melody Blue's place. As a trapeze artiste she would know exactly how the act worked, how important was the split-second timing.

Then again, if it wasn't Chiara, who could it be? And might the killer strike again. I shivered at the thought.

As I drove through Ardbeg towards Rothesay I began to wonder about Brannan. I knew little about him. Was he as innocent as he appeared? Was engaging me to spy on the circus no more than a smokescreen? Maura might be able to tell me more about him. If he'd been her neighbour she must be able to give me some background.

My mind a muddle of possibilities I reached the mini roundabout in Rothesay and slowed to a stop to let a tractor lumber across my path.

Concentrate on driving, I told myself and proceeded more cautiously through Rothesay and up the High Street to the Meadows. What's more, I'd no plan of where to begin. Brannan had suggested my pretext was that I was checking the stock of programmes. That might work, but I didn't see it being a cover story more than once unless everyone believed my numerical abilities were strictly limited.

The playpark at The Meadows was quiet except for a couple of toddlers on the roundabout, their mothers engaged in chat as the children whizzed around, screaming in delight. The Big Top looked deserted when I came in, puzzled that the tent flap opened easily. Surely there was some form of security? It didn't appear so. If safety was so lax, that would explain why it had been easy to tamper with the trapeze.

Without the blaze of coloured lights, the Big Top was eerie, the low safety lights along the edges of the rows of seats hardly penetrating the gloom. I shivered at what might be lurking in the shadows. It was hard to believe that only last night the arena had been lit up with flashing lights of blue and pink, the Big Top echoing to the sound of laughter as people enjoyed the magic of the show. The smell of the circus lingered – greasepaint overlaid with the acrid odour of canvas scenery – more noticeable now the Big Top was deserted. But I didn't want to linger here in the semi-darkness and walked quickly around the perimeter of the ring, keeping my eyes fixed on the entrance to the backstage area.

As I pulled aside the flap I almost collided with someone coming out. It was Joffo.

'Look where you're going,' he said crossly.

'Sorry,' I said regretting my words at once. It was as much his fault as mine.

He glared at me. At least I think he did. As he was in full costume and make up it was difficult to tell. Once again, this close up, how different a clown looked – the white paint around the eyes, those bushy black eyebrows, the slash of red for the mouth, the sickly yellow undertone to his greasepaint. Threatening rather than comic.

'What are you doing here, anyway? There are no performances so I don't see the need for you to be creeping around.' Again it struck me how shrill his voice was. This wasn't what clowns were supposed to be like, surely, no matter what Brannan said?

At this remark I bristled and drew myself up to my full height. Not that I'm tall but standing on tiptoe brought me almost level with him and gave me more of an advantage.

'I'm here at Brannan's request. He asked me to check the stock of programmes.' I stopped as he continued to stare at me. 'In case he has to order more,' I ended lamely.

'More likely he'll have to give them away for free,' Joffo scoffed. 'How can we reopen any time soon? And we're stuck here while the police investigate. The chances of making Glasgow in time for the next stage of the tour are slim.'

'But once Health and Safety report you'll open again. Or so Brannan seems to believe.'

'He's nothing but a fantasist.' Joffo sounded angry. 'Clearly the chain on the trapeze wasn't checked properly before the performance. The blame for that lies with Brannan. If he hadn't been skimping on support staff it might never have happened. Now everything depends on how quickly Health and Safety clear us. If they do.'

This was interesting. If Joffo believed it had been an accident it might be worth probing further.

'So you don't think it was deliberate? That someone sabotaged the trapeze?'

'Don't be ridiculous.' He gave a hollow laugh. 'Who would want to do that. If the circus doesn't run we're not paid and if we're not paid we don't eat.'

This was what Brannan had said but there might be undercurrents neither was aware of.

'Yes, but there might be someone with a motive – a grudge against Fabio or Melody Blue – one of The Flying Volantes.'

Joffo snorted. 'The only one to gain from this is

Chiara. She's now got Melody Blue's place in the act. Don't you think that happened rather quickly? One minute the act couldn't go ahead without her, the next Chiara and Fabio were working together as though nothing had happened.'

I had to ask. 'You don't think Chiara had anything to do with Melody Blue's death, do you?'

Joffo shrugged. 'She has Melody Blue's place in the trapeze act now, doesn't she?'

'And you think it was deliberate?'

'Who knows? Although whoever did it would have made certain that the chain snapped when they were at maximum height in the arena. Made certain she'd be killed outright. A Dead Drop for sure. That's what would have happened.'

'But she didn't survive,' I said. 'Was that accidental? Someone wanted to injure her rather than kill her? Make sure she couldn't continue with the act?'

Joffo moved away in the direction of the exit without replying, leaving me staring after him. He might be right. Even if the trapeze chain had been sabotaged it might have been designed to injure, not kill. This was a new take on the event.

How easy would it be to judge the timing of this act? The perpetrator might have thought he or she had loosened the chain sufficiently to cause injury rather than death but misjudged the drop.

And if it was deliberate, who was responsible? Joffo's mention of Chiara might be no more than the spiteful musings of someone who didn't seem to get on with many of the circus folk. Or he might be correct. Chiara might have been so desperate to replace Melody Blue in The Flying Volantes that she was the one responsible. Having seen her with Fabio there was no doubt they had what could only be called an interesting relationship. But was that enough for her to attempt to make sure her rival would be so injured she would have to give up her place in The Flying Volantes? If that was the case it was a plan that had gone horribly wrong.

SIXTEEN

Why I'd imagined the performers would be around in the changing area at the back of the Big Top when there was no show I can't imagine. A stupid mistake.

I had to be honest. There was another reason for deciding to come along to Kanzi's. It wasn't only because I'd promised Brannan I'd do what I could to discover the truth about Melody Blue's accident. Being here gave me an excuse for avoiding any difficult scenes between Alan and Maura. I hoped that when he'd caught up with her somehow they'd managed to have an amicable discussion, resolve their differences. But was that likely, given what Maura had said about their situation? And how she'd been behaving?

I went to look for the large cupboard at the back where Brannan had shown me the programmes for each performance were stored.

Now I was here I might as well do what Brannan had suggested and count them. Though what difference would that make? I'd no idea how many were usually ordered or if what was left was enough for the remaining performances – assuming there would be any.

It was rather clever how the back part of the Big Top had been divided off by sections of canvas and chipboard to make a series of rooms. Although the performers initially dressed in their caravans some, such as the clowns, who had several adaptations of costume, put on their main outfit in the caravan and then used these makeshift rooms for speed. So much of a modern circus depended on a slick delivery, especially by the clowns who made so many appearances during the show.

One such makeshift room housed a series of cupboards. These were also constructed of chipboard, sturdy enough to see out the season but easily dismantled for moving on. Each was clearly labelled with the contents. I must say the organisation of the company was admirable. Brannan had certainly done well there, taking over from Jonas, even on a temporary basis. Everything would have gone without a hitch if the trapeze incident hadn't happened.

Thinking about Jonas reminded me there had been no further word about him. Kanzi's circus indeed seemed to be having a run of bad luck. The question was what would the new owner, Nicolas, decide to do? Until a decision was reached I'd a feeling Brannan was determined to act as if the future was secure.

As I pulled at the cupboard door I discovered it wasn't locked and only just managed to grab the loose programmes before they came tumbling out. This lack of security, especially when Brannan had emphasised how much it cost to produce these glossy editions, was of some concern.

The remainder of the programmes were stored in unopened boxes, each containing fifty, and it didn't take long to do the tally.

Once finished, I closed the doors carefully, after placing the loose programmes far back on the top shelf where they'd be less obvious to anyone opening the cupboard. What could I say to Brannan? I could hardly keep coming back day after day with the excuse of counting the programmes on the off chance

I might overhear some snippet of information that would give a clue to the circumstances of Melody Blue's death.

As I was about to leave I heard voices. No more than a murmur at first but gradually they became louder. I stood still, scarcely daring to breathe. With only a flimsy piece of canvas between me and whoever was talking I could hear the conversation though I couldn't make out every word. Creeping as close as I dared to the canvas wall, I recognised the voices as those of Fabio and Chiara, the new Flying Volantes team, and it sounded as if they were having an argument.

'You promised me it would work out.' That was Chiara speaking.

There was a mumbled reply from Fabio. All I could hear was 'unexpected…hopeful…try later.' Fabio must be further away.

'That's all very well for you but I'm living with…Melody…no answer.' Chiara had also moved away.

This was frustrating. Chiara had mentioned Melody Blue. They must be discussing the accident and this might be my opportunity to find out more.

Chiara spoke again. 'Melody Blue was…or so I've heard. That might not be…'

Once again part of the sentence was lost.

What could I do? I was trapped. If I revealed myself they would know I'd been listening in. So much for undercover work. On the other hand this might be the only chance to obtain useful information.

I edged right up against the canvas wall, leaning in close. If only they wouldn't keep moving about as they spoke I might be able to make out more of their conversation. Perhaps foolishly, I'd a conviction that whatever they were talking about was of vital importance. And what had Joffo said? He was sure Chiara had designs on The Flying Volantes, wanted to take over Melody Blue's role. But was Joffo to be trusted – spreading malicious rumours seemed exactly the kind of thing he'd do.

More murmured voices then Chiara said in a loud voice, 'I was promised. You always said…'

There was the sound of sobbing and Fabio saying in a rough voice, 'You knew the risks. It is not my fault.'

This was unbearable. I could hear enough to suspect they were discussing what had happened to Melody Blue but I couldn't make out the details. I leaned against the canvas again hoping this would help. Bad mistake. Although the general structure of the Big Top was strong, secured with huge guy ropes and heavy metal pegs, these interior walls were much flimsier.

Unfortunately I moved too quickly and stumbled, making a dent in the canvas wall.

'Who is there?' Fabio called and a moment later he came rushing in to where I was standing, too afraid to move, closely followed by Chiara.

'What are you doing here?' he demanded coming over and putting his face close up to mine.

I instinctively shrank back before an idea struck me and I grabbed several loose programmes from the cupboard. 'Counting these,' I managed to squeak holding up the pile, realising how pathetic an excuse that sounded.

Chiara came over and placed herself squarely in front of me, her hands on her hips. 'Oh, really?' she said.

If looks could kill, I might be next to have a nasty

accident.

My mouth felt dry and I tried to stop myself shaking. It was important to appear to be in control, though I'd never felt less in control in my life. All I could think of was, What if it hadn't been an accident? What if Joffo was right in his suspicions and Chiara had been responsible for what happened to Melody Blue? It had to be someone in the circus troupe who had tampered with the chain. This was the only solution that made sense.

As this flashed through my mind, I swallowed and managed to say in a shaky voice, 'Brannan wants everything to be ready to start quickly when the Health and Safety committee give the all clear. He told me these souvenir programmes are a good way of making money.'

The question was, would they believe me?

I could feel a surge of relief as 'That is true,' Fabio said, putting his hand on Chiara's shoulder. 'And Brannan will have to recover the losses somehow. We do not know when we will be able to leave the island and start up again in Glasgow.'

'I suppose so.' She didn't sound convinced but continued to glare at me.

Attempting to defuse the situation I said, 'I was sorry to hear about Melody Blue's death. Has there been any word about what happened – if the chain was faulty?'

Would everyone know that the chain had been deliberately tampered with?

Fabio hesitated, casting an anxious glance at Chiara as he replied, 'We know no more than anyone else. It is a police matter.' Then seeing the look on Chiara's face, he added quickly, 'It was a terrible tragedy for sure. We are lucky Chiara was able to step in at such short notice.'

This at least raised a smile from his new partner, but it was a smug self-satisfied look.

'It must've been an accident,' she said in a low voice. 'Anyone who thinks otherwise is making mischief. I don't care what they say.'

Fabio shuffled his feet. In spite of Chiara's protest, they gave me the impression they knew it had been no accident. 'Well…' his voice faded.

Emboldened by Fabio's attitude I said, 'But surely the Sixtus troupe will miss you, Chiara?'

Chiara shrugged. 'It's not a problem. I only joined the troupe last year. Before that there were only five of them called the Tarlinn Acrobats. I can't go on doing both acts for much longer. I've been helping while on Bute so they don't have to change their name again but after this venue, if we continue, they'll go back to their original name. And I'll remain with Fabio.'

'And what did you do before you joined the Tarlinn Acrobats?'

There was a gleam in her eyes as she said, 'I was a high wire acrobat and for a time I worked the trapeze. Why do you ask?'

'No more than curiosity,' I said, attempting to sound indifferent. 'It's interesting how people make choices about a career. I would have thought the circus acts would have been particularly specialised. Performers wouldn't…' I stopped, aware I was gabbling.

Fabio broke in, having regained his composure. 'We are all highly trained athletes.' Exactly what Brannan had said. 'Though to do high wire or trapeze work you do have to have a head for heights. You can lose your fitness easily. That is why we are training still, despite the circus being closed.'

'Saying which we should get back to rehearsing.' Chiara pulled at his arm.

'I hope all goes well with your act,' I said as they walked away.

'And good luck with counting those programmes,' said Chiara turning her head. 'I'm sure it's a challenging job.'

They linked arms and walked off to the arena giggling quietly.

Let them make mock as much as they liked. My only concern was that they believed my cover story. They appeared to do so, but the way things were I didn't trust anyone in this company. I waited for several minutes before popping my head out. All clear. After replacing the programmes in the cupboard and closing it securely I went out into the arena, up to the tiered seating area and waked quickly towards the stairs leading to the emergency exit.

I turned back to watch. Fabio and Chiara were in the middle of the arena – though the trapeze was no more than a few feet above ground level. I assumed there were strict rules about this while the Health and Safety investigation continued. Strange though that they had been so emphatic about continuing to practise. There was no sign of anyone else having the same inclination. Despite Brannan's story that the performers had to continue training to keep up their levels of fitness, I'd seen none of the other acts in the arena since Melody Blue's accident had been confirmed as murder.

As I slipped out of the Big Top I heaved a sigh of relief. Was I misjudging Chiara? Surely she wouldn't have deliberately set out to get a place with The Flying Volantes by injuring her rival? If that was her intention it had backfired spectacularly. Melody Blue wasn't injured but dead. And far from creating a situation where she would no longer be able to continue and could be replaced, the future of the everyone in the circus was now in jeopardy.

There were too many possibilities to consider. And apart from this slender suspicion about Chiara I was no further forward in determining the truth of Melody Blue's death. What's more, I'd no idea how I could continue returning to the circus while it was officially closed to audiences. I might have to call Brannan and tell him his idea I could investigate was nonsense. There were only so many times you could use the excuse of counting the programmes as a way of loitering around the Big Top.

SEVENTEEN

Back at the cottage there were more problems. Engrossed in the troubles of the circus, I hadn't given Maura and Alan a thought for at least an hour. But as I drew up outside suddenly this family crisis came to mind again. What would they do? Was there any chance Alan had managed to convince Maura they should give their marriage another chance?

When I came in it was to find Simon on his own. The television was on but this time it appeared to be a programme about renovating houses and I'd had enough of that recently in refurbishing the cottage. A task which had taken a lot of time and money.

Simon was poring over a nautical catalogue, open on his knees.

'What do you think, Alison? It might be worth buying an extra set of sails for Hoppity the Third.'

Ignoring this question, 'Where's Maura?' I whispered.

'Why are you muttering?' Simon said. 'She's not here. She's gone out with Alan. They came back briefly and then headed off.'

'Where did they go?'

'No idea and I didn't ask. Leave it be, Alison. It's up to them to sort it out. I'm only sorry we seem to be in the middle of it.' He sounded upset.

He was right. Whatever was wrong they had to decide how to sort it out without interference.

'We should go out,' I said. 'You can't spend all your time indoors watching daytime television.'

‘I wasn’t really watching it,’ he said, indicating the catalogue. ‘Anyway, I thought you were too busy with all this circus nonsense. Trying once again to solve a problem that’s really nothing to do with you.’

Oh, did I detect an aggrieved note in his words? ‘I’m here now and it’s a lovely day. We can go into Rothesay. I want to look at carpets. If we’re still here in the autumn we might need more than this rug to keep the room cosy.’

Simon stood up, stretching his back. ‘You’re right. It’s a bit too easy to sit around all day. I’ll check out buying spare sails for the boat later.’

Ten minutes later we were in the car and on our way to Rothesay. We’d decided, or rather I’d decided, it was too easy to let things drift and I worried Simon would end up filling our small house with sailing equipment before he had the opportunity to use his boat. Certainly his injured wrist caused a difficulty but there was also the problem that he was watching too much television for my liking.

We browsed the selection of carpets in the shop beside Montague Street, chatted to a few people we knew and in spite of Simon’s reservations about the weather forecast for rain, decided it would be a pleasant walk along the promenade beside the bay.

‘Let’s have a few minutes here,’ Simon said, sitting down on a bench in one of the shelters. We sat in silence, watching the waves lapping on the shore, calmed by the swishing sound of the water. The MV Bute came in sight and we watched its stately progress down to the ferry terminal.

‘It must have been an amazing sight when Rothesay was the resort of choice for most of the population of Glasgow during the Fair Fortnight,’ I said. ‘This whole area would be crowded with holidaymakers.’

‘That was some time ago. The nineteen fifties were the last heyday,’ Simon said. ‘There’s been a revival in recent years but many of the tourists now are day trippers.’

It was proving difficult not to talk about Maura and Alan and there were several lapses in the conversation as we tried to keep away from that subject.

Finally Simon said, ‘We have to go back at some point, find out what’s happening.’

Reluctantly I stood up. He was right. We couldn’t delay any longer. We had to face the outcome of the meeting between Maura and Alan.

We walked slowly along the promenade and as we reached Guildford Square a long line of cars came rolling off the ferry.

‘I see what you mean about the island being busy,’ I said.

On arriving back at the cottage I helped Simon from the car, being careful not to knock his injured wrist, and went ahead of him to open the front door. ‘Hello,’ I called. ‘Anyone there?’

Silence. Alan and Maura hadn’t returned. Trying to stay positive, I said as Simon came in, ‘They’re not here. Perhaps this is a good sign and they’ve made up, decided to put aside their differences.’ I certainly hoped so.

Simon was too intent on manoeuvring himself into a comfortable position in the chair to reply. Finally he seemed to have found a position to suit him and said, ‘They haven’t come back?’

‘No. Oh, wait a minute.’ I hurried into the kitchen in case Maura had left a note. But there was nothing except a couple of empty mugs on the draining board to indicate they had had coffee before going off again.

‘Looks like Alan caught up with her and they came

back here,' I said going through to the living room.

Simon grunted and reached for the remote. The television sprang into life. I bit back a comment.

'I'm going into Rothesay again,' I announced. 'I won't be long.'

'But we've only just come in,' Simon said in a puzzled voice.

'Yes. I meant to do some shopping at the Co-op while we were out and forgot.' Not strictly true.

'From what I can see we've plenty of food.'

'We're out of a few essentials.' I grabbed my bag and hurried to the front door before he could reply.

I started to drive towards the town with no real idea in mind. I'd have to buy some groceries in the Co-op – we could always do with more milk – but that would take a matter of minutes and I needed a longer break. A walk around the Rothesay Castle and back down Montague Street would pass some time. I parked at the Albert Pier – the walk to the Co-op would take another few minutes.

As I passed the Coffee Stop I spied an empty table. I'd had more than enough coffee for the day but a cup of tea was welcome.

The table was by the window and I could watch the comings and goings as I sipped my tea and ate the cake I'd been persuaded to buy. Or rather had spotted when I'd ordered my tea.

My glance fell on a couple walking past Rothesay Castle. I blinked. Yes. My eyes weren't deceiving me. It was Maura and Alan but it was difficult to see the expression on their faces from this position. He'd caught up with her then.

Instinctively I stood up, almost spilling my tea in the process.

'Is something wrong?' One of the waitresses came

over.

'No, nothing. I saw someone I thought I knew.' I sat down again. The last thing Maura and Alan needed was my rushing out to speak to them.

There were any number of reasons why they'd come into town and I turned my attention back to my tea. But I was in no mood to finish it and after paying the bill I left.

Now I had to get back to my car in Guildford Square without being seen. Else they might think I'd followed them into town.

Keeping close to the wall, looking neither to left nor to right, I hastened down to the corner and into Guildford Square to collect my car.

I breathed a sigh of relief as I started up the engine to drive back to the cottage, my mind turning over and over the possibilities of what Alan and Maura might be doing.

Simon was still in the same position as when I'd left him, still watching the same programme or something that looked very like the same programme, still with the catalogue balanced on his knees, though worryingly it was open at a different page.

He looked up as I came scurrying in. 'Is everything okay? You looked anxious.'

'Fine, I'm fine,' I said.

He glanced over and I realised I was empty-handed. 'I thought you were going shopping?' he said.

Drat! In my hurry to get away from Maura and Alan I'd forgotten the reason for my trip into town had been for groceries. I hadn't even remembered to buy milk.

EIGHTEEN

Maura returned late, long after Simon and I were in bed. I heard her footsteps as she crept slowly up to her room. A reminder we hadn't got around to fixing the creaky stairs.

Although I strained to hear, there was only one set of footsteps. Alan hadn't returned with her then. Had he gone back to Kent? But I'd seen them late afternoon in Rothesay. Unless he was staying over in Glasgow before heading south and had managed to catch the last ferry.

After that there was no possibility of sleep and at five o'clock I decided I'd be better up and doing something to pass the time rather than lying in fretful wakefulness.

But what? That was the question. I was beginning to regret I'd abandoned my writing career. Several times over the past few months ideas had flitted into my head, but I'd firmly dismissed them, reminding myself that this was time for Simon and me to enjoy together. But I needed something to distract me from my current problems.

I went into the living room and, switching on the radio, sat down to listen to the early morning programmes. The inevitable happened. A few minutes later I was sound asleep and only woke up with a start in time to hear the beginning of the seven o' clock news.

Half-asleep, I was about to go through to the kitchen to make breakfast when I was stopped in my tracks by a news item about Jonas Gastrell.

I waited, hoping for an update but disappointingly there was no new information. Police investigations were continuing and there was another appeal for witnesses. How had I managed to become involved in the problems at Kanzi's? Jonas Gastrell's accident was no concern of mine but, with a sinking feeling, I thought about Melody Blue's death and Brannan's plea for me to investigate. I could understand his anxiety, wondering what the future held. Funny, he'd said no more about Nicolas Gastrell coming to take over the running of the circus.

Simon would be awake soon. He was fretting about his boat and several times he'd gone along on his own to check it was safe in the Marina – which of course it was. He hadn't mentioned asking Brannan for help. That would have to wait until he was fit enough to sail Hoppity the Third. I still thought it was a peculiar name for a boat but Simon was determined not to change it.

'You're up early,' he said, coming into the kitchen and sitting down opposite me.

'I couldn't sleep after I heard Maura come in last night. I was sure Alan wasn't with her,' I said.

Simon shifted in his chair. 'I didn't have much sleep either, to tell the truth. I hope they've sorted out their differences.'

Unwilling to be involved in another speculative discussion I said, 'There's coffee in the pot. I'm going to get dressed.'

And before he could quiz me about my plans for the day, I hurried off.

Trouble was, I'd no idea what to do. I might have to try contacting Brannan, explain how hopeless was the task he'd set me. I could hardly go back to the circus to count the programmes again. He'd have to come up with another reason for my being around when no more performances were planned.

I took my time getting ready, dawdling over what to wear. The weather had changed and a glance out of the bedroom window revealed grey skies, the clouds scudding across the bay as the wind got up. Not exactly the day for a walk, though in that usual island way the evening would probably be glorious. And though dull, it would be warm enough. Finally I settled on summer trousers and a long sleeved top, adding a jumper and an umbrella to my bag for good measure.

In the event the problem of finding a new excuse for my involvement with the circus was solved. My phone rang. It was Brannan and it was a moment or two before I could make out his garbled message.

'Slow down,' I said. 'What is it?'

'There's been a development. I can't believe it. Just when...' he broke off and I could hear him choking back a sob.

'Tell me. What's happened?' But I sensed what he would say.

'It's Melody Blue. The preliminary Health and Safety report is back and it's clear the chain used by The Flying Volantes had been deliberately tampered with. There's no room for speculation. It was murder.'

'What happens next... to the circus, I mean.'

'I've no idea. Melody Blue's death is a matter for the police. How long will their investigations take? We'll need your help urgently, Alison. What have you managed to find out?'

I had to confess to a lack of success. 'How can I help? Sorry, Brannan, it was a mad idea. If the circus isn't running there will be no need to sell programmes. I've been over, counted them, tried to listen in but it's not as simple as you seem to think. And this is serious, Brannan, if it's a murder enquiry.'

He broke off suddenly, saying, 'Give me a minute, Alison.' I heard him say in a low voice, 'Yes, what is it?' and then there was a muttered conversation before he came back to me.

'Sorry about that, Alison. A minor problem. Now where was I?'

I might think there was no way to help but I hadn't reckoned on the showman Brannan was. He'd had an idea.

'I thought…'he hesitated. 'I thought we might try selling programmes even if we can't sell tickets. I could offer them at a special price. And could you ask Maura to come with you? We need two people at least. I thought the best place to locate you would be at the entrance to the Big Top – set up a separate stall.'

My head told me this was yet another crazy idea but I was sorry for him, understood the difficulties he faced. 'I'm happy to discuss the idea,' I said reluctantly, 'but I'm not sure about Maura.'

'She seemed happy enough the other night,' he said. Then dropping his voice to a whisper, 'When the accident happened.'

'She's busy right now,' I replied, wanting to remind him it had been no accident. I didn't tell him she had enough to worry about without adding this silly idea about selling programmes to her list.

'Oh, that's a pity.' He added with no trace of humour, 'You'll have to work twice as hard.'

'I'll come along in good time tomorrow night,' I said, against my better judgement, preparing to sign off. ‘But only to chat about it. Much depends on what you have in mind.’

‘Oh, could make it this morning? Nicolas Gastrell is due to arrive soon. It would be good if you could meet him along with the rest of the troupe.’

I was sure I wasn’t important enough to merit Nicolas Gastrell’s attention but with no other plans for the day, I might as well join the others to meet the new boss.

‘I hope he’s not sailing his own boat here to Bute,’ I said in an attempt to lighten the atmosphere. ‘One disaster with his father Jonas was enough.’

‘Oh, why would you think that, Alison?’ Another sign of Brannan’s lack of humour. ‘I don’t know if he possesses a boat. And if he does it’s likely to be one of those huge yachts designed for sailing on the Mediterranean, not the Firth of Clyde. He’s a most successful businessman from what I hear. He has other interests apart from managing the finances of the circus.’

‘It was a joke,’ I said. ‘I expect he’ll drive and then come by ferry.’ Brannan’s request now made sense. He wanted to create a good impression, hoping the rich Nicolas Gastrell would be prepared to support the continuation of the circus.

Brannan sounded puzzled. ‘I don’t think so. I’ve been told by his PA that he’ll be piloting his private plane. He’ll be landing at the Bute airfield shortly after eleven o’clock this morning.’

Nicolas must be doing well if he had a private plane. This might be a good sign for Brannan as far as the circus finances were concerned. If Nicolas could afford a private plane he must have the kind of money the circus required. I merely mumbled a reply and, ‘See you later, Brannan.’

Popping my head around the kitchen door, I said to Simon, 'I'll be back at lunchtime,' and grabbed my jacket and bag from the coat rack in the hall before he could ask any questions.

Not that it was likely as he was yet again engrossed in one of his maps, spread out over the kitchen table.

Little spits and spots of rain started as I drove off. No matter how bad the problems at the circus, it was a distraction from the problems at home.

And I'd be back soon. I didn't see Mr Gastrell taking much interest in a lowly programme seller. Especially a temporary one.

NINETEEN

As Brannan had predicted, Nicolas Gastrell arrived at the Isle of Bute airfield out at the road to St Blane's. I'd passed the site several times on various trips around the island but hadn't realised it was an airfield. It was no more than a huge field with a hut at the entrance and this time I noticed the large windsock.

'I believe the locals call it Bute International,' El Gran Fuego, the fire eater, whose real name was Rhys Bolan, had informed me as I came into the arena. 'A bit of Bute humour.'

The circus performers were gathered there, in groups of two or three, ready to leave for the airfield.

There was a palpable air of excitement as we chatted about this latest development. Brannan was holding forth in a pompous manner but that may have been nothing more than nerves. So much depended on what the new owner had to say and everyone knew the continuation of Kanzi's circus depended on decisions made by Nicolas Gastrell. 'The information I have is that Mr Gastrell will be arriving at approximately eleven o'clock so if we leave in the next half hour we should be there in time to greet him.'

Brannan had asked me to come along to meet the new boss but I wasn't sure I wanted to be part of the reception committee to greet him on his arrival at the airfield.

'Do I have to be there?' I asked.

'Of course.' Brannan seemed surprised by this question. He thrust his hands into his pockets. 'Mr Gastrell has to meet everyone. After all, the souvenir programmes are an important source of revenue so you're an essential part of the company.'

My immediate reaction was to take a firm stand, refuse to accompany the rest of the performers but then I thought, what did it matter. And I was curious to see this new owner of the circus. Not to mention how he'd manage to land his airplane in the field.

Brannan directed us in groups into the available transport and I found myself crammed into one of the jeeps, squashed between El Gran Fuego and Stoffo, while Joffo and Boffo sat in front beside Brannan. Interesting that everyone was in costume. This might be to make an impression on Nicolas Gastrell, show him how dedicated they were as a performers.

'Is Joffo always like this?' I whispered to Rhys as Joffo was leaning forward to make some complaint to Brannan who chose to ignore him.

Rhys winked. 'Keeps everyone on their toes, or so he says.'

Joffo was indeed strange but it was none of my business and as Brannan started up the jeep, I sat back, resolutely staring ahead. There was no way I wanted to engage in conversation with the morose Joffo.

Our convoy, with Brannan in the lead, progressed in a stately fashion down the High Street from The Meadows to turn right at the ferry terminal and head through Montford and Ascog towards Mount Stuart. Suddenly I realised why progress was so slow. Each of the vehicles was emblazoned with the name of Kanzi's circus and Brannan was using this as a publicity stunt, a way of letting everyone know about the circus. He never missed an opportunity, that was for sure. If Kanzi's Circus could be saved, Brannan was the man to make it happen.

There was little conversation on the journey, something I found difficult. I can't abide silence but I'd no intention of starting a chat only to have Joffo make some sharp reply.

As we passed the Kingarth Inn a few customers were braving the drizzle of rain, sitting under sturdy umbrellas. One of them looked up and waved as our convoy passed and Boffo returned this greeting with a salute before we turned left at the graveyard to take the road leading to St Blane's.

A little way down the road Brannan and edged the jeep on to the verge, announcing, 'This is our destination, everyone.' The vehicles behind us followed his example but as there wasn't enough space for so many, the last two had to park awkwardly, half on and half off the road. I hoped a farm tractor wouldn't come lumbering along because at this point the road was too narrow for more than one vehicle.

We scrambled out and walked behind Brannan across to a large field where a small wooden hut sat at the entrance and a windsock was fluttering in the breeze.

'So this is the airport,' I said to Rhys, gazing around at the empty space.

'Yes, indeed.' He pointed to the wooden hut. 'Have a look at the plaque on the side. It commemorates one of Bute's famous sons – Baird.'

'Famous for…?'

'Andrew Blain Baird was a Bute blacksmith who in September 1910, at Ettrick Bay on Bute, flew a plane of his own design and manufacture to record the first

All-Scottish Heavier-than-air Powered Flight,' he said, emphasising each word. He grinned. 'The Wright Brothers aren't the only ones with a claim to fame.'

'Of course. I've seen the bronze model of an airplane on the plinth outside the tearoom at Ettrick Bay. How did you learn about him?'

Rhys said, 'One of my aunts lived here on Bute and I spent many holidays here. If you look to the right of the entrance to Bussey's carpet shop on the High Street you'll see an inscription commemorating Andrew Baird. That was where he had his blacksmith's shop – where the prototype was built. There are several claimants who are reputed to have made the first flight but I think Baird is up there with the best of them.'

I nodded. I was familiar with the story of Baird, but Rhys was so keen to tell me about it, I thought it better to act as if it was new to me.

Any further discussion was cut short as Brannan began to run around excitedly, trying to usher the straggling performers into his idea of a reception committee.

'He's on his way. He should be here in the next few minutes.' He pushed his hands into his pockets and took a deep breath.

Reluctantly, under Brannan's direction, the circus people began to form into a semi-circle, shuffling about as they tried to find the best spot. Everyone was aware of the need to make a good impression, though some were keener than others.

'Don't you think we should move back a bit?' Rhys looked doubtful at Brannan's attempts to organise everyone. 'We don't know how much of a run he'll need to land safely.'

Brannan frowned but he did as Rhys suggested and waving his arms to indicate where we should stand eventually succeeded in imposing an order of sorts.

And that was it for the next fifteen minutes or so. We scanned the skies eagerly but there was no sign of Nicolas Gastrell's airplane.

Some of the group began move restlessly, wandering around, one or two beginning to walk down the field despite Brannan's attempts to bring them back into line.

Chiara and Fabio had a whispered conversation before wandering off to cross the road to have a look at the Standing Stones, one of several sets on the island. Recent felling of the trees around them had left them clearly visible to the passer-by. Last time I'd been here they were invisible from the road, in the middle of a dense copse of trees. So dense I'd become lost.

As soon as he noticed their departure, Brannan began to run after them, calling out, 'Come back, come back. Mr Gastrell will be here any minute.'

But Fabio and Chiara ignored this plea as Fabio called out over his shoulder, 'We'll be able to see him coming. Don't worry we'll be back in plenty of time. We've a clear view of the airfield. It will take him more than a few minutes to touch down.'

Brannan looked unhappy, but he now had to contend with mutterings from the clowns, huddled together beside the hut. The smirr of rain earlier had developed into a proper shower.

'This is madness, Brannan,' Joffo said. 'Our costumes will be soaked through if he doesn't arrive soon.'

'Soaked through,' repeated Boffo.

'If he doesn't arrive soon,' echoed Stoffo.

‘Oh, for goodness sake!’ Brannan had lost any pretence of calm. ‘Don’t you recognise how important this is for us. We have to create a good impression. And that’s why we’re here. We must let Nicolas Gastrell understand how vital it is that he continue the circus. Don’t you understand our jobs depend on it.’

Doubt about the new owner’s desire to continue with the business was more than a rumour then?

Stoffo and Boffo looked suitably chastened, shuffling their feet, but Joffo said, ‘That’s very well, but Mr Gastrell will be more upset if he has to shell out money for new costumes and…’

But then there was the drone of an engine overhead and we turned from this dispute to see a speck in the distance, gradually looming larger as a plane approached.

‘Do you think that’s him?’ I said, squinting upwards trying to see through the misty rain.

‘I don’t see how it could be anyone else,’ Rhys replied. ‘I mean, it’s hardly likely to be a busy airfield, is it?’

Chiara and Fabio came sauntering over from the Standing Stones. They appeared to be in no rush – possibly making a point. However they did stand beside Brannan who was now unable to contain his excitement, scratching his head, wiping his hands on his jacket. He was nervous, that was for sure.

A few minutes later the plane came in low at the far end of the airfield, the undercarriage came down and with a couple of bumps the pilot successfully landed. There was a pause for a few moments as we waited for the plane to come to a final stop.

As the aircraft cockpit came up the pilot jumped out and Brannan strode forward eagerly, hand outstretched to greet the arrival.

But Nicolas Gastrell ignored this gesture and Brannan was left to say, ‘Welcome to Bute, Mr Gastrell. We’re delighted to meet you.’

Nicolas Gastrell eyed Brannan coldly as he took off his gloves before scanning the group of circus people before him. He was suitably dressed for flying in tight-fitting black overalls and it was clear his clothes were of the best quality and created the impression (which I’m sure was deliberate) of what he was – a successful businessman. He pushed a lock of his blond hair back from his face before unwinding the silk scarf he wore around his neck.

There was a buzz of anticipation, then one by one everyone fell silent as we waited to hear what he had to say. Surely he would acknowledge Brannan’s words of welcome? Brannan had gone bright red and it was clear he’d no idea what to do next.

We stared at Nicolas Gastrell and he stared back, his gaze again sweeping around everyone in the group.

He directed his reply to Brannan. ‘Thank you for your welcome to Bute. I’m taking over from my father but I’m afraid you won’t be so pleased when you hear what I have to say.’

Oh, oh, this didn’t sound promising. And I was right. He narrowed his eyes as though daring anyone to challenge him as he continued, ‘This trip to Bute will be a farewell for Kanzi’s circus. There will be no more tours.’

TWENTY

It was a subdued and gloomy group of circus performers making their way back to The Meadows. A few people were talking in low voices but most were silent, bewildered by Nicolas's announcement.

'I'll come with you,' Nicolas said and Brannan had no option but to escort Nicolas to his car. Everyone edged away, reorganising the transport. No one was in a mood to travel in the same car as Nicolas. I managed to squeeze into a large jeep with The Sixtus Troupe – who might soon be the Tarlinn Acrobats once more if Chiara elected to partner Fabio permanently.

'What do you think Nicolas means?' one of the troupe asked. Apart from Chiara they were related and I didn't know them well enough to distinguish one from the other. Not that they were identical but they were from one family and had a distinct resemblance except in height.

'It means we're out of work,' the tallest of them said bitterly. 'Where are we going to find another job at this time in the season? It was difficult enough to get a regular job with Kanzi's. There are so few circuses left in the UK.'

I could contribute nothing to this discussion though I could understand why they were so concerned. But why had Nicolas Gastrell decided to close down the circus so soon? From what I knew the circus was doing well and people were clamouring for tickets. Brannan had said the advance sales from the other venues were highly satisfactory. Was Nicolas concerned because of the murder of Melody Blue?

Staring out of the window, I tried to tune out the excited chatter of those squashed into the jeep with me, tried to think of other matters. But that was worse. All that came to mind was Maura's predicament. Maura! I'd told Simon I'd be back by lunchtime. I scrabbled for my bag, wedged between me and the sturdiest of the Sixtus Troupe, to find my phone. He wriggled about on his seat but we were so tightly jammed together I had to pull and push to extract it.

About to call Simon, I decided to text instead and promptly put my phone on silent before contacting him. I didn't want to have to deal with a reply.

The journey seemed endless and on our arrival back at The Meadows it was a very muted group who dispersed to their caravans, while I stood by the Big Top waiting for Brannan to arrive.

He made an appearance at last, escorting the grim-faced Nicolas Gastrell. I wondered what they had talked about during the journey. If they'd had an uncomfortable conversation about Nicolas's disastrous plan to close the circus.

'Have a late lunchbreak everyone. We'll gather in the Big Top at two thirty and we can go over our routines for the performance for Nicky tonight.' He tried to sound upbeat but failed miserably as he saw the expression on Fabio's face. Chiara and Fabio might be a force for Nicolas to reckon with. I didn't see Chiara giving in without a fight.

Nicolas winced at this use of a nickname as Brannan's words drifted off into the wind that had sprung up. Brannan didn't seem to notice this reaction from his new boss.

‘You won’t need me,’ I whispered to Brannan as he passed me. ‘I should be going home. I promised Simon I’d be back by lunchtime and…’

Brannan grabbed me by the elbow. ‘For goodness sake, Alison. Stay here. Of course I need you, need all the support I can get. We have to try to make Nicolas change his mind about closing the circus. It would be a disaster for the performers. And we’d have the problems of sorting out the tickets bought in advance for the other venues.’ He was sounded determined and I wondered if there was another reason for his concern. If money had come in from advance ticket sales had that been used to support the present run on Bute?

I hardly thought as a programme seller I’d be able to persuade Nicolas Gastrell that he’d made the wrong decision but I felt a certain loyalty to Brannan. And there was another reason for my hesitancy. Simon had mentioned again that he intended to phone Brannan in the next few days to ask about helping with the boat.

‘Why does he want to close the circus? Did he give you a reason?’

Brannan looked glum. ‘It was only a brief conversation in the car on the way back. It’s partly to do with costs but it’s also because he can’t devote the time to this business. Or so he said. I’m not sure I believe him.’

‘But you’ve been running the show – literally. Wouldn’t he delegate that to you?’ Nicolas’s proposal didn’t sound like much of a justification. There must be some other reason.

‘That’s what I’ve been trying to say to him but he’s resolved it’s better we close for good. There’s something odd going on. I’ll have to find out what it is.'

This seemed a cruel decision when there was no need, given the success of the show on Bute. The island venue had been a way of testing interest and it had worked spectacularly well.

'You could try for a stay of execution. Ask him to let you run the rest of this season instead of closing down so abruptly. Doesn't he realise the problems you'll have with the other venues you've booked? How much work that will be, returning the ticket money and disappointing so many people.'

Brannan appeared to consider this for a minute, stroking his chin thoughtfully. 'Would you come with me? You can talk to him. He might listen to you. You don't have the same involvement in the circus as the rest of us.'

This wasn't the reaction I'd expected – or wanted. 'I don't think so. I'm only on the periphery of this. All I've been doing is selling programmes and that has come to an end now that the Bute run is over.'

'That's exactly my point,' Brannan said eagerly, ignoring my reservations. 'That's what I'm trying to say. You don't have a vested interest so you can act as an independent. To you it doesn't matter if the circus stays open or closes for good.'

That this might influence Nicolas's decision seemed a far-fetched possibility but how could I let Brannan down – or indeed the others in the circus? It was awful to think that after their success on Bute they might be out of work.

'I'll give it a try,' I said. 'But if Nicolas persists with his plan, there's nothing I can do.' And following him across to his caravan, I gritted my teeth for what lay ahead, though I'd no idea how to approach the problem, what to say. What's more I was sure Nicolas was the kind of person that having once made his mind up would be reluctant to change.

Nicolas was sitting in the chair by the window in Brannan's caravan as we came in, his head bent over a bundle of papers.

'A word, Nicky?' Brannan grabbed my arm as he opened the door, almost certainly in case I had a change of heart and tried to flee.

Nicolas looked up from the papers he was studying. I squinted at them, trying to read upside down. From what I could see they seemed to be a set of accounts. Ah, was that the main reason he was determined to close the circus? Was Brannan too optimistic about the money the circus was making? That would be a sound reason for a businessman like Nicolas to close Kanzi's. And I'd some vague idea Nicolas might be intent on asset stripping – selling off what was profitable and jettisoning the rest. But I wouldn't suggest that possibility to Brannan.

Nicolas looked up. 'Any word about who was responsible for the death of that trapeze artist? Let's hope the family don't sue us.'

If there were financial problems, and a worry these could be made worse by the death Melody Blue, that might be behind his decision. Concerns about what a lawsuit would cost. And Brannan must have been aware of this. Annoyed that he'd involved me without telling me the whole story I opted to remain silent unless asked a direct question.

Nicolas waved the set of papers towards Brannan. 'These don't look good.'

Brannan blustered, 'It's not as bad as it appears. You're looking at the worst quarter for our finances. After Christmas people don't have money to spend. Theatres, cinemas, all the Arts suffer a downturn in

January. That's why it's important to keep going at this time of the year. I'm sure we'll do better. Already bookings for the next venues on the tour have been good.'

There was merit in his argument but, 'That's as may be,' Nicolas said, crinkling up his eyes. 'Exactly how many tickets have you sold for Glasgow, for example?' He lifted his hand as Brannan began to speak. 'Yes, I know the show has been successful here but on an island there's not much in the way of entertainment. People will sign up for anything. I'd want some concrete evidence of future takings before I changed my mind. If we sell off the circus assets that will make enough to cover any losses. You have to understand I'm in charge now.'

I bit back a reply. But my guess had been correct. Jonas was either already dead or so incapacitated by his stroke he'd be unable to return to run the circus. A savvy businessman like Nicolas would almost certainly have power of attorney for his father. And now he was only interested in how much money he could make from selling off the circus. And his guess about Bute was wide of the mark. He knew nothing about the many activities available to people who lived on the island. The circus wasn't the sole form of entertainment he imagined.

Brannan replied, 'We've sold lots of advance tickets for the forthcoming venues – Glasgow in particular. And besides you wouldn't want to let people down, destroy the good name of the Kanzi family.'

Nicolas frowned as this plea by Brannan came to an end. 'Yes, but Kanzi isn't my name, Brannan. My grandfather bought the name with the circus because it seemed easier.' He drummed his fingers on the table before saying, 'I'd need exact numbers about ticket sales, Brannan, not some vague guess.'

There was a pause before he added, 'Although I suppose I could try to sell the circus as a going concern. That might be a solution. If we could find someone to buy it, that is.'

'I'm sure that would work,' Brannan responded eagerly, leaning forward in his chair. 'The permanent performers are excellent, dedicated. Besides, as many of them are contracted there would be financial implications if you were to close.'

This notion made Nicolas frown and taking advantage of the situation, Brannan said, 'If you don't want to continue to manage Kanzi's, selling the circus as a going concern would be the best option. Have you anyone in mind?'

Nicolas didn't appear entirely convinced by his own suggestion, though he was certainly wavering.

The problem was, could he sell the circus as a going concern? There was always the possibility whoever bought it would do exactly as Nicolas had proposed and sell everything off to make money. Some of the equipment must be valuable.

Brannan nodded to me. Then, when I didn't respond, he coughed loudly and stared at me.

Oops, my cue to help if I could.

Taking a deep breath, I said, 'As an outsider I can tell you the initial response has been superb. The islanders who managed to come to the performances before Melody Blue's unfortunate…unfortunate accident have said how enjoyable the event was. And while it's awful about what happened to Melody Blue, Chiara is an excellent substitute…'I tailed off, wondering if Nicolas was listening to me.

Suddenly swivelling around to stare at me, he said, 'But that's the point, isn't it. What happened was no accident. It was murder. That might put buyers off for a start. Have you any suggestions about how we overcome that? That's why we may have to sell Kanzi's off piecemeal. Make as much money as possible.'

So much for my helpful suggestion. My argument wouldn't convince anyone, certainly not Nicolas, especially as I didn't have the opportunity to finish what I wanted to say.

Nicolas bundled the papers together with little concern for order and stowed them in the briefcase beside him. 'I'll have to go through these in detail, check everything. Only then will I be able to give you a decision about what happens next.'

'That's fine. Of course.' Brannan jumped in. 'Meanwhile I'll see if I can come up with a plan to cut costs for the rest of the tour. It would be a good use of the time while we have to wait here on Bute,' he said eagerly.

'Cut costs, but don't cut corners.' Nicolas stood up. A reference to Melody Blue for sure. 'I'm booked into the Stuart Hotel in the High Street. If you could take me there now. When is this special performance you promised?'

'Tonight. Seven o'clock. Everything's ready. I'm sure you'll be pleased.'

Brannan ushered Nicolas out, talking all the while about the great acts they had, about how well they'd been received, leaving me standing looking after them.

I hoped Brannan could pull off this attempt to persuade Nicolas to change his mind, give the circus another chance. But I wasn't too sure anything would convince a hard-headed businessman like Nicolas.

But if he didn't want the circus to continue and if he

thought it would be difficult to sell it as a going concern, what other option was there? Only to follow through on his plan to sell off the assets piece by piece. How would Brannan break that news to the performers?

TWENTY-ONE

I left Brannan to have a meeting with the circus acts to stress how important the special performance would be and how hard they had to work to impress Nicolas Gastrell. I hoped he'd have a strategy to make sure the audience whose tickets had been cancelled for the last night didn't hear about this performance and think the circus was back in business.

'Are you certain everyone understands how crucial this show tonight will be?'

Brannan was dismissive of my concerns. 'I've made sure everyone is aware of how much depends on this performance, Alison. Don't fret. Besides,' there was a gleam in his eye, 'if we have to be on Bute for a bit longer we might get the all clear from Health and Safety. We could run the cancelled show and put on another couple of performances.'

'How would you do that? How would you let people know the circus was open again?'

'Easy. I'm sure we could have a couple of spots on Bute Island Radio and we could send the small van with the loudspeaker out around town morning and afternoon. Salome is an artist of some talent and could design a flyer for us to distribute copies widely around the island.'

He seemed buoyed up by this plan. 'It's important to show Nicky that we're able to keep the business running. That Kanzi's circus has a future.'

'You seem to have all bases covered,' I admitted, exhausted by so many discussions that were seemingly leading nowhere. 'I must go now. I'm needed at home.' And I hurried off before he could prevail upon me to help with anything else. Which I was sure he was about to do.

I wasn't making an excuse. I genuinely had to find out what was happening with Maura and Alan despite Simon's constant refrain of 'Don't interfere.' It was easy for him to say that but it ignored the possibility one of them, or both of them, might need support.

I took a deep breath as I drew up outside the cottage, trying not to let my imagination run riot.

There was no sign of Simon or of Maura when I came in. The cottage was silent, that quiet of a warm summer's afternoon. The earlier heavy rain had cleared and now the sun streamed in through the living room window, little dust motes dancing in the air. A bee buzzed at the window, struggling to escape. I opened the window and after a moment of confusion it flew off letting in a waft of warm air, the promise of a hot afternoon, one of those balmy interludes seldom occurring on the West Coast.

In the kitchen I opened the fridge door and a welcome blast of icy air hit me. What could I have for lunch? There was some cheese and a couple of tomatoes. It would have to be a sandwich.

While I was busy preparing this modest repast, the telephone in the hall rang. This was unusual. These days most people call me on my mobile and putting down the knife I was using to slice the tomatoes I went to answer it.

It was Maura.

'Hello. Why are you using the landline?' I said.

'Because your mobile is going straight to voicemail,' she said.

Oh, drat. I'd put it on silent while we went off to

meet up with Nicolas and had forgotten to change the setting.

'How are you? And where are you?'

'I meant to leave a note for you but it was such a rush. Alan and I are on the ferry. We're heading to Glasgow airport and going back home.'

That could only be a good sign and my heart leapt. 'So you've sorted out your problems?' I said breathlessly.

'Not exactly. Alan has persuaded me the best way to have a sensible discussion about our future is to go back home with him.' There was a tremor in her voice. 'And I do miss the children.' Her decision to return home with Alan must be a good sign. 'I'll keep you posted. Have to go. That's the ferry coming into Wemyss Bay. I'll be in touch later.'

The line cut abruptly, leaving me standing staring at the receiver. What was going on? Had she and Alan patched up their differences and gone home for good? Or possibly this was a temporary truce while they decided what to do.

I replaced the receiver and ran upstairs to the spare bedroom. As soon as I opened the door, I could see Maura had taken everything with her. The wardrobe door swung open, empty apart from a few coat hangers. She didn't intend coming back anytime soon. Or was this wishful thinking on my part?

TWENTY-TWO

While I was in the Bute Tool Company later that afternoon, buying a new garden spade, a text came through from Maura, saying only that they had arrived at Glasgow Airport and their flight would be taking off soon. Thankfully she hadn't changed her mind.

I considered giving her a quick call then decided against it. There would be time to talk later. They could surely work something out and my fears were nonsense, I told myself. Maura and Alan were both sensible people.

My gloomy imaginings were interrupted as my phone rang. It was Brannan. He sounded more upbeat than I'd heard him for some time.

'Wanted to let you know the good news, Alison. Nicky has come back to me with a suggestion he might be willing to consider the Glasgow tour can go ahead and he'll make a final decision after that. That gives us a breathing space to prove to him that the circus has a secure future.'

He sounded so much happier I didn't want to voice my suspicions – that Nicolas knew it would be better to have some money coming in from the ticket sales in Glasgow while he investigated selling the circus for the best price possible.

His next words were unexpected. 'Of course that leaves me with a problem.'

'Mmm,' was my only comment, wondering what he would say.

'Chiara seems to think she's now a permanent member of The Flying Volantes. She won't be happy about stepping down,' he said. 'I've the feeling this is the opportunity she's been wanting for ages.'

'Why should that be a problem? I thought she was doing well.' I didn't add how well she appeared to be getting on with Fabio.

'It's the Sixtus Troupe. They were agreeable to making an adjustment to their act in the short term but now they're making noises about having Chiara back. She's one of the key members – you've seen how well she performs with Fabio. She's a skilled acrobat.'

'I think you're making too much of this,' I said. 'Joffo told me that most circus performers are adaptable. Is there no one else in the company who could step up?'

He sighed. 'I suppose I could check that out. But that would still leave me having to tell Chiara.' I could understand why this was a task he would dread. From the little contact I'd had she wasn't someone I'd like to tangle with.

'I must get back to work. As Nicolas Gastrell is coming to the performance tonight we must make sure it's absolutely brilliant. Though it's going to be difficult to generate the atmosphere without a full house.'

He rang off, leaving me staring thoughtfully at the screen. Brannan was right. If the Sixtus Troupe insisted on Chiara returning to their act that would be a problem – but not an immediate one. Being part of The Flying Volantes for this performance for Nicolas was critical and the issue of the Sixtus Troupe could wait till later.

Everyone has problems, I thought.

When I reached home Simon was in the living room, sitting in the chair, lifting and lowering a book.

'What are you doing?' I said, staring at this strange performance.

'I'm trying to get back to normal,' he said. 'Do some exercises. That boat won't sail itself. Just my luck to have this happen as soon as I bought it.'

Feeling sorry for him I suggested, 'It's a lovely afternoon. Why don't we walk along to the Marina.'

He seized on this suggestion eagerly. 'You're right.' Then his face fell. 'But it will be difficult to get on board, won't it, as moving my wrist easily is still difficult?'

Determined to encourage him, I said, 'Let's see how you cope. I can go onboard and check everything if you find you can't manage. But you seem much better now.'

At first he seemed reluctant to agree. Not because he didn't want me help him, but because he wanted to be first on the boat.

As he hesitated I said, 'You've been doing the exercises. It's a good idea to find out what progress you've made.'

In a happier tone of voice he said, 'You're right. Let's try it. If I can't manage on board you can do it. The walk will do me good.'

'And you'll feel better once it's been checked again…inside as well as outside.'

This plan appeared to satisfy him and a few moments later we set off for the walk to the Marina a short distance away.

I'd a feeling he was rather self-conscious but there was no one around. At least not until we came to the village shop which serves as tearoom, shop, and Post Office.

The tables outside were busy and as we came past a loud voice called, 'Good to see you out and about again, Simon. I heard you'd had an accident on the golf course. Out of practice, were you?'

Every head swivelled around to stare at Simon.

It was Mervin Dawd, whose nickname was Titch – because of his height in that perverse way people have of giving nicknames. We'd first met Mervin when renovating the cottage. As he spoke I thought, Was nothing secret on this island? Then I remembered we should be grateful to him for stepping in when our first builder let us down.

'I'm getting better,' Simon said through gritted teeth. 'It was an unfortunate accident.'

Mervin appeared not to notice his unwillingness to have a conversation. He stood up, pushed his chair aside and came over.

'Aren't you working?' I said. 'I thought builders on the island would be too busy to have time to sit around in the cafe.'

Mervin gave a loud laugh. 'Even a builder has to have a time off. I'm doing up a house at the top of Quay Street and I've finished for the day. How's the cottage?'

Remembering again we owed him a debt of gratitude for the excellent renovation work he'd done, I said, 'We're so pleased with it.'

'Still jobs to be done,' Mervin said, shaking his head. 'Those creaky stairs should be fixed and there's going to be a problem with…

But at that point Simon hissed to me, 'Let's go.'

I smiled at Mervin and we moved off, trying to ignore the murmur of conversation behind us. The last thing we heard was him saying in his loud voice to the other customers in the café, in case they hadn't picked up the first time, 'He did it playing golf, you know. That course at the Port is a real test and…'

The sound of his voice faded as we made our way past the Coronet Hotel, which looked busy with summer visitors. A small group waited outside, surrounded by suitcases, probably waiting for the tour bus to pick them up.

'Let's cross over,' Simon said and we made our way over to the prom. The tide was out and the shingle beach was covered in seaweed, the salty smell drifting towards us on the breeze that had sprung up.

We stopped at the mini quay which projected out over the water, leaning on the iron railing to watch a family of ducks move up and down far off on the water.

'Are you feeling okay?'

'Yes, fine. I'm sure I'm well on the mend.' He moved his wrist with some ease.

'It must take a lot of work to plant these baskets every year,' I said, pointing to the troughs of flowers adorning the buildings along the front. 'How pretty they make the village look.'

We stood in silence for a while before setting off on the last part of the walk to the Marina. A walk that in normal circumstances would have taken us no more than ten minutes. So far it had taken us twenty-five, not because of Simon's injury but there didn't seem to be any urgency. It was good to be out on a lovely day like this.

There was a little queue at the bus stop and we nodded to one or two people we recognised as the single decker West Coast bus for Kilchattan came trundling along.

I was beginning to feel more and more at home here and the prospect of returning to the city was quickly losing its appeal. I wouldn't say anything to Simon yet but if the boat was a success (once he could use it) that might help us come to a decision.

As we approached the Marina Simon stopped suddenly.

'What's wrong?' I said.

'Look. What are the police doing here?' He pointed to the parking spaces outside the portacabin where a police car sat.

'Could be any number of reasons,' I replied. 'Maybe they've caught someone smuggling, bringing in contraband. That would make a story to tell in the Anchor Tavern.'

Simon didn't appreciate my attempt to make light of the situation as his attention was drawn to a little group at one of the pontoons. 'Wait a minute. There are a couple of police officers over at my boat. What's going on?'

'Really?' I followed the direction of his gaze. Sure enough there was a small crowd where his boat was berthed, including two policemen.

Putting on a spurt which surprised me, Simon headed straight for the pontoon.

I came up close behind him as he said, 'Can I help you?'

One of the policemen turned as Simon spoke and I recognised Sergeant McQuoid of the Rothesay Police. Oh, dear, I'd had dealings with him on several occasions in the past and I thought it prudent to hide behind Simon in the hope he wouldn't notice me.

The younger policeman frowned. 'Can I help you, Sir?' he said with a strong emphasis on the "you".

Just then I spotted an elderly man standing beside him.

'The Police are dealing with it,' the elderly man

said in a sharp voice. 'The fewer people here the better.' This said as he glared at the curious group of spectators standing a little way off.

'Dealing with what?' Simon sounded annoyed.

'There's been a complaint by this gentleman, Mr Spinks, about his boat,' said the first policeman introducing himself as Sergeant McQuoid. Thank goodness – he didn't recognise me then. 'But it's no business of yours, Sir. We're dealing with it.'

The constable I recognised as P.C. Brevin – I'd also met him before.

Although he sounded polite Sergeant McQuoid was clearly warning Simon not to interfere.

But Simon was having none of it. 'I'm here to check out my boat,' he said. 'Hoppity the Third.'

'Your boat?' Mr Spinks sounded astonished. 'I'm sorry, whoever you are, but this is my boat.'

This stunned Simon into silence but only briefly. 'There must be a mistake. I purchased this boat from Damien Loughty. It's all in order.'

'Perhaps we'd be better to see the paperwork, Sir.' The sergeant lifted his hand to silence Mr Spinks whose face had gone bright red as he clenched his fists into a ball.

'It's in the cabin,' Simon said. 'If you follow me.'

Now that there was an important reason to be on board, Simon managed to do so, though with some difficulty, and after several minutes, dismissing any offers of help. The boat's cabin was too small to accommodate Simon, the elderly man and two police officers so after some discussion (reluctantly agreed to by the elderly man) Simon and Sergeant McQuoid climbed on board and disappeared down into the cabin. I watched with some trepidation. What was this about? How could this Mr Spinks think he owned

Simon's boat?

A few minutes later, Simon and the sergeant emerged, Simon clutching a folder.

He opened it and pulled out a form. 'See,' he said, thrusting the paper towards the sergeant. 'Proof of ownership.'

'Let me see.' Mr Spinks moved forward to grab the document from Simon's hand, almost tearing it as he did so.

'Whoa. I think I should have a look at this,' the sergeant said, taking the document from a reluctant Mr Spinks. He frowned as he began to read slowly, scanning the documents twice as the tension grew.

Now Simon appeared concerned, his earlier confidence vanishing as the sergeant continued to examine the documents in silence.

Finally he said to the elderly man, 'Let me see your documentation again, Mr Spinks.'

Mr Spinks handed over a bundle of papers, glaring at Simon as he did so.

We waited expectantly as the sergeant moved away to confer with his junior colleague, trying to listen in to their mutterings with little success.

At last the sergeant came over and spoke first to Simon.

'How did you acquire this vessel?' he said.

'I bought it from a reputable source,' Simon replied but he was beginning to sound doubtful. 'Damien Loughty. He runs a boat selling business out of Inverkip Marina. He specialises in selling second-hand boats for the amateur sailor. He's well-known. You can see that from the document. He's been in business for over twenty-five years.'

A hollow laugh came from Mr Spinks. 'What did he look like, this Damien?'

Briefly Simon described him, with a little help from me. Or rather a lot of help. Simon had been too engrossed in the boat to notice much about Damien's appearance.

Mr Spinks slapped his thigh and chortled. 'Told you so,' he said to the sergeant who ignored him but spoke again to Simon. 'And how did you get in contact with this Damien? Did you go over to Inverkip?'

'Well, no,' Simon admitted. 'I saw an advert in Yachting Together, you know, the monthly online magazine. I'd been thinking about buying a boat and when I saw this it seemed too good an opportunity to miss. So I went online to the link and saw this. It was the size of boat I wanted and the right price.'

Not too sure about that, I thought, but now wasn't the time to mention Simon's disappointment with the boat he'd purchased.

'You've been had,' Mr Spinks sniggered in the background.

'What do you mean?' Simon had gone pale. 'How have I been had?'

The sergeant waved the document Simon had produced. 'We'll have to do more investigation but it looks as if we're dealing with a scam.'

Simon said stubbornly, 'I don't know what you mean. How can it be a scam. Damien Loughty had lots of reviews from satisfied customers on his website. Surely someone would have mentioned it if there had been a problem.'

'Did you check any of those out properly? Apart from reading the reviews online? Contact anyone who'd had dealings with this seller.' The sergeant pursed his lips.

'No, of course he didn't.' This was Mr Spinks again

and I was beginning to find him extremely annoying. As were the police officers, I suspected.

We appeared to have reached an impasse. 'What happens now?' I said, reluctant to believe Simon had parted with his hard-earned money in a swindle.

'We have to double-check all the paperwork, but as far as I can see, if it's the same person, this isn't the first time this man has carried out such a scam. We've been tracking him all over Britain in partnership with other police forces. He doesn't stay long in any one location, changes his name and his appearance. He's a wily character.'

'But how on earth would he get hold of Mr Spinks's boat?' I said.

Before the sergeant could reply, Mr Spinks jumped in. 'I needed some work done on the boat. There was a bit of trouble with the engine. I found this Damien whatsit online working out of Inverkip Marina and he said he could do the repairs for a good price. I sailed over to leave it with him. Should have known it was too good to be true.'

'That was foolish,' I said, determined to defend Simon. He wasn't the only one who'd been a victim, then. 'How did you find out about your boat?'

Mr Spinks eventually growled a reply after Sergeant McQuoid nodded to him. 'He contacted me a couple of times to say he was having difficulty getting the spare parts. Eventually I pinned him down to a date for completing the work. He didn't return the boat when he said he would and there was no reply to his phone. That's when I contacted the police. And today they contacted me to say they'd found it.'

'Probably he was using a burner phone,' explained P.C. Brevin helpfully.

'What happens now?' I turned to the sergeant.

‘We’ll have to impound the boat while we carry out further investigations. I’m sure Damien Loughty isn’t his real name. As I said, there have been reports of similar scams in different parts of the country.’

If Simon was unhappy with this suggestion, Mr Spinks was furious. ‘It’s my boat, mine,’ he said. ‘I want it back.’

‘Sorry, Sir, there’s nothing I can do. We have to impound your boat while we carry out our enquiries.’

Mr Spinks lapsed into a sullen silence and beside me I sensed Simon taking some satisfaction from the decision not to hand over the boat to this man who claimed to be the owner. Not without further investigation.

It wasn’t much consolation but at least Simon wasn’t the only one who’d been scammed. The perils of buying online.

TWENTY-THREE

The walk back to the cottage was difficult. Simon refused to discuss the possibility of being duped about the boat and eventually I lapsed into silence. I could only guess he was furious about being so easily taken in.

Once inside the house, he rallied. 'I can't believe this has happened, Alison. He seemed so genuine, this Damien.'

'That's what scammers are good at,' I shrugged. 'And Damien, or whoever he is, is clearly very good. What do you think happens now?' I didn't say that the price being asked for the boat should have made him suspicious. Judging by even the most modestly priced boats for sale in the Marina, the one Simon had purchased was far too cheap. That should have been a red flag.

'No idea.' He sat down on the sofa. 'We have to leave it to the police. Though I guess I'll never see my money again.' He sounded despondent.

I couldn't disagree. This scammer was clearly good if he'd managed to evade the police for so long. And if he was eventually caught it wasn't likely any of the money would be recovered. However I was more concerned with how disappointed Simon was, that his dream of owning a boat had come to nothing. And what would he do with all the sailing gear he'd bought?

I tried to cheer him up. 'Perhaps Mr Spinks is also a con man. Maybe he's in league with Damien.'

‘You think so?’ He raised an eyebrow. ‘Most likely that’s your writer’s imagination at work again.’

The remainder of the afternoon stretched before us and I couldn’t face sitting in the cottage going over and over the problem of the boat. There was nothing we could do until the police completed their investigations and decided who owned the boat. And that could take some time. Even worse, from what we’d heard, the decision was unlikely to be in Simon’s favour.

‘I’m going over to the circus,’ I said, watching for Simon’s reaction. ‘Most of the performers should be around rehearsing. This is so important for them.’

‘But the performance isn’t till this evening, you said.’

‘Yes, but they might need help. If it doesn’t go well Nicolas Gastrell may well close the circus for good, not even allow them to fulfil their agreement to perform in Glasgow.’

Simon sniffed. ‘I don’t see how you can help with that. A programme seller isn’t going to make much impression on the owner.’ Then he added, ‘No matter how many you managed to sell during the past week.’

I ignored this comment, putting it down to Simon’s disappointment about the boat. Life in retirement wasn’t working out as either of us had planned. My friend, Susie, had warned me. She’s been a friend for many years and although she now lives in California we’re in regular contact. In our last call she’d cautioned me, ‘You’re both too young to retire. I know you’re freelance, can pick and choose (as if, I thought) but Simon is going from a busy working life to doing nothing. Mark my words. Simon will regret his decision.’

And she was right. Now that the plan for the boat

had fallen through, he'd have to find something else to occupy his time. I wasn't sure he'd plan to go back to the golf course any time soon.

'Why don't you walk along to the Anchor Tavern? There are bound to be people you know there.'

Leaving him mulling over this suggestion, I made a quick escape to The Meadows.

Although there were several hours before the performance started, the circus was a hive of activity. In one corner of the arena the acrobats were rehearsing while a little too close for comfort and safety, I thought, El Gran Fuego was going through his act. His assistant, Nobilia (though that wasn't likely to be her real name considering El Gran Fuego was called Rhys) was standing ready to help with the flaming torches, but she wasn't wearing her glamorous costume.

I stood watching them for a minute. Surely Nicolas Gastrell would be impressed by these performers. And then I thought, everything depends on tonight. Everyone would want to be on form.

Leaving the performers to rehearse, I went in search of Brannan. I seemed to remember his caravan was on the far side of the field and that's where I found him, so engrossed in the pile of papers on his desk that he didn't hear me knock and enter.

'Hello, Brannan,' I said. 'I came over early to see if there was any way I could help.'

Brannan looked up and I was shocked at the change in his appearance – he was pale and hollow-eyed. He gave a mirthless laugh.

'I doubt if you – or anyone else – can help.'

'What's wrong? I've come from the arena where some of the acts are busy rehearsing. I'm sure it'll go well tonight. Nicolas Gastrell is sure to be impressed.'

'You think so? It's not as easy as that. Read this.' And he thrust a newspaper clipping into my hands.

Quickly I scanned the article. 'Where did you get this?'

'It was sent to me by a 'friend' if you could call him that. You see what it means?'

I reread the piece. It appeared to be from a newspaper gossip column and claimed that Nicolas Gastrell was about to sell the circus, or at least the Kanzi name, to a foreign buyer.

'But Nicolas said tonight's performance would be important? And that he was willing to consider the Glasgow part of the tour before a final decision?'

'Oh, that's what he said, Alison. It's now clear he's no intention of saving the circus in its current form. He wants to get a good price for the name. That will allow a foreign rival to gain a foothold in Britain. And most probably want to bring in a whole new set of performers.'

'But there are lots of areas – theatres, cinemas, variety – where there are several companies. You have nothing to fear from a rival. Your circus is well-regarded.' I'd no idea if this latter comment was true but my intention was to make him feel less despondent.

Brannan shook his head, took the clipping from me, and gazed at it. 'That's where you're wrong. The circus has been in decline for years. You might remember that in the old days there were lots of animal acts – tigers and bears and elephants – that drew people in. Not to mention the horse acts. At Kanzi's, Delia the bareback rider was a particular favourite from what I've heard. We have to work hard now to have enough daring acts to substitute for those.'

'A good thing, surely. Some of those animal acts were cruel.'

'Whatever your opinion the truth is there isn't room for more than one big circus company in Britain at the moment.'

What could I say? Any other words of comfort I could give would be no more than that – words. Instead I said, 'No matter what you think, tonight's performance is still important. You have to prove to Nicolas Gastrell that he can gain a lot by keeping Kanzi's going.'

'I guess so.' He stood up and pushed the clipping under a pile of papers. 'Don't want to leave this lying about where it might be spotted. You're right. It's no more than a rumour at the moment. Damn reporters always ready with a story, whether or not it's true. '

He straightened up, adjusted his jacket and said, 'Let's go and find out what's happening over in the arena.' He shot me a warning glance. 'I don't want the others to know about this. Best to let everyone think there's still hope the circus will continue. That Kanzi's will give pleasure to people for years to come.'

I followed him as he strode across the grass, trying to keep up.

In the Big Top El Gran Fuego had disappeared to be replaced by the clowns, rehearsing an act which involved a lot of water, though the smell of smoke lingered in the air.

Brannan and I stood watching as the three clowns went through their paces, mimicking tossing the water, rather than throwing it over each other. Too close to the performance to get their costumes wet.

Joffo spied us and raising his hand to stop the others came hurrying over.

‘What’s the latest?’ he said. ‘Do you think Nicolas Gastrell is going to close us down? Or is it an idle threat?’

How quickly news travels. I wondered if Joffo had been the ‘friend’ who had sent the clipping to Brannan.

Brannan shrugged. ‘You know a lot depends on tonight’s performance. If he likes it, he’ll think Kanzi’s circus has a future. If not, well…’ His voice tailed off.

Joffo waved his hand in the general direction of the arena. ‘What will happen to this? All the equipment?’

‘Don’t you understand? I’ve no idea, Joffo. Now, instead of speculating it’s far better to continue with the rehearsal.’ He glanced at his watch. ‘There’s not much time left before Nicky Gastrell arrives. I’m going over to the Stuart Hotel soon to have dinner with him and then bring him back for the performance.’

Again I thought one way to help might be to call him Nicolas instead of Nicky, given the use of a nickname appeared to annoy him. But I didn’t say so.

Sighing loudly, Joffo turned on his heel and shouted to Stoffo and Boffo, ‘Let’s take it from Stoffo’s entrance.’

‘I’ll be back later,’ Brannan said. I could see he was upset. If the circus was closed, sold on, he’d be the person who’d have to break the news to the performers. Not a pleasant task.

‘I’ll collect one of the programmes for Nicolas,’ I said.

‘What? Oh, yes, of course. Make sure it’s there for him as soon as he arrives.’

There was nothing else I could do to help. The investigation into Melody Blue’s death was best left to the police. And for the circus there were greater stakes at play.

As Brannan marched off, I walked slowly to the back of the arena. The arrival of Nicolas Gastrell had been a tremendous upset for everyone – small wonder tempers were frayed.

This back section of the arena was busier than I'd seen it and I quickened my pace to the cupboard where the programmes were stored, avoiding talking to anyone. But as I pulled aside the flap to reach the cupboard, Rhys came out from the other side.

'Why if it's not our programme seller,' he said with a laugh. 'Pity you won't sell any tonight – we need all the money we can get.'

'Were you expecting a large crowd here tonight?'

'Sold out. And we could have sold the same number of tickets again. It's awful we've had to cancel.'

'You see,' I said, 'people are interested in coming along to see a professional troupe. I'm sure once you're cleared to reopen you'll be successful. I gather Brannan is hoping to put on some performances here on Bute if that happens.'

Rhys grimaced. 'I wish I could agree with you, Alison. But I think the attraction now might be what happened to Melody Blue. Perhaps those who buy tickets for any extra performances hope they'll witness another accident.'

This sounded harsh – another example of how depressed everyone was. I could only hope they'd be able to rise above this uncertainty and put on the show of their lives to impress Nicolas. And Melody Blue's accident wasn't likely to be repeated. Then again, many of these acts were dangerous, including Rhys's.

'I have to pick up a programme for Nicolas

Gastrell,' I said, moving past him. 'Everyone has to pull their weight tonight.'

As I started to open the cupboard, I noticed my hand was trembling. The sooner tonight was over the better. I pulled open the door then stopped. I closed my eyes tightly before opening them very slowly.

My eyes weren't deceiving me. The cupboard was empty and the programmes had disappeared.

TWENTY-FOUR

My first instinct was to go in search of Brannan. There must have been a reason for moving the programmes and surely he would know where they were. Then again he would have told me if he'd decided they were better stored elsewhere. There were already piles of boxes taking up space in the office caravan – why add to these?

And if he didn't know about this, who did? There was no one else with this responsibility.

Then I remembered he'd gone to the Stuart Hotel to have dinner with Nicolas. Somehow I didn't think phoning to tell him about the missing programmes would be a good idea.

Then it struck me – Gloria. For some reason she must have decided there was a better place to store them. She might have put them in the kiosk. It was a long shot, but the only answer I could think of despite the lack of space to store the boxes.

Gloria should be around somewhere. Although she wouldn't be opening the kiosk tonight as a member of the company she'd be required to be on duty. I tried the kiosk first, peering in through the window, but there was no sign of her. And although I pulled and pushed at the door, it wouldn't budge.

What to do? I had to find the programmes. I ran over to the area behind the arena then realised I couldn't go rummaging through all the cupboards in the makeshift rooms.

As I stood pondering my next move, Chiara came

in.

Why I asked her I don't know but anything was worth a try. 'Have you by any chance seen the boxes of programmes?'

'Why ask me? I thought you were in charge of them.' She sounded more hostile than ever.

'Sorry,' I mumbled. 'I can't seem to find them. They should be in the cupboard in the room on the far right but they aren't there.'

'Ask Brannan,' she said and flounced off.

This encounter left me with a bad feeling. The circus performers weren't the one big happy family Brannan would have us believe. Under all the glamour and the apparent bonhomie there were hostile undercurrents. Was it to do with the possibility of the circus closing down? Was that upsetting everyone? Or was there something else going on?

Whatever the problem my immediate difficulty was locating the programmes. I hurried out of the Big Top and across to Brannan's caravan, hoping he'd have arrived with Nicolas. But there was no sign of him.

I was at a loss. In under two hours the performance was scheduled to start. The programmes were an important source of revenue as Brannan had constantly reminded me. And I'd been the last person to see them. How stupid not to have greater security for something so valuable. That certainly wasn't my fault.

If someone had taken them, what could be the motive? Unless, unless. I thought about Melody Blue's death. The police had given no information about possible suspects in the murder investigation but they must have a strong suspicion someone in the company was responsible. Someone who knew how to tamper with the chain. No one outside the group of performers would know how to arrange it so the chain snapped at exactly the right moment. That required specialist knowledge.

Yet how could that be anything to do with the programmes? It wasn't possible. There must be a simpler explanation.

My first thought was to go again to the back of the Big Top and check out the other temporary rooms. I crept in, mindful some of the performers might be there but every room was empty. Of course. They would be in their caravans, preparing for tonight. Many of the costumes they wore were highly elaborate and a full make up was essential under the brightly coloured lights. This would take time – time that allowed me to check out the rooms at the back without being seen. But I'd have to be quick.

My guess came to nothing as I ran from room to room. In the first one, apart from a long wooden rack holding a colourful array of costumes and several tables with well-lit mirrors above, there was nowhere large boxes of programmes could be hidden. And though I searched in every corner there was no sign of the loose programmes either.

I sat down on one of the chairs, stared into the mirror and as quickly looked away again. The bright lights surrounding this mirror were far from flattering. This was hopeless. What would I tell Brannan? The truth, I told myself sternly. This was no fault of mine. The cupboard should have been locked. Even so, I'd a sinking feeling in the pit of my stomach as I left, unable to think of where else I might search. I'd have to hope Brannan had returned from the Stuart Hotel by now and that I could have a word with him in private. As I crossed the field to his caravan, I heard a loud noise and the Council bin lorry came rumbling along the narrow road beside the entrance to The Meadows.

I stood and watched as the workmen began to empty the large green bins. Anything to postpone the moment when I had to face Brannan.

As I was about to turn away, I heard one of the men say, 'Blooming ridiculous to put these heavy boxes in the bins,' and I turned in time to see him heave a large box out of the nearest bin.

There was a familiar look about it. Of course! It was a box of the programmes.

Without a moment's hesitation I ran over to the bin lorry, shouting, 'Stop, stop,' at the top of my voice.

Clearly astonished, the binman dropped the box. Unfortunately it landed on his foot and he began hopping about shouting, 'Ouch, ouch.'

'Sorry,' I said, as I arrived, breathless, beside him. 'I …need that box – and… there should be others.'

Probably annoyed that my yelling had caused him to drop the box, he growled, 'We're not allowed to do that. Once the box is in the bin, it's the property of the Council.'

'Please,' I pleaded. 'Someone has put the boxes in here by mistake.' I stood on tiptoe to peer into the bin. Sure enough I could see another three large boxes occupying the space.

The binman appeared reluctant but I kept insisting until he said, 'I'll have to speak to the boss.'

He trudged over to the bin lorry and I saw him chat to the driver in the cab, all the while gesticulating over to where I was standing with my fingers crossed.

After a long consultation the binman came back to me. 'He says,' he jerked his head in the direction of the cab, 'he says you can take them.'

Now that he'd had the approval of his boss, the

binman seemed more amenable. 'I'll get them out for you.'

Accepting his offer gratefully, I stacked the boxes one on top of another as he brought them out.

Now I was faced with the difficulty of transporting them back to the Big Top. As the bin lorry drove away, leaving me looking helplessly at the stack of boxes, I heard a voice beside me say, 'What are you doing here, Alison? And what are you doing with the boxes of programmes?'

It was Brannan. Thank goodness the day was saved. After giving him the briefest of explanations at which he looked grimmer and grimmer, he took out his mobile and summoned help from the crew responsible for setting up the arena.

'What do you think happened?' he asked me as the last of the boxes was taken away by a couple of the technical crew.

'I've no idea. All I know is that the programmes were in the cupboard last time I checked.'

'It was lucky you were here when the bin lorry arrived.'

'Goodness knows what would have happened,' I gulped.

'They'd be making their way to landfill by now. That's what would have happened.'

He put his arm around my shoulders. 'The main thing is that you rescued the boxes. To lose those would have been a catastrophe. I've asked the crew to put the programmes in the office – there's a lockable cupboard there that I can use meantime.'

'I'll collect one for Nicolas,' I said, still shaken by this turn of events.'

Brannan gave the briefest of smiles. 'Let's get on with making sure this performance is the best one possible. That's the most important thing now – to convince Nicky Gastrell that the circus is worth saving. He's waiting in my caravan. I came out to check the Big Top before bringing him in for the performance. It'll do him no harm to wait there a little longer.'

I followed him back to the caravan that served as the office, my stomach churning, aware how close we'd come to losing the programmes. The boxes were saved, but there had been twenty-five loose programmes when I'd done the last count. I wasn't going to mention that to Brannan. Or not yet. He'd enough to worry about.

There was only one conclusion I could draw from this latest incident. Someone was trying to sabotage the circus. But who could it be? Surely not one of the performers?

TWENTY-FIVE

The show was a great success, as I recounted to Simon when I arrived home late that night exhausted. 'Nicolas Gastrell appeared to enjoy the performance, though reluctant to admit it. I caught him trying to suppress his laughter on several occasions. I think he was surprised by circus acts, didn't realise how great they were.'

'That can only be good news,' Simon said. He was listening politely but I suspected the problem of his boat, or rather Mr Spinks's boat, was preoccupying him.

Undeterred by his lack of interest, I went on, 'From my vantage point at the entrance I was able to see Nicolas watching every move. The clowns were on top form. From time to time his face broke into a thin smile as though against his will.'

'Let's hope you're right and the future for the circus is more secure.'

'I caught up with Brannan at the end of the night. Nicolas found himself surrounded by the performers before he could escape. Brannan was convinced Nicolas had enjoyed himself. Small wonder. The performers gave one hundred and ten per cent. There's nothing more Brannan can do to persuade him.'

I related this to Simon and he poured me a glass of wine as I flopped into the chair by the fire saying, 'I'm not sure if I should have this. I'm so tired I'll be lucky to make it upstairs to bed.'

Simon grinned. 'Come on, tell me more about it. Was Nicolas pleased with the glossy programme you gave him? That was the highlight of the evening, surely?'

Too tired to rise to the bait, I said, 'Everyone did so well – the performances were slick, all the technology worked. El Gran Fuego was a special hit as were the clowns.'

'What about the trapeze artists – what were they called again?'

'The Flying Volantes. Yes, it went without a hitch.' I didn't say that Brannan had come over to stand beside me at the corner of the ring and say, "I'll be glad when this one is over."

Of all the performers Brannan had been the least successful. A couple of times he fluffed the introductions. Clearly a case of nerves but I daresay Nicolas didn't notice. It was only because I'd seen several performances that I spotted he wasn't on form.

Then I added, 'It was a pity there wasn't an audience. That would have made it more enjoyable.'

Taking a sip of wine, I said, 'There was one strange thing that happened,' and I told him the story of the missing programmes.

'Perhaps someone made a mistake – thought they were rubbish.'

This wasn't likely – the boxes of programmes were stored in a cupboard, not left lying around. But I was too tired to think about that right now.

Simon said, 'You were lucky to be able to put on a performance, given the circus is still unable to reopen.'

'Mmm…if there's a difficulty Brannan might claim it was a rehearsal.'

‘Could still be a problem.’

‘But not my problem,’ I said, adding, ‘I’ll have to go to bed,’ and putting my glass down on the table. I’d hardly touched it. Standing up, I stretched to ease the stiffness in my neck. Simon was right. If word got out about this ‘special performance’ the circus might be in trouble.

‘Before you go, Alison, there’s something I’d like to discuss with you.’ He looked serious.

I sat down again saying, ‘It’s not Maura is it? Has she been in touch?’ The expression on his face could only mean one thing – Alan and Maura had failed int the attempt to patch up their relationship.

‘No, no, it’s not Maura. Let’s assume as far as Maura and Alan are concerned no news is good news.’

‘It’s the boat, then. Have the police contacted you?’

‘I wish you would stop jumping to conclusions, Alison. It’s nothing to do with Maura and it’s nothing to do with the boat. I’m resigned to not seeing the boat – or my money – again.’

What else could it be? I quickly ran through other possibilities but nothing came to mind.

‘Can’t it wait till the morning?’ I was too tired to be capable of rational discussion.

‘I’d rather you knew now.’ Then he said, ‘I’ve had a phone call.’ He looked at me over the rim of his glass.

‘Yes? Go on.’ Now, despite my tiredness, I was intrigued.

He hesitated, taking another sip of his wine.

Sighing, I said, ‘Simon, why don’t you tell me about it.’

‘I had a call from my old boss at Scottish Alignments Limited,’ he said slowly. ‘They want me to take on some work and...’

'But you've only just settled into retirement,' I interrupted. 'I thought we'd agreed we'd spend the summer here together. I've turned down a couple of commissions.' I didn't add I'd refused them because they weren't particularly interesting. Visions of Simon departing overseas again sprang to mind. Over the past few years he's spent a lot of time working in Washington. This wasn't what we'd planned.

Simon held his hand up. 'If you'd let me finish.'

I reluctantly lapsed into silence.

'The offer is for a six-month contract based in London. I haven't said I'll accept it yet. I wanted to discuss it with you first.'

What could I say? The idea of retirement was fine, but the reality was different. Susie was right. Someone like Simon who'd had several busy careers wasn't suited to this life of idleness.

'When do you start?'

'In four weeks,' he replied. 'I mean if I decide to take the job and if you agree.'

'Of course I agree,' I said. 'If it's what you want.'

A look of relief spread across his face. 'Are you sure? I would like to do this and it's only for six months. You could come down some weekends and …and…we could keep an eye on Maura and Alan. And other weekends I could come back here to Bute.'

I wasn't sure that Maura and Alan would be happy with this suggestion of "keeping an eye on them" but I didn't say so.

'Anyway,' Simon added, 'I don't have to confirm I'll take the job until the end of next week. That gives us time to make a final decision.'

It was clear Simon was eager to take up this offer but further discussion had to be held over as my phone rang. It was Brannan. 'What now?' I muttered.

At first I couldn't make out what Brannan was saying. He sounded hysterical.

'Slow down,' I said. 'Say that again. You're not making sense.'

I listened as he repeated his words then said, 'Okay. I'll come over if it will help you.'

'What's happened?' Simon said.

'I can't believe this. There's been another incident at the circus.'

'What is it this time? If the performance is over surely it can't be anything to do with that.' He was looking far from pleased.

'No.' I shook my head. 'This happened after the performance had ended. It's Chiara. She's been attacked. Brannan wants me to go over. They've no idea who the attacker was.'

'What help can you be? The police will deal with it. Besides I don't want you putting yourself in danger.'

'It's because I'm not part of the circus that he wants my help.'

Simon shook his head. 'I don't understand. If there's an attacker on the loose you shouldn't be anywhere near the circus. And you said you were exhausted.'

But in spite of Simon's warnings I felt I had to go. And of course I did want to find out what was going on.

So, promising I'd be careful, and feeling revived, I left Simon both bemused and cross and once again drove to The Meadows. Just as well I hadn't touched my glass of wine.

TWENTY-SIX

A scene of confusion greeted me when I arrived at the Circus. People were running here and there and the noise was deafening. A police car was parked at the entrance to The Meadows and as I arrived an ambulance drove away, siren blaring. This must be serious.

I caught up with Brannan inside the Big Top. He was addressing the performers and I arrived in time to hear him say, 'Remember. No interviews with the Press. Not until we've established the facts. There's too much speculation already.'

'We have to say something,' Rhys mumbled.

Though he spoke in a low voice, Brannan heard him. 'If you feel you must reply, how about saying "No comment". Refer everyone to me.'

At this Rhys looked embarrassed and moved further away.

I did a quick check. Yes, they were all there, clustered around Brannan. But of Nicolas Gastrell there was no sign.

As the performers slowly dispersed, murmuring to each other, and casting a glance back at Brannan from time to time, Joffo came forward. 'Where's the boss?' he said in that high-pitched voice of his. 'Why isn't Nicolas Gastrell here?'

Brannan shuffled his feet and, avoiding looking directly at Joffo said, 'He's back at the hotel. I took him straight there after the performance ended. I've phoned him of course to tell him what's happened to

Chiara.'

'Can't see much possibility of Kanzi's staying open now,' Joffo said.

'Surely you have to be more positive.' I couldn't resist coming into the conversation.

But Joffo ignored me and walked away.

'What's wrong with him?' I turned to Brannan. 'You'd have thought he'd be anxious to keep the circus going.'

Brannan shrugged. 'I don't think it's worth worrying, Alison. Nicky Gastrell is certain to want to close the circus now. First a murder and now this attack. It's too much.'

What could I do but agree with him. Despite Brannan's attempts to keep the Press at bay, the story was sure to leak out soon. This would be more bad publicity for the circus.

'What happened?'

Brannan looked at me and bit his lip. These terrible events were taking their toll.

'No. Chiara was going back to her caravan after the performance when someone crept up behind her and knocked her to the ground.'

'But surely there would be plenty of people around at that time. The crew would have to clear up and many of the others would be lingering in the area.'

'It happened late at night. She went back into the arena for her mobile – she'd left it in the back dressing room. So she was alone when she came out.'

'Is she badly hurt? What does this mean for The Flying Volantes?'

'Badly enough hurt not to be able to continue with the performances even if Nicky decides we can continue to Glasgow, that's for sure. Fortunately one of the technicians was coming back from a darts match in The Golfers' Bar else she might be dead rather than injured.'

This was terrible news. The Flying Volantes was the most important act, the showstopper that provided a thrilling finale. "Always leave them with something great to go away with. Something they'll tell their friends about," Brannan had said to me when I first started. Well, there would be plenty to talk about now.

Then I remembered a previous conversation with Brannan. 'But didn't you say there was a problem with Chiara continuing with The Flying Volantes? That the Sixtus Troupe wanted her back with them?'

'Yes, that's true. But I'd hoped to persuade them to let her continue for the Glasgow run, if it came off. It takes time to train someone up to the level needed for that kind of act.'

'This is terrible news,' I said, unable to suggest a way of helping.

'I have to go to the hospital,' Brannan said abruptly. 'Find out how Chiara is.'

'Which hospital has she been taken to?'

'She's in the Victoria Cottage Hospital on the High Street and luckily her injuries aren't serious enough for her to be transferred to one of the mainland hospitals.'

'Has there been any word from Nicolas?'

Brannan gave a hollow laugh. 'Apart from a few terse words about the circus being closed down before there's yet another disaster? No.'

He curled his lip. 'He's said he'll be in touch and that I shouldn't contact him.'

'I hope he makes his mind up soon. It's not fair to keep the performers in suspense.'

But Brannan ignored this. Possibly he'd rather not

have dealings with Nicolas right now.

'If you do manage the Glasgow tour how will you cope if The Flying Volantes are unavailable?'

'We'll announce at the beginning that The Flying Volantes won't be making an appearance. The Sixtus Troupe can step up – though without Chiara obviously – and the clowns have another routine they can incorporate – though that one involves me.' He looked miserable at the thought.

Brightening, he said, 'At least the attack on Chiara was nothing to do with the circus. It could have been a random attack.'

'Was anything stolen?'

'No…,' he admitted. 'But whoever was responsible may not have realised she wasn't carrying anything of value. It was dark in that part of the field between the caravans and the Big Top.'

He sounded as if he was trying to convince himself. As for me, I'd a feeling the attacker must have known Chiara and that the assault was unlikely to be as random as Brannan thought.

'There is another problem, Alison. We'll have to maximise our takings – and that includes selling as much merchandise as possible. Gloria will deal with the light sticks and the clown hats but I'll need an experienced programme seller. Would you consider coming with us? I know I can rely on you and it would be for no more than a couple of weeks.'

This was unexpected and I couldn't think of an answer immediately. Did Brannan really believe I'd be willing to follow them to Glasgow? Then I remembered Simon was going off shortly to take up his new job. Why shouldn't I go?

'Take time to consider it,' Brannan said. 'I do need someone I can trust after what's happened to Chiara and the incident with the boxes of programmes yesterday.'

And without waiting for an answer he strode off in the direction of his caravan, leaving me staring after him. There was something far wrong in this company. Someone must have a motive for targeting The Flying Volantes. No one else had been hurt. I felt sorry for the company but most of all I felt sorry for Brannan, bearing the weight of this disaster.

Could I help? Do something short of travelling to Glasgow with them? Could I find out more about The Flying Volantes? Someone must know the truth about these calamities at the circus.

TWENTY-SEVEN

Still no word from Maura.

'I'm going to phone her,' I said to Simon. He shook his head. 'Let them be. They'll be in touch soon enough. They'll have a lot of talking to do.'

Simon was more cheerful. Even the confirmation the boat did indeed belong to Mr Spinks did little to dampen his mood, though he'd muttered now and again about selling off the equipment he'd bought. After several discussions we'd agreed it was best if Simon took up the offer of a job and the start date for his contract had come through. Suspiciously quickly, I thought. Had he been planning this for longer than he'd given me to understand? His wrist certainly seemed to have improved since he'd first mentioned it.

Before he could persuade me otherwise, I rang Maura's number. At first it appeared my call would go to voicemail, but suddenly Maura cut in.

'Hello, Mum,' she said. She sounded brighter than I expected but I knew I had to choose my words carefully. 'I thought I'd let you know Dad has accepted a new contract.'

'He's going back to work?' She sounded astonished. 'I thought this idea was that you'd both retire, walk off into the sunset together.'

'Not quite,' I replied crisply. 'We're not that old yet.'

'No, no,' she blustered, 'I thought with dad having a boat and everything that you'd be happy…'

I cut in. 'There's a story about the boat but that's for later. I'm phoning to find out how you are.'

There was an embarrassed cough at the other end. 'I did mean to phone you, Mum, but I wanted to be sure.'

My heart sank. Sure about what? That their marriage was over?

Her next words did nothing to reassure me. 'I'm meeting with Alan at the weekend. He says there's something we should discuss. Whatever it is he believes it will clear the air.'

'I do hope so. This state of limbo is no good to either of you – or to the children.'

'I know, I know,' she sighed. 'But it's so difficult. Alan is staying with his parents meantime and the children and I are at home.'

'How are you coping?'

'I'm spending time in the garden,' she said. 'That visit to Ardencraig gave me lots of ideas.'

While this was frustrating I could tell she'd no intention of continuing the conversation about her marriage and, changing the subject, I told her about the latest problem at the circus. That was a mistake. She echoed Simon's words, 'I wish you wouldn't become mixed up in these crises, Mum.'

'Don't worry. It'll be fine,' I said and after a few more promises about keeping in touch, Maura rang off, leaving me to go over what she'd said.

The consolation was she and Alan hadn't broken off negotiations entirely. With a sigh I turned my mind back to current problems. Thank goodness the circus would be gone before Simon left for London. I didn't always listen to his advice but I did value his support. I'd now decided no matter how hard Brannan tried to persuade me I wouldn't be going to Glasgow with them. Even if Simon's new job meant I'd be living on Bute on my own.

I walked out into the garden at the back of the house. I'd been full of good intentions when we'd arrived – how as soon as the winter was over I'd transform the bare flower beds, plant some shrubs and even a row of trees at the boundary wall. Sadly none of that had happened. I'd gone as far as buying several packets of seeds and planting them but the soil was poor and the only signs of life were a few straggling plants desperately seeking to make an impression. With little success. It was too late now to make much of the garden but I determined autumn would see me set to and plant lots of daffodil bulbs.

Meantime the local garden centre, Mill Cottage, must have some pots and hanging baskets I could buy to brighten up the garden for the remainder of the summer.

Simon declined to accompany me. 'I've a few phone calls to make,' he said. 'I can do those while you're out.'

So much for the new job not starting yet. He was at work already and had commandeered the spare bedroom as an office, resurrecting a desk stored in the garden shed.

Mill Cottage was quiet. There was only one other customer, carefully sifting through the packets of seeds on display on the rack beside the entrance.

As I browsed what was left of the summer stock of flowering plants, a voice beside me said, 'Why, hello, Alison. How are you?'

I turned to face a young woman wearing overalls emblazoned with the name of the garden centre. Her face was familiar but I couldn't place her.

'Why, hello, how good to see you,' I said slowly,

trying to remember her name.

She laughed. 'You don't recognise me, do you?'

'I know I should,' I admitted.

'I'm Kelly. I used to work at the new Kyles Hydro Hotel – the one in Port Bannatyne.'

Of course. 'Seeing you in a different location puzzled me for a minute,' I said. 'What are you doing here? Aren't you at the Kyles Hydro Hotel any longer?'

Kelly smiled. 'I decided I had to do something more productive with my life before I was too old. I'm starting an agricultural course in the autumn and I'm working here over the summer.'

As she lifted her hand to brush away a lock of hair that had fallen over her face, I noticed a sparkle from the finger on her left hand.

'You're engaged!'

She put out her hand to let me have a better look at her ring. 'Yes, another reason for a change of career. Murray is from farming stock and we hope to find a place of our own. Hopefully on the island but if not we'll look elsewhere.'

'Isn't farming a hard business these days?'

'That's why we have to diversify. Oh, I don't mean set up in competition to Mill Cottage but lots of people want help with designing their gardens. The idea is I'll partner with the garden centre – beneficial to both of us.'

I could do with that kind of help, I thought as she said, 'And what brings you here, Alison?'

Briefly I explained about buying the cottage at Port Bannatyne and my problems with the garden.

'It looks so bare. But I know it's too late in the season for summer plants. I thought I'd try to get ahead for autumn.'

'Might be better to wait a month,' she said. 'Why don't you try these.' She gestured to a display of pots containing a variety of summer flowers.

We pondered the merits of busy lizzies against fuchsias, marigolds against begonias. Eventually I settled on three pots close by the entrance displaying a colourful mixed selection and I followed her into the well-stocked shop to make payment.

'I'll ask Johnny to help you to the car,' she said, deftly removing the price tags from the pots. 'He's in the back shop.' As she moved away to find Johnny she said, 'Awful business that at the circus.'

'Yes,' I agreed not wanting to add to the many rumours already in circulation.

A look of disappointment crossed her face as she realised I was unwilling to speculate about events at Kanzi's. She tried again. 'Strange that both Melody Blue and Chiara should be targeted.'

'What do you mean?'

'Both partners of Fabio. Don't you think that's strange?'

'Mmm.' I waited for her to continue. I did think it was strange, but I'd no intention of saying so. How had the news leaked out? Even for a small island this news had spread exceptionally rapidly. Someone at the circus must have been gossiping.

Kelly chuckled. 'Someone doesn't like Fabio's partners. Then again, I've heard he's a bit of a ladies' man. Gets romantically involved with his partners. Won't be a minute.'

As I watched her walk away I thought about what she had said. Working as closely as The Flying Volantes did I supposed there was likely to be a strong connection but was it possible Fabio had been Melody Blue's lover and had so quickly transferred his affections to Chiara? I tried to think of any signs I'd noticed about Fabio and Chiara then remembered how he'd been with her. A picture came to mind of Fabio with Chiara after Melody Blue's death, how intimate they were.

Then there was the spat I'd witnessed with Joffo, but I'd no idea what had caused that. Unless Joffo was concerned about Melody Blue? I'd no idea why that might be.

Kelly came out of the shop accompanied by a short, stocky man whose spectacles kept slipping down his nose as he bent to lift two of the heavy pots with no difficulty.

'I'll come back for that one,' he said as I bent down to pick up the last one. 'Where's your car?'

Ten minutes later, after a further exchange of pleasantries, I was on my way home with the pots safely stowed in the boot. Hopefully I'd be able to unload them by myself. Although almost recovered Simon wouldn't be able to risk helping me in case he damaged his wrist again.

But as I drove away I kept thinking about what Kelly had said. Should I try to find out more about the possible relationships between Fabio and his circus partners? Or should I take the sensible option and stay back. A dilemma. Or rather, another dilemma.

TWENTY-EIGHT

I kept remembering what Kelly at Mill Cottage had said. Of course it could be no more than a rumour. The island would be abuzz with stories about what had happened. True, there must be a motive for Melody Blue's death but that was for the police to discover.

This left me with an option. Should I tell Brannan about the conversation with Kelly? Despite the statement that the chain on the trapeze had been tampered with and that it had been no accident Brannan refused to face up to reality. His stubbornness in not wanting to acknowledge the truth was the most likely explanation for his determination to keep going no matter what. Nicolas might have other ideas.

When I returned to the cottage Simon watched me fuss about where to place the pots in the garden, all the while saying, 'I could try to help.' For very good reasons I declined this offer and it took several attempts before I was satisfied with their positions in the garden.

'I'm not sure they make much of a difference,' I said, standing back to view them. They had looked sizeable at Mill Cottage but now placed in the emptiness of the garden, small as it was, they weren't as attractive.

Simon put his arm around my shoulders. 'They cheer the garden up meantime and you can take time in the autumn to plant bulbs. Think what it will look like in the Spring.'

As we walked back into the kitchen he said, 'Oh, I forgot to say there was a phone call from Brannan while you were out.'

'Why didn't he phone my mobile?'

'He said he did, but there was no reply. It went to voicemail.'

Drat – I must have put it on silent again and forgotten to switch it back on. I'd have to be more careful about checking it. I clicked my phone on. Sure enough there were several missed messages from Brannan.

'He wants you to go over earlier tonight. Something about a question to do with the trapeze act.'

'No more details?'

'No. And I didn't ask. I'm not happy about you being involved in this mess. It was fine when all you were doing was selling programmes but now that there have been two incidents…' he made quotes in the air and let his voice trail off. He didn't say, but I knew he was thinking, One of which was murder and one might have been attempted murder.

'I'm not sure what's going on but you can be sure I'll be careful. There's nothing else I can help with.' I hoped adopting a firm tone of voice would convince him. He knew little of the background to the problems at the circus apart from what I'd told him. Better he knew nothing about Brannan's eagerness for me to investigate.

Fortunately Simon was preoccupied with his new contract. He seemed keen to begin.

'I've been on the phone to the new office at Scottish Alignments Ltd,' he said. 'Are you sure you don't mind me starting so soon? We had plans for the rest of the summer on Bute.'

‘Not at all. You’ll be back at weekends while the summer lasts. And then I can come to join you in London. I know how bored you’ve been, Simon. The problem with your wrist didn’t help. And once you’re settled we can think about where we want to live permanently – Bute or the mainland.’

This contract might revive our interest in house-hunting. And the fiasco of the boat could be shelved meantime. Neither of us had mentioned it recently.

‘I guess so. As long as you’re certain.’

I stretched up and kissed him. ‘Now, I’d better go over to the circus and find out what Brannan wants.’ Though I knew exactly what he wanted.

‘Fine. I’ve a few papers to read.’ Then, ‘I could cook. Try out one of those recipes I’ve seen on TV.’ He held up his arm. ‘My wrist is much better.’

Torn between a desire to let him go ahead and a knowledge of what the kitchen would be like in the aftermath, given he would be working almost one-handed, I settled on agreeing he would provide something simple for our meal. He’d be able to bring something out of the freezer and put it in the microwave if all else failed.

Simon’s return to work would be another change for us. The truth was the idea that two busy people such us could settle to a life of inactivity had been nonsense. We’d given it a try, though admittedly not for long, and the offer to Simon of a new contract was a spur to both of us. Already ideas were flitting through my mind, proposals I could work up and pitch. This would be a better use of my time, and of my skills, than selling programmes for the circus. Soon Kanzi’s would leave Bute, possibly to close down forever. And Simon would leave to take up his new post. Who knew what the future might hold for me? That in itself was exciting.

With a guilty start I realised I hadn't given Maura a moment's thought all day but I pushed the desire to phone her to the back of my mind as I drove to The Meadows.

As I parked beside the Leisure Centre a fine drizzle of rain started. The playpark was deserted. I picked my way across the field to the Big Top mindful that even a little rain could turn the ground boggy.

The lights inside the tent were dimmed, only the emergency lighting illuminating the arena while the tiered spectator seats were in complete darkness. I stood for a minute before groping my way forward as my eyes became accustomed to the gloom.

Suddenly I heard a sound over in the far corner. At first I thought it was my imagination but then it came again – chink, chink.

'Hello,' I called out, stopping at the edge of the arena, listening intently. Chink, chink it came once more. A sound I couldn't identify.

No response to my call.

I spoke again, louder this time. 'Who's there? Is that you, Brannan?'

This time there was a scuffling noise. Too loud to be a rat I convinced myself with a shudder and taking a deep breath I strode into the Arena and across to the source of the noise at the back of the ring. What danger could there be here? Brannan would be along any minute.

As I came up to the changing area, I caught a glimpse of a figure scurrying away towards the corridor that led to one of the emergency exits. It wasn't one of the performers. Whoever it was was slim, with a mop of short blonde hair and although I couldn't be certain I'd a strong feeling it was the woman I'd seen going into Joffo's caravan.

Perhaps I'd been wrong about a relationship with Joffo. Security at the circus was so lax she might well be an opportunistic thief, coming over from time to time to see what she could pick up. But Joffo hadn't, to my knowledge, reported anything missing. Yes, the costumes were valuable but too identifiable to be easily resold. Some of the specialised equipment must have cost a great deal but again where could it be sold? And much of it was too large and cumbersome to be easily moved.

It was too late to find help and steeling myself for an encounter with this intruder I quickened my pace to the emergency exit. Too late – I arrived as the door slammed shut and when I yanked it open to look out there was no sign of her.

Should I tell Brannan about this? He'd enough to worry about right now and there was little concrete information I could give him. Better to ask around, try to find out if anyone had noticed items missing.

As if on cue, Brannan came striding into the Big Top, stopping when he saw me. 'Why, Alison, what are you doing here in the dark?' He went over to the console at the side of the arena and the circus ring blazed into light, the pink and blue brightness dazzling me.

'I've only arrived a few minutes ago,' I said. 'You wanted me to come over early.' When he didn't reply immediately I said, 'What's happening with Nicolas Gastrell? Has he given you a reprieve? Or even a temporary stay of execution?'

He shook his head. 'Not really. He said he'll wait until the end of this week before making a final decision. By then we should have more news from the police about Melody Blue's murder. Not that it's much help. It will only give the performers a week's notice if we are to close. And there are plenty of rumours swirling around already. The Sixtus Troupe told me this morning they've decided to go back to their old name of the Tarlinn Acrobats and they've managed to secure a contract with a stage show at The Hippodrome in Southsea. One of the acts there has had to pull out because of a family crisis and I suspect The Sixtus Troup, or rather the Tarlinn Acrobats, will leave us before the end of the week. He looked disheartened. 'Leaving another gap in the running order.'

'That's too bad,' I said. 'But how will they manage without Chiara?'

'Fine, now they've reverted to their old name, The Tarlinn Acrobats. Chiara is making good progress but much depends on her decision about The Flying Volantes.'

'But you still have a good core of acts left. That must count for something.'

'We can just about manage as long as no one else leaves suddenly. El Gran Fuego was muttering when he heard about The Sixtus Troupe. Though,' he brightened a little, 'Rhys's not likely to find it as easy to secure another booking.'

'Really? I thought his act was popular?' Almost as popular as The Flying Volantes.

Brannan smiled. 'Oh, it is, it is. But given the kind of act it is – pretty dangerous – the insurance costs are sky high.'

This made sense. Then I reminded him. 'You asked me to come over early?'

'Yes. There's something I want to ask you.' A hesitation. 'Have you noticed anything odd about what's been going on here?'

Apart from one suspicious death and an attack on Chiara, I was tempted to say. Instead I murmured something inconsequential and waited for him to continue.

'It's that someone seems to be targeting The Flying Volantes. At first I thought it was bad luck that both events occurred with their act. But now we know Melody Blue's death was no accident, I have to believe that Chiara's attack was meant to be more serious than it was. In fact it was intended to be fatal.' He paused, waiting for my reaction.

'You could be right,' I admitted. It appeared he was at last facing reality. 'But what conclusion does that lead you to?' Better to give him the opportunity to say what was on his mind before answering.

'I know this may sound far-fetched and that's why I wanted to ask you before I go back to the police.'

'If you have suspicions so will they,' I said firmly. 'It might be dangerous to become involved.' And I've no intention of doing so, I said under my breath.

'How long will they take to come up with an answer? To find the culprit? They don't know the circus as you do.'

This was a step too far. 'I can't say I know the circus well,' I said. 'I've only been working for a short time. I can't pass an opinion.'

'This is a matter of grave concern for me. Don't you understand, Alison? By the time the police come up with an answer, find the culprit, we may be closed for good. I need to have a solution sooner than that.'

I sighed. 'What is it you think the police are missing? That they can't find but you can?' laying emphasis on the "you".

Sensing a weakening of my position he said, 'Don't you see? Melody Blue's death and Chiara's accident could only have one motive – to cause problems for Fabio. He's the one being targeted.'

This suggestion wasn't the first time I'd heard it. Now I was curious about why Brannan also believed this. 'If you think it was Fabio who was the intended victim, why is he still alive? Indeed without a scratch?'

'That's what I don't know.' Now he sounded impatient. 'If only we could come up with a reason that would be a step forward.'

Seeing the look on my face, he went on hastily, 'I don't mean we should think about catching the killer. But if we could identify a motive that would help the police I'm sure.'

Even so, this sounded too dangerous. I'd been involved in so many incidents in the past where I'd started out 'helping' before ending up in deep trouble. Simon's words, 'Don't get involved' rang in my ears again as I said, 'Sorry, Brannan. This is best left to the proper authorities. It's becoming too dangerous.'

His face fell. 'I thought you'd be more helpful, Alison. I'm not asking you to do anything hazardous. Merely to watch or to listen out for anything that might give us a clue about the culprit.'

He sniffed. 'Honestly, I wouldn't ask if I thought you couldn't help. But as a programme seller you're in a unique position to listen to any gossip.'

'I'm not a programme seller any longer if you remember. And I won't be coming to Glasgow with you. I've made my decision.'

'Yes, that's fine, that's fine. I understand, though I am disappointed. But you can pretend you're still going to be part of the company. Please, Alison. I need your help.'

Then I thought about the strange intruder I'd seen

earlier and once more I wondered if I should tell him. I decided not to. Another mistake.

TWENTY-NINE

The sense of frustration was palpable.

'Why can't Nicky make up his mind,' Brannan groaned putting his head in his hands. 'Surely he must see how well the Circus is doing. I've managed to pull together the information about advance sales in Glasgow, including the block bookings which will be a nightmare to cancel.'

There was little I could say to cheer him up. And I had this sinking feeling that there were undercurrents at Kanzi's that Brannan might not be aware of. The question was what should I do about this – if anything?

Rehearsals continued as usual. I admired the dedication of these circus people – how they persisted despite the uncertain future that lay ahead. As the performers went through their acts in the first half I scrutinised each one carefully, trying to identify any of them as the interloper I'd spotted earlier. But there was no one who looked even slightly like the slim, blonde stranger. Once again I wondered if I should tell Brannan but he was so despondent I didn't want to trouble him. Besides it could be nothing. The Meadows was a public space and it might be someone who'd wandered into the circus out of curiosity, wanted to watch one of the rehearsals.

I slipped into one of the seats in the bottom row and settled back to watch as El Gran Fuego and his assistant came running into the ring.

As he lit the first torch and launched into his act,

tossing the lighted torches in the air, and catching them as they burned steadily. I decided I was making too much of the woman I'd seen. It was probably of no consequence and I settled back to enjoy the rest of the acts as they followed in quick succession, interspersed by performances from the clowns. Their act had been extended to help fill the space left by Chiara's accident and the loss of The Flying Volantes from the programme. Joffo, Boffo and Stoffo certainly worked hard to entertain the audience and their routine would delight any children in the audience – if they were ever able to perform again. As the last performer, Timor, the trick cyclist, ended his act I remained in my seat waiting for Brannan to appear.

But it wasn't Brannan who emerged from the back of the arena but Fabio. He came striding across to where I was sitting. At first I didn't recognise him without his costume and make up. How handsome he was. I could see how his finely chiselled features and his dark looks would appeal to women.

'Hello,' he said, moving beside me.

'Oh, Fabio,' I said. 'I'm so sorry about what has happened. How is Chiara?'

'She will be fine soon,' he said in halting English. 'She was lucky. But she may not perform again with me again. The Sixtus Troupe – they are anxious that she returns to them. If that happens our act is finished. Pouf!' He made a cutting motion across his neck.

I stared at him. Would Chiara prefer to give up the opportunity to work with Fabio? Not from the way I'd seen her behave with him.

And he clearly didn't know The Sixtus Troupe had already decided about their future. One that would leave Chiara free.

THIRTY

The police had been to see Simon.

'There seems no doubt that boat sale was a scam,' Simon said. 'The money's gone. There's no chance of getting it back.'

'But how did Damien, if that's his real name, manage to pull it off? Surely a boat of that size isn't something you could hide?'

'That was the clever part. I wasn't the only one taken in. He advertised himself as a company specialising in low-cost repairs and maintenance, and once he'd been contracted he took the owner's boat into the local Marina where he had a temporary berth. Then he advertised the boat online for a quick sale. After he'd collected the money, he made off, changed his name, and moved to another part of the country. With so many aliases it's taking the police some time to track him down. Though they assured me they would catch him soon. They've had a tip off.'

'I suppose the problem is that no one can resist a bargain.'

'Yes. When I think of all the times I've warned others about not being taken in…'

It was dreadful that Simon had been duped and I felt sorry for him – and for the other victims of the scam – but there was something funny in that Simon, usually the most prudent of people, had been deceived.

'Anyway,' he said briskly, 'how did you get on at the circus? Did you tell Brannan you wouldn't be accompanying them to Glasgow to sell programmes?'

‘Yes, but I’m not sure he understood. I’ve a feeling he’ll try again to persuade me.’ I didn’t mention the intruder I’d spied. Nor did I mention what Brannan had asked me to do. I could imagine what Simon’s reaction would be. And it didn’t seem to be worth causing an upset. Nothing would come of Brannan’s request.

He sighed, ‘Surely that’s you finished with the circus now, Alison. You’ve helped them as best you can.’

Changing the subject, I said, ‘Any more word of your new job?’ in case he quizzed me more closely about why I kept going back to the circus.

He visibly perked up. ‘Yes, Scottish Alignments Ltd phoned today. I go to London for a briefing next Monday. They’ll sort out temporary accommodation for me until I can find a flat.’ He grinned. ‘Which the company will pay for. With the price of property in London I wouldn’t take on the contract otherwise.’

‘Do you think this will turn out to be a long-term job? That we’ll have to consider moving there?’

He shook his head. ‘This is a short contract. Six months at the most. I don’t think I’d like to go back to living in London permanently. Not with what we could afford for a house.’

This was a relief. He said, ‘It might be difficult to rent in London. Even if the company pay. If it’s too difficult I can stay with Maura for a while. She’s on an excellent trainline.’

Given the problems Alan and Maura were facing I didn’t think having your father/ father-in-law to stay was a good idea but I kept my own counsel. Best to take it step by step. After all, Simon might find being back at work wasn’t the exciting prospect he envisaged. He’d become used to having the time to do as he wanted…even if that was nothing.

We discussed the arrangements we might make for the weekends once Simon started work and there was so much to talk about we ended up having a late dinner. As we finished, Simon said, 'There's a programme I'd like to catch. It's on in a few minutes.'

As the programme was a documentary about the First World War it didn't interest me and I slipped out to the kitchen on the pretext of clearing up before bedtime. I'd had an idea. Taking a pen and a notebook from the kitchen drawer where we keep all manner of odds and ends, I began to make a list. If I wrote down the names of all the circus performers and went through them one by one, perhaps there would be a connection between one of them and the mystery intruder.

It was a slow process. I didn't know or in some cases remember the names of all the individuals – the Sixtus Troupe I only knew as a group and ended up listing them as 1 to 6, then crossed out 6 as I remembered Chiara had left to join The Flying Volantes.

An hour later I'd considered every one of the performers twice but was no further forward. The woman I'd seen didn't belong to the circus. Nor could I think of a reason for her being there, skulking about in the back of the arena unless she was a thief. She might have been responsible for the attack on Chiara but she couldn't have interfered with the chain that caused Melody Blue's death. And there might be a perfectly good reason for her being at the circus. One I hadn't thought of. Still, it was a puzzle.

I was back to considering the performers. But why would any of them want the circus to be closed? What about Brannan? That was even more unlikely. He was trying by every means possible to persuade Nicolas to continue with the tour.

There was a creak on the stairs. Simon must be going to bed. A glance at the kitchen clock told me it was after one a.m. Hastily I put the pen and notebook back in the drawer before Simon could come in and ask what I was doing. I switched off the light.

Time I was also in bed. Tomorrow might bring some answers. I could only hope that I'd sleep, given the many questions whirling around in my mind.

THIRTY-ONE

The next day Simon was occupied with preparations for his new job. Although he didn't start for a while yet there appeared to be a lot of preparatory paperwork and after breakfast I left him to it. Since he'd accepted this new post he'd been much happier. Susie was right. What on earth had made us think early retirement would suit us? Now I had to find something I wanted to do. It wasn't continuing with the circus, that was for sure.

Simon was so engrossed he scarcely registered my departure, giving an inaudible reply in response as I shouted, 'Goodbye'. This suited me – I didn't have to go into a lengthy explanation of my movements for the day.

My first stop was the Rothesay Library. I wanted to find out more about Kanzi's Circus. I'd a memory of Brannan saying the family circus used to visit Bute for two weeks each year from its first beginnings in the early 1900s. If that was so, there was sure to be some information in the sadly missed island newspaper The Buteman. While much information was now digitised, there was still information on microfiche and after a few tries I remembered how to use the system. I set to, intending to check any references to the circus. This would give me background which could help Brannan. I might not be able to identify the person who'd been skulking around the circus last night or find out who'd caused the accidents to Melody Blue and to Chiara but I could put together information Brannan could use in his discussions with Nicolas. Even as a hard-headed businessman surely he wouldn't want to let the traditions of Kanzi's fail after so many years of success.

I was in luck and within five minutes of scouring the first newspaper of 1900 there it was – an advert for Kanzi's Circus, taking up half a page of the middle of the newspaper.

In those days it was rather different from the circus currently in The Meadows. Many of the acts involved animals – elephants and performing tigers (how dangerous was that, I thought), a chimps' tea party with the poor creatures dressed as humans and the bareback rider Brannan had mentioned. While modern circus acts were still dangerous, it was a different kind of danger.

Subsequent newspaper archives showed Kanzi's circus had come every year to Bute until the outbreak of the first World War and after the war ended there had been a gap. They hadn't resumed until the mid-1920s.

And of course the second World War had created a further break with what appeared to be a smaller circus starting up again in 1951. This was a major event for the island and this time there was a full page spread about the return of the circus with a photograph of the smiling owner – Murray Gastrell. This must be Jonas's father and Nicolas's grandfather. He'd purchased the circus on the death of Emilio Kanzi but had decided to keep the original name – "such a long tradition deserves to be maintained," he was quoted as saying. Animal acts were still advertised but they were fewer in number than before the war.

This was interesting but there was nothing helpful emerging from my research. And although the Gastrell family had owned the circus for many years it wasn't the same as being able to claim that they had been the original proprietors.

As I sat back considering this information, Tina, one of the librarians, came over.

'Do you need any help?' she said. 'Oh, it's you, Alison. I might have guessed. You're one of the people who uses the microfiches most regularly.'

Gesturing to the screen, I said, 'I'm looking at the reports on the history of Kanzi's circus in the local paper.'

'Are you searching for anything in particular?'

I shrugged. 'I don't know what I'm looking for to be truthful. Brannan who's the current Ringmaster has been left in charge of the circus and with the threat of closure hanging over them…' I stopped, aware this was a piece of information I shouldn't have disclosed. I didn't want to encourage further rumours.

Either Tina didn't notice this slip or she already knew about the difficulties because she replied, 'Yes, awful about what's happened, isn't it? I can see why everyone is so upset.'

Then she said, 'Funny that.'

'What?'

'Well, the son, Jonas's son Nicolas, he has a bit of history.' She appeared to be taking time to consider her next words. 'There was a story about his being involved in some financial dealings which were rather shady.'

Gossip as usual, I thought, feeling rather sorry for him. Her next words took me by surprise. 'Yes, I'm sure it was mentioned in one of the articles about

Jonas. I'm one of the many people on the island who regrets the closure of The Buteman. My mother read it cover to cover every week and I'm sure she mentioned something about a scandal to do with Kanzi's circus.'

'And that was…'

'I'd have to check back,' she said. 'Oops, sorry, there's someone looking for help.'

She pointed to an elderly woman who was waving frantically to her. 'I'm on my own today. Kieran is ill and won't be back until tomorrow.' As she hurried away to deal with the concerned customer she said, 'I'll try to find it for you and let you know.'

I stood up to go after her, taking a card from my bag to scribble my phone number. Best not leave this to chance. This information might prove useful.

I came out of the library into brilliant sunshine and paused to look over at Rothesay Castle. How many changes to the island had this 14th Century fortress seen? It was hard to imagine now, as I gazed down the High Street leading to the ferry terminal, that the waters of the Firth had come right up to the castle walls.

As I set off to collect my car from where I'd parked at Guildford Square, I continued to think about what Tina had said. Was there something in the history of the Gastrell family that would help explain what was behind Nicolas's reluctance to continue with the circus? Somehow I doubted it. There was most likely a simple explanation. Nicolas wanted to sell the circus – either as a going concern or by selling it off piecemeal to make money.

Disappointed by my lack of success, I decided to walk along Montague Street and call in at the Electric Bakery to buy a cake – I doubted Simon's culinary expertise would stretch to dessert.

The street was busy with holidaymakers. A family stood outside the Bute Tool Company, their two children discussing the choice of yellow or blue or red buckets and spades for the beach. The windows of The Dressing Room had attracted a group of young women admiring the stylish display of summer outfits and I edged past them to go into the Electric Bakery. The shop was crowded and my choice at this time of day was limited. I settled on a rhubarb tart and as I came out, my mind still on what had happened at the library, I almost collided with someone coming in. It was Rhys's assistant. For a moment her name escaped me as I said, 'Sorry,' but when she smiled I suddenly recognised her. 'Ah, it's Tegan, isn't it? Are you a fan of this bakery also?'

She smiled. 'Rhys is. He says it's one of the pleasures of working on the island.'

This I could understand.

I couldn't resist asking, 'How is everyone? It's been a difficult few days.'

At first I thought she wasn't going to reply but then, making a face, she said in a low voice, 'It's awful. No one knows what's going to happen next. There are so many rumours floating about. One minute the circus is going to be closed for definite as soon as this run is over. The next Nicolas is going to invest money to make sure Kanzi's is the best circus on the planet. We're all stressed out by it.' She added, a frown creasing her forehead, 'It's not good for morale and it's not good for the performances. You have to be on top form, be calm and in the right frame of mind to perform well. Can you imagine what would happen if Rhys let his concentration slip – even for a second? Whoosh!' She illustrated this last comment with a wave of her hands.

Shuddering I said, ‘I’d hate to think about it. But these are professionals, surely.’

‘You would hope so. But we’re on our guard, that’s for sure. Sorry, I’d better collect my order before everything is sold out.’

And sure enough as lunchtime approached, the queue had been increased by the arrival of a gaggle of youngsters from the Rothesay Academy, jostling and laughing as they came in.

As I walked away, my mind was a jumble of thoughts. Was there the remotest possibility that Nicolas could be persuaded to invest in Kanzi’s, make the circus world class? The rumours were contradictory. Was it possible Nicolas was telling one story to some of the performers and another story to the others?

Between what Tina at the library had said and now Tegan, there was no option but to wait patiently for news.

THIRTY-TWO

My determination to avoid the circus – at least until the librarian came back with more information – didn't last long. In my anxiety to help Brannan I decided I had to find out more about this story of Nicolas Gastrell. If there was a scandal it must be recent. He was still a young man.

What age would Nicolas be? If his grandfather bought the circus in 1900 he must have been a young man, judging by his photo. I did a rapid calculation, remembering he'd been at school with Alan. A time span of the past twenty years should be enough to look for any scandal. From what the librarian had said it had to be something to do with money. A scam of some kind, I wondered, thinking of Simon's recent experiences with the boat.

Or perhaps he embezzled money from a firm he was working for? Whatever it was he had been found out, which probably meant arrest, trial, and a prison sentence. A story which would surely have been carried by the major newspapers. I considered returning to the library but I could as easily go home and check the newspapers on the internet from there. Whatever had happened he'd recovered enough to be doing well with his own company. And a lucrative one at that, if the private plane he owned was a sign of his success.

Then I remembered Simon had offered to organise the evening meal – better that I didn't return home before late afternoon. I'd leave him to it.

As I turned the options for finding out more about Nicolas over in my mind, I wondered if anyone at the circus might know the story. I'd a strong feeling some of the performers might be aware of it, but which one of them could I ask? The Sixtus Troupe? But how would I choose one of them? Then there were the clowns – Joffo, Stoffo and Boffo. I certainly wouldn't approach the surly Joffo and I didn't know either Stoffo or Boffo well enough to ask them. Fabio from The Flying Volantes was rumoured to be in a state of deep depression – understandably. So he was out. What about Rhys, El Gran Fuego? Tegan, his assistant, was too young but Rhys had been with Kanzi's for some years. Surely he would have some inkling about Nicolas's misdemeanours? It was worth a try.

I started up the car and set off once more for The Meadows, hoping Rhys would be there. If he'd sent Tegan into town to the bakery, it seemed likely he was back at the circus.

There was one parking space left at the Rothesay Leisure Centre on the far side and I squeezed in with some difficulty. As I walked behind the Big Top towards the caravans that were home to the various performers I realised I'd no idea which one was Rhys's.

Then I remembered the name of each performer was on their caravan. Yes, here was the caravan belonging to El Gran Fuego in the middle of the row and I knocked on the door.

At first I thought I was out of luck as there was no reply. I knocked again, more loudly this time. A moment's pause then the window to the side was pushed opened abruptly and El Gran Fuego stuck his head out.

‘Yes?’ he said in a grouchy voice, a cigarette dangling from his lips. ‘What do you want?’

Oops! He’d been asleep and wouldn’t welcome my disturbing him.

‘Sorry to bother you, but I wondered if we could have a word.’

He peered more closely at me and rubbing his eyes and yawning said, ‘It’s Alison, isn’t it? The programme seller?’

‘Yes, that’s me.’

‘How do you think I can help with that? It’s your job.’

‘No, no,’ I cried as he made to shut the window. ‘It’s not about the programmes. It’s about,’ I went closer and lowered my voice. ‘It’s about Nicolas Gastrell.’

This didn’t improve matters.

‘That shyster,’ he snorted. ‘I’ve no time for him.’ He closed the window with a bang.

Had I lost my opportunity? I moved over and pounded on the glass. ‘It won’t take much time. But if you could answer a few questions it might help save the circus. It really is important.’

This appeared to change his mind and the next minute the door opened and he stood there, tying the belt of his dressing gown.

‘I always try to have a nap at this time of day,’ he said, sounding more awake. ‘When you finish a performance the adrenaline is still going and it can take ages to unwind. I don’t sleep well at night and you have to be at the top of your game to do my act.’

Behind him I could see a table with a couple of tumblers and an empty whisky bottle. Another couple of empty bottles sat on the floor beside the overflowing rubbish bin. Surely with the kind of dangerous act Rhys did, he wasn't a big drinker? But Rhys's drinking habit was not my concern.

Looking around to make sure we wouldn't be overheard, I said quietly, 'I wanted to ask what you know about Nicolas Gastrell. More specifically what you know about his past?'

'Why do you want to know?' Now he sounded bemused.

'I'm trying to help Brannan,' I said. 'There's every likelihood the circus will close after this spell on Bute. Surely you don't want that to happen, to jeopardise employment for so many of the circus acts. Including yourself and Tegan.'

Rhys hesitated before saying, 'I think you'd better come in.' And standing aside he ushered me into his caravan and motioned me to a seat.

It was difficult to know where to sit. Every available space was taken up. There were two banquettes along the sides with a table in the middle but both were strewn with clothes and piles of old newspapers. At the far end there was a tiny kitchen area, the worktop piled high with empty cups and plates. Presumably because there was no more room in the sink. A pervasive air of stale food and smoke hung over the room.

'I keep meaning to tidy up but I never seem to have time,' Rhys said, doing so by the simple method of lifting everything from the seats and tossing it on the floor, leaving me to pick my way over to the far corner and sit down gingerly.

'Now what was it you wanted to know?'

He looked expectant, a wry smile on his face, as though I might come out with some foolish question.

'This is rather difficult,' I began cautiously. I didn't want to say that Brannan had asked me to investigate.

That was meant to be kept under wraps. Besides I'd no idea how Rhys might feel about the idea I was spying on them. 'After what's happened – the death of Melody Blue and the assault on Chiara and now the threat of closure I wondered if there was a reason Nicolas Gastrell was so keen to end what has been a long and proud tradition.'

Rhys appeared non-plussed. 'I'm not sure I'm the person you should be speaking to.'

'But you've been part of Kanzi's for a long time.'

'Not that long,' he protested. 'Only ten years. And this act of mine is quite recent. Like many circus folk I've changed my act over the years. Anything for money.' He put his hand to his face to disguise a grin. 'Well, not anything, obviously. It's not exactly a well-paid career. And audiences want more and more dangerous tricks.'

He nipped the stub of his cigarette before bending down to lift a packet of cigarettes from the floor. Then reaching into his dressing gown pocket he pulled out a lighter and proceeded to light up. A dangerous habit but probably no more so than his day job.

My roundabout way of asking about Nicolas Gastrell wasn't having the right result and clearly Rhys had no idea what I was talking about. I decided to come straight out with my question.

'The truth is…' I said, leaning back and then quickly sitting forward again as I felt a sharp pain in my back. I reached behind me and pulled out a small radio which Rhys grabbed. 'Ah, that's where it was,' he said, putting the offending object on the shelf behind him.

'I've been in the Rothesay Library going through back copies of the former local paper The Buteman, looking for references to Kanzi's Circus,' I said.

Rhys blew a couple of smoke rings into the air and watched as they faded away. 'And what did you find?' he said.

'Apart from the fact the Gastrell family bought it in 1900 and that except for the interruption during the two World Wars it's been a feature of island life every summer.'

Time to come clean. 'But it's Nicolas Gastrell I'm interested in. I've heard a rumour that he was involved in some shady dealings in the past.'

Rhys tapped the ash from his cigarette roughly in the direction of an ashtray and missed. The ash landed on the floor but this didn't appear to bother him.

'And why would you be interested in Nicolas Gastrell? I thought you'd been taken on as a programme seller – temporarily – hardly a worry if you lose that job, is it?'

'Okay. Here's the thing. I'm a writer (or was, I said under my breath) and research is my main interest. Brannan thought I might be able to help, find out more about Nicolas, perhaps persuade him that the circus should be saved.'

Rhys raised his eyebrows. 'Blackmail him you mean?'

This conversation was going in the wrong direction. 'No, no, not at all.' Then I thought, perhaps that's what Brannan is intending and he's roped me in. Not a good idea.

Rhys stubbed out his cigarette and stroked his chin thoughtfully. 'As it happens I do know about Nicolas. I'm from as long a line of circus folk as the Gastrells. Longer in fact. My family started when circuses first became popular in the 1800s. Animal acts, that's what we did. My father was a lion tamer as was his father.

We've always lived dangerously.'

He paused as though lost in memories then said, 'Nicolas was always in trouble as a youngster. But as he grew older his crimes became more serious. Had to do something to fund his gambling habit.'

'Is there one particular crime, I mean incident, you remember? Or know about?'

At first he seemed reluctant to answer then he shrugged. 'I suppose it's easy enough to find out if you know where to look. He and a friend set up a scheme for people to buy shares in a company that didn't exist. And he was stupid – how did he think he'd be able to get away with it?'

'What happened?'

'His father had to bail him out. Raised every penny he could by getting a loan on the Circus. Kanzi's nearly went under. Luckily his father managed to find a generous sponsor – someone who'd an interest in keeping the circus going.'

'Did Nicolas go to prison once he was found out?'

Rhys laughed. 'No, that would have been a bigger scandal. The money was paid back and then Nicolas's part in it was hushed up.'

'That must have left a huge debt. How did they think no one would discover what they were up to?'

'Nicolas's pal was the mastermind behind it all. Their plan was to sell shares as quickly as possible – I think they put a two week limit on it to create interest – and make off to South America.'

'Sounds like a mad idea. The money they'd make surely wouldn't last them long? What happened to it?'

'His partner made off with it, leaving Nicolas to take all the blame. There was a theory that his partner had this in mind all along. Use Nicolas as the stooge and take the money.'

This explained a lot and clarified the rumour I'd heard but it didn't throw any light on what was happening now.

'And what happened after that?'

'He should have been cast out. Disowned. But he was an only child, the only one who might take the circus on after Jonas, keep the name going. He showed remorse, or so I've heard. Took on some of the lowliest jobs, worked his way back into his father's affections. Not that that was difficult. His father doted on him.'

'And now he's inherited. But he works elsewhere and is doing well, from what I gather. And from the style in which he arrived on Bute. You must be doing well to have a private plane.'

Rhys pulled out another cigarette and I began to cough. I wondered if he'd mind my asking him to open a window.

'Yes, you're right. That kind of lifestyle takes money.'

'But his job – that pays well.'

'No, I don't think you understand. Despite his appalling track record his job is looking after the circus finances and his father's investments. Set up a company to handle everything. Now what do you think he'll do?'

This was startling piece of news and not what I'd expected. 'I understand he's likely to sell up or try to find a buyer for the circus name.'

'Of course he will.' He rubbed his fingers together. 'You must know what's going on.'

'I'm not sure I do.'

'It's all about the money, Alison. At least as far as Nicolas is concerned.' He looked at me through narrowed eyes as the smoke drifted upwards. ‘Money is important to everyone.’

‘Surely what happened to Melody Blue and to Chiara isn’t anything to do with Nicolas? Though I realise that has given him a reason for getting rid of the circus.’

‘No, of course not. I’m sure Nicolas had decided about the fate of Kanzi’s before these events happened. He was waiting for Jonas to die and then…’ he waved his cigarette in the air, scattering more ash. ‘So when this incident on the yacht happened much sooner than he could have anticipated, it let him do as he wanted.’

‘So Nicolas isn’t responsible?’

‘Of course not. He’d prefer the circus to be in good shape so he can sell it as an entity. There’s someone else behind these “accidents”. If that’s what they were,’ he said before pulling out another cigarette, lighting it from the stub of the previous one. He took a long drag, coughed, and thumped his chest. ‘Someone with a different motive.’ He raised his eyebrows.

‘You have an idea who that is?’

He put his finger to his lips and despite my phrasing the question in several different ways he refused to say more. If he did know anything Rhys wasn’t about to tell me.

‘I have things to do, Alison.’ He stood up, a signal it was time for me to go.

I said goodbye and stood up to leave the caravan.

At the door I stopped. ‘One last thing, Rhys, has anyone mentioned they’ve been burgled?’

Rhys coughed again, then wheezed, ‘Burgled? No one’s said anything to me.’

‘You haven’t noticed anything missing?’

At this he laughed. 'Alison, what would make you think I'd notice?' he said.

I left with more questions than answers. If the woman I'd seen wasn't a thief why was she at Kanzi's?

Rhys might not know about the intruder but I was convinced he knew the identity of the killer. Then again, if he did, why wouldn't he go to the police? There was more to this story than I could have imagined. If Rhys was to be believed there was a killer on the loose in the circus and whoever it was might strike again.

THIRTY-THREE

Disappointed at being little further forward after my meeting with Rhys, I went in search of Brannan. I'd little to report but the few snippets of information I'd had from Rhys might be of interest.

Unfortunately the first person I encountered was Joffo. Literally. As I came in through the flap that served as the entrance to the Big Top he was coming out and we collided.

'Oops, sorry,' I said, stepping back.

He ignored my apology even though the fault was as much his as mine.

'Have you seen Brannan?' I said.

'No. I'm also looking for him. What do you want with him?'

'Just… a…a question about the programmes.'

'You're making a meal of this job, aren't you? I wouldn't have thought there was much to discuss.' He was so curt, so dismissive.

This annoyed me even more but trying to keep my temper under control I said in a moment of inspiration, 'We may be running low on stock. I want to make sure there are enough programmes for the rest of the tour.'

'Well, we won't need them after we finish on Bute, that's for sure. We might not even need any more here.'

'Have you heard something? About the closure of the circus I mean?'

'What concern is that of yours?'

Really this Joffo was a nasty piece of work. Everything about him annoyed me – his preference for always being in his clown outfit, his high-pitched voice, his surly attitude.

'I'm trying to help, as Brannan asked. He's had so much to contend with – the death of Melody Blue, the accident to Chiara. He's lost one of the most important acts of the show – The Flying Volantes – and now Nicolas Gastrell is threatening closure. Aren't you worried?'

Joffo looked down at his feet and it was then I noticed he wasn't wearing his usual oversized shoes but a pair of rather smart black slip-ons which made his feet look tiny. 'I'm worried, of course I'm worried. But we're versatile in the circus – we can take on all kinds of roles with the right kind of training. There's bound to be something else come up.'

'So you weren't always a clown?'

But, ignoring my question, Joffo merely mumbled something and moved away, leaving me staring after him.

Brannan wasn't anywhere in the Big Top, nor backstage. A trip across to his caravan proved fruitless but eventually I tracked him down in the caravan at the end of the row which served as the canteen for the performers and the crew. It was bigger than the living quarters, set out with a kitchen at one end and several tables and chairs squeezed in to the rest of the space.

He was sitting with what looked like a book of accounts in front of him and an empty plate at his side. He snapped the book shut as I came in to sit down opposite him. At least the catering staff had some regard for others as all the windows were open to dispel the smell of food.

There was no one else there, not even the catering staff, so we could talk freely without danger of being overheard.

'I'm making no progress with finding out what's going on,' I said. 'I think I'm the wrong person for this job. You'll have to find someone else.'

'Nonsense,' Brannan said heartily. 'There is no one else. I can hardly ask any of the circus employees to do it and I must find out what we can do to save our jobs. What do you think will happen to everyone if Nicky sells up?'

'Joffo certainly isn't worried. He seems to think he can turn his hand to anything.'

Brannan laughed. 'I think he's putting on a brave face. Or else he's refusing to face facts. How many circuses do you think there are? How many opportunities?'

'No one is interested in helping,' I said peevishly. 'I've just spent time with Rhys but he won't say much, though I'm sure he knows more than he's saying about recent events. And as for Joffo…he's so grumpy. I know there's this theory that clowns aren't necessarily the happiest of people. Was he always like this?'

'I'm not sure,' Brannan said, stroking his chin. 'I don't know much about him. He only joined last year. Boffo and Stoffo were the original two.'

'Was he always a clown? I spoke to him a few minutes ago and he hinted this hadn't been his first choice.'

Brannan shrugged. 'I didn't hire him. I was perfectly happy with two clowns but it was Jonas Gastrell who hired him. One day he was just there. There was a story about him being down on his luck, having to change career and that Jonas took pity on him. Boffo and Stoffo weren't pleased but it seems to have worked out in the end.'

I turned to other matters. 'I don't see what more I can do to help you, Brannan.'

'Give it another couple of days,' Brannan pleaded. 'I've a meeting with Nicky Gastrell then – that's when he'll make his final decision.'

Brannan was being too optimistic. This was a lost cause. If Rhys was right and the sale of the circus was about making money for Nicolas Gastrell I couldn't see him backing down. Until the awful incident with Melody Blue, there had been a full house at the circus every night. But I'd no idea if that was enough to make a good profit.

Grudgingly I agreed. 'You may think I'm the right person to do this,' I said, 'but, as you'd expect, the circus people have closed ranks.'

I left him with his accounts book, sure it wouldn't make happy reading. And certain I wasn't going to make progress any time soon.

As I came out of the caravan I noticed someone slipping away. It was Joffo. Had he overheard our uncomplimentary remarks about him? I hoped not. This would make relations worse.

Then I thought – why worry? In a short time the circus would have left Bute and I'd have no further responsibility whatever Nicolas Gastrell decided.

THIRTY-FOUR

I was glad to be home. With his wrist now recovered, Simon's addiction to cookery programmes on daytime television had paid dividends and the meal was delicious – lamb casserole with dumplings followed by apple crumble with cream. Perhaps not the best choice for a warm summer evening but I wasn't going to complain. And I quietly put the rhubarb tart in the back of the fridge.

'There are plenty of leftovers,' Simon said as he cleared away the plates. 'I didn't check the quantities before I made it. I thought it was rather a lot.'

'What did the recipe say?'

He looked abashed. 'Actually it was a recipe for eight people.'

'Not a problem,' I said, not wanting to discourage him. 'What's left can go in the freezer.'

We wandered out into the front garden to sit on the bench outside the front door and watch the sun set over the bay. This time of evening in summer is my favourite – what is called 'the gloaming' – neither day nor night when the sun slowly disappears over the horizon and the stars peep out one by one. When it isn't raining, that is. And tonight was perfect.

'Are you absolutely sure you're happy about this new contract of mine?' he said.

In that half-light I couldn't read the expression on his face. 'Are you having second thoughts?'

'No, not at all,' he said hurriedly. 'I want to be certain you're okay with it.'

‘It’s only short term,’ I said, shivering a little as the air cooled.

We sat in silence until Simon said, ‘Let’s go. It’s getting cooler.’

Indoors, as Simon stacked the dishwasher, I decided to phone Maura. Although it was only a few days since she and Alan had left it seemed forever. Frustratingly she didn’t pick up and my call went straight to voicemail.

‘Why are you sitting in the dark, Alison.’ Simon switched on the lamp as he came in.

‘It’s Maura,’ I sighed. ‘I wish she would contact us.’

‘In her own time.’ Simon kissed the top of my head.

I wished I could be as logical as he was and spent the rest of the evening hoping she would phone but by the time we went to bed she hadn’t yet replied.

The result was yet another restless night and next morning I found it hard to focus.

‘I’m going for a walk,’ I announced at breakfast. ‘I’ll pick up the local paper while I’m out.’

‘While you’re out I’ll look through some documents Scottish Alignments Ltd sent over,’ Simon said. I could only imagine he was glad of an opportunity to escape to his study. I began to wonder if the proposed six months might extend longer than he imagined. Or was telling me.

That’s what I should be doing, I thought. Sitting down and trying to come up with a proposal for a new project. Instead I was stuck with the problem of Maura and the problem of the circus. I couldn’t concentrate on anything else.

The village was quiet at this time in the morning. The shop cum Post Office was opening up and along by the Marina a dog walker came striding out. The island could be busy with tourists at this time of year but Port Bannatyne was still an oasis of calm.

After walking around Kames Bay, I went past the Lodge House of Kames Castle to sit on one of the benches with a view across the water to the village.

How easy it had seemed, making our choice to come here. Perhaps even to make it our permanent home. We had friends here, including my long-standing friend Tara who lived out at Straad. But Simon was restless and I had to respect his need for something more challenging than idling our days away on the island.

As I sat in contemplation a voice beside me said, 'Still here, then?' It was Mervin the builder, this time accompanied by his dog, a frisky collie that strained at its leash despite Mervin's attempts to keep it under control.

'Yes. I thought I'd come out and enjoy the morning. Summer is so short here you have to take advantage of every opportunity'

'Very wise. There's rain forecast for tomorrow,' he said gloomily.

This wasn't likely to cheer me up. 'I thought you'd be at work. Didn't you say you're renovating a house in Quay Street?'

'Yes, but all work and no play, you know. I'm having today off. We've finished that house in Quay Street. There's nothing so urgent it won't wait a day or two.'

'Have you another project on?' I said to break the silence as we both gazed out over the bay.

'Yes, funnily enough we've been asked to do a renovation for that guy at the circus.'

'Brannan?' I said. This was strange. He hadn't said anything about a renovation.

He shook his head. ‘No, no, that guy who arrived in the private plane a few days ago.’

Nothing escaped the islanders. They would know all about this arrival.

‘You mean Nicolas Gastrell?’

‘That’s him. Odd kind of character. Seems to want everything done yesterday.’

He’ll soon learn that’s not possible, I thought, but aloud I said, ‘What is he having renovated?’

‘It’s a building on the far side of Ettrick Bay – the north side. It’s a manor house but it’s lain derelict for years. Used to belong to one of those Victorian shipping magnates who lived in Glasgow and brought his family here for the summer. When he died the family inherited but couldn’t keep it up so it fell into disuse. It’s a big job. Everything needs replaced. I’ll have to call in some favours to get it finished in time. If it ever does get finished. I’ve heard there might be money problems.’

‘It might be simpler to knock it down and build something modern on the spot.’

Mervin looked horrified at this suggestion. ‘It might need a lot of work but it’s part of the island heritage.’ He stood up. ‘Anyway. Must get on. Can’t sit about chatting all day. The wife wants to go over to the mainland to do some shopping. So much for a day off.’ He appeared gloomy at the prospect. ‘Come on, Tricky.’ The dog, who was at last lying quietly by his side, sprang to its feet and they walked off in the direction of the village.

That was strange. If Nicolas Gastrell wanted to sell the circus because he needed money, why would he be spending what must be a considerable sum of money on renovating a derelict house? Or perhaps that was why he needed to sell.

Unless he had other plans.

THIRTY-FIVE

An early morning phone call startled me into wakefulness. After several nights tossing and turning I'd at last managed to fall sleep immediately. Aided no doubt by the couple of glasses of wine I'd consumed at dinner time.

It took me a couple of minutes to focus as I reached out to the bedside table to switch on the light and grab my phone.

'Who's calling at this hour,' Simon grumbled, pulling the duvet over his head.

The caller was Brannan and at first I couldn't make sense of his garbled message.

'Slow down, slow down,' I said. 'What's wrong.' I glanced at the bedside clock – four a.m.

'It's Rhys,' Brannan gasped, panting heavily as though he'd been running.

I sat up in bed, fully alert. 'What about Rhys?'

'There's been an accident…it's awful. I can't understand it.'

Oh, no, I thought, not another incident at the circus. This was too much. And what did Brannan expect me to do?

'Slow down, Brannan. What kind of accident?'

'There's been a fire – a fire in his caravan. It's all but destroyed. This is awful.'

A picture of the inside of Rhys's caravan flashed into my mind: papers and other flammable stuff everywhere. And his habit of chain-smoking. The slightest spark would have set it off. I remembered seeing the whisky bottle – had he been drinking and smoking and dozed off with a lighted cigarette?

Best to let Brannan do the talking. 'Do you know what happened? Is he okay?'

Brannan choked back a sob. 'No, by the time anyone got to him, the caravan was completely ablaze. There was not the slightest chance he'd make it out alive. The fire was too intense. Timor tried to get in but the flames beat him back – there was nothing he could do. The fire service came really quickly but it was too late. And it will be a while yet before they can risk going in to check…to bring his body out… given what the caravan is made of.'

Of course. Being metal the caravan would be red hot – it would have to be cooled down before any of the firemen could go in to investigate.

Before I could stop myself, still groggy from sleep, I said, 'Do you want me to come over?' Then I thought, Why on earth did I suggest that?

'Oh, that would be great.' Brannan sounded relieved. Too late to change my mind.

There was nothing I could do to help poor Rhys but I could support Brannan. For all his faults these problems weren't of his making and this latest disaster could only bode more ill fortune for the circus. Nicolas would have yet another excuse for closing it and selling on the name.

I pulled on some warm clothes – at this time of the morning there was still a chill in the air – and telling Simon I wouldn't be long, I shut the front door as quietly as I could behind me. From the mumbled reply I doubted if Simon registered I'd gone but there was no sense in waking the neighbours by banging the front door.

I drove quickly through the deserted streets as dawn

was breaking with the promise of a fine day despite Mervin's gloomy predictions. As well he was a builder and not a weather forecaster. But I'd no time to stop and admire the vista of Kames Bay and the boats bobbing at anchor. I had to reach The Meadows as quickly as possible.

Black wreaths of smoke filled the air with an acrid smell as I jumped out of the car and ran towards the site of the performers' caravans. Even from a distance I could see Rhys's caravan was a blackened shell. No one could have survived a fire as fierce as that.

'Stay back,' one of the firemen said as I approached. 'It's still very dangerous.' He moved in front of me, blocking my view.

'Have you found whoever was trapped inside?' It was too terrible to think about.

Brannan came up beside me. 'Awful. Absolutely awful,' he said, shaking his head. 'Can anything else happen? This will be the end. That's another act down.'

While I had a degree of sympathy for Brannan's predicament I was more concerned for Rhys rather than the loss of his act to the circus. 'Poor Rhys. What an awful way to die – trapped like that in a burning caravan.' I patted Brannan on the arm. 'We can only hope he knew nothing about it. He'd be quickly overcome by the smoke. He probably died in his sleep – he wouldn't have suffered. He wouldn't know anything about it.'

'What do you mean – he wouldn't know anything about it?'

'I saw him yesterday – and saw the whisky bottle on the table. And he smoked non-stop. You must know what happened to him. It's the only explanation.'

'Mmm. Let's hope you're right. I don't want to

think of the alternative.' He shuddered.

'Who raised the alarm?'

'Timor, the trick cyclist.'

'An early riser?'

'Late to bed more like. He'd been in town in one of the pubs – a lock in. As he was coming back he saw the smoke, realised what was happening and tried to force the caravan door but it was no use. The fire had taken too much of a hold by then. He phoned the Fire Brigade and then ran round the caravans wakening us.' He paused. 'It was impossible to help. If only Timor had come back earlier before the fire took hold…' his voice drifted off and he looked grief stricken. Perhaps he wasn't so uncaring after all. Rhys had been one of the more reliable acts of the team.

He looked distraught. 'So by the time Timor reached the caravans, saw that Rhys's caravan was on fire it was too late. There was nothing anyone could do. We were beaten back by the flames.'

One of the firemen came over, pulling off his gloves to wipe his brow. 'We're hoping to move in shortly. We're just arranging another hose to dowse the caravan with water. Then the team can go in with breathing equipment.'

We moved away to the far end of the row as he instructed us but continued to watch from a distance. We could do no more than keep a vigil, waiting for Rhys's body to be recovered and brought out. Not a pleasant thought. I tried not to imagine how little might be left of his body, how charred his remains would be.

'Have you told Nicolas?' What would be his reaction to this latest news?

'Oh, bloody hell. No. I suppose I'd better phone him.' Brannan looked around wildly as though

Nicolas might suddenly materialise.

'I think it would be a good idea to tell him as soon as possible.' What I didn't say was that he should have phoned him earlier – as soon as he discovered the fire. The circus belonged to Nicolas and he should have been the first to know. But I guess in the confusion his only thought had been for Rhys.

Brannan pulled out his phone and moved off. I could hear little of the conversation and I turned my attention back to the smouldering caravan the firemen were continuing to dowse with water. My heart began to thud. I'd no desire to wait here to see Rhys's body being brought out but something compelled me to stay. It was hard to believe that only yesterday I'd been sitting with him in this caravan, discussing Nicolas and the future of the circus. How I wished I'd pressured him for more information about Melody Blue's killer because I was certain he knew or had a strong suspicion.

Lost in thought I didn't register when someone came up beside me and said in a loud voice, 'What the hell has happened here? What's going on?'

A shock went through me as I turned abruptly to see Rhys standing beside me. Whatever anyone had thought, Rhys hadn't perished in the caravan fire. He was very much alive.

THIRTY-SIX

For a moment I thought I was about to faint. I blinked several times in case this was a figment of my imagination. No, it was most certainly Rhys.

'What…what are you doing here? How did you get here?' My words tumbled out as I tried to adjust to the sight of Rhys being alive.

'Never mind that. What's happened to my caravan?' He sounded angry.

'We thought you'd been burned to death… that you were dead. How are you still okay? How did you escape?' This perhaps wasn't the best way to answer his question but I was stunned by his sudden appearance.

Rhys made to dart forward but one of the firemen held out his arm. 'Keep back, Sir. This caravan is still dangerous.'

For a minute it looked as if Rhys was going to push the fireman aside but thinking the better of it, he took a step back, muttering to himself as he pulled out a packet of cigarettes.

Brannan came strolling over, frowning at his phone, stopping abruptly when he saw Rhys.

'What are you doing here?' he said. 'Where have you been? We thought you were trapped in the caravan.'

Rhys scowled. 'Alison's already asked that question. I was coming back to my caravan. That's what I was doing. Only to find there's not much of it left. What's going on. Will someone kindly tell me.'

It was then I noticed he was fully dressed.

'We thought you were inside. We're waiting for your body to be brought out.' Brannan kept staring at Rhys as though he couldn't believe his eyes.

'Well, you're in for a disappointment. I'm very much alive as you can see. Now, for the umpteenth time is someone going to tell me what happened?'

Briefly Brannan told him the story of the fire but then he said, 'Where were you if you weren't in the caravan?'

'Somewhere else,' Rhys growled.

'That's pretty obvious.' Brannan sounded as if he was beginning to lose patience. But that might have been the shock of finding Rhys was alive.

Rhys was saved from having to explain why he hadn't been burned to death as there was a gasp behind us and we turned to see Tegan.

'OMG,' she screeched. 'What have they done to your caravan, Rhys?' She ran up and buried her face in his chest and he put both arms around her, hugging her tightly.

Brannan and I exchanged a look. It would appear that El Gran Fuego had more than a professional relationship with his assistant.

'Thank goodness you weren't there last night,' Tegan continued looking up. 'If we hadn't gone to that hotel…' She stopped and clamped her hand over her mouth.

'Exactly. There wouldn't be much of me left if I had been here.' Rhys stared at us as though defying us to make a comment.

But Brannan was so relieved that Rhys had hadn't been in the caravan– which meant the act was also saved.

'Yes, yes, that's certainly something to be thankful

for. We'd better get you away from here. Let's go into the catering caravan.' He began to guide Rhys by the elbow, but Rhys shook him off. 'What about my costume for the act?' he said. 'Cost a fair whack, that did. Not to mention the full bottle of whisky. I hope I'll be compensated for that as well.'

'Perhaps you should have a rest for a day or two? Take some time. We'll be on the island for a few days yet.' The soothing tone Brannan adopted was a sign he very much hoped Rhys wouldn't decide to desert Kanzi's as the Sixtus Troupe had.

'He'll be fine,' Tegan piped up. 'There are spare changes in the back dressing room where the props are stored. He can wear one of those while we organise replacement costumes. Don't worry, Brannan, we can go on as soon as we restart in Glasgow.'

She tugged at Rhys's elbow. 'We can't stay here,' she said.

'Cursed is what this circus is,' muttered Rhys as Brannan said, 'You need to sit down. Come over to my caravan.'

This matter settled, though Rhys continued grumbling, the trio began to walk away towards Brannan's caravan, leaving me on my own.

The fire at Rhys's caravan had been extinguished but wisps of black smoke continued to curl up into the early morning air.

'Thank goodness this is all we have to carry out,' said one of the firemen, showing me a pile of soggy bits of paper and the remains of some soaking wet and badly singed seat cushions.

Better than a charred body, I thought though I merely nodded.

The rest of the contents of the caravan already lay

scattered around on the grass in front: piles of smouldering clothes, charred seats and bedding, all the detritus of a life. It was a job now for the forensic team to discover the cause of the fire.

It was strange. If Rhys wasn't in the caravan my theory about how it had caught fire was wrong. Someone must have been responsible for setting the caravan on fire. Was this linked with the accidents to the trapeze act?

A problem for others to ponder. I'd had enough. I began to shiver – delayed shock. And the stench of the charred items strewn outside the caravan filled my nostrils, making it hard to breathe.

No point in waiting here: I could join the others in the catering caravan or else I could head home. I glanced at my watch. Six a.m. Still time for a couple of hours sleep.

But I wasn't to escape so easily. The police had arrived and we were all asked to wait to give statements. In vain I protested I'd arrived too late to be of help. They were searching for any clue about what had happened, how the fire had begun and the sooner that was dealt with the better.

Brannan spent some time with them and as I waited for him to return, crammed into the catering caravan with most of the other performers, Stoffo came over to sit beside me.

Or rather someone came over to sit beside me and introduce himself as Stoffo. Out of costume he looked so different: a stoutish middle-aged man, balding and pale-skinned.

'Right mess this, isn't it?' he said. 'Do you want a cuppa?'

This was the best news I'd heard since I'd arrived. 'I'd love one but…' looking around, 'there doesn't appear to be anyone on duty.'

Stoffo winked and stood up. 'Don't worry. I know where the supplies are kept. Might even be able to rustle up a biscuit.'

Were the other two clowns here, I wondered. A scan of the others in the caravan revealed someone who might be Boffo – he was the only one I didn't recognise.

But of Joffo there was no sign. Most likely he was with the police, giving his statement.

Stoffo returned with two large mugs of tea. 'Wasn't sure if you took sugar but I put in one in case. Good for shock they say.' He produced a packet of biscuits from his dressing gown pocket. 'These won't be missed,' he grinned.

As he sat down opposite me his expression changed. 'Terrible business this, coming on top of everything else. I don't think we can survive this.'

'Any chance it was an unfortunate accident?' I tried to sound optimistic although I didn't believe this for a second.

He shook his head, his expression grim. 'We'd like to think that's what it was – an accident. But the rumour is they've found an accelerant – probably petrol.'

'Good gracious.' This was serious. 'So it looks as if it was deliberate.'

Stoffo nodded. 'There's a possibility whoever did it knew Rhys wouldn't be there. But I can't think of a reason why he, or his caravan, would be targeted.' He frowned and took a long gulp of his tea. 'This on top of what happened to Melody Blue and to Chiara is too much. I wouldn't be surprised if more of the performers want to leave. Once you have a run of bad luck like this you wonder if you'll be next. We're a superstitious lot if the truth be told.'

I racked my brains for something to say that would comfort him, but I couldn't think of a single thing. And I could well understand why the others were becoming twitchy.

'Do you think there's a link between what happened to Melody Blue and to Chiara and this latest incident at Rhys's caravan?'

'How could there be? There's no connection surely?'

Suddenly I felt overwhelmed by tiredness. After draining the last of my tea, I stood up. 'I'm going to find out who's in charge and hopefully I can go home.'

Stoffo barely acknowledged my departure but continued to stare gloomily into his mug of tea.

Outside I stopped for a moment before striding over to one of the policemen on duty. He agreed I could leave "as long as you give contact details," and I made my way back to my car before he could change his mind.

Brannan could deal with giving Nicolas an update. Thankfully this time it was good news.

When I arrived back at the cottage, worn out with the stress of the fire at the caravan, Simon was up and dressed.

'What was all the commotion about?' he said. 'Why did you have to go out so early?' He sniffed. 'Is that smoke I can smell?'

Briefly I explained what had happened at the circus as his face grew thunderous. 'Alison, this is nothing to do with you. Please stay out of it.'

'Don't worry. I intend to. Another few days and the circus will have left the island.'

'Let's hope they manage to complete the tour. At

this rate there won't be enough acts left to warrant the circus staying open.'

'Let's not exaggerate,' I said but in my heart I knew he was right. What was worse I had this dread that the fire at Rhys's caravan wouldn't be the last incident. Meantime my only thought wish was to have a shower to get rid of the smell of smoke.

THIRTY-SEVEN

Simon had a business meeting in Glasgow. Something to do with the new contract though I didn't enquire too closely. He offered to take me with him. 'I'm sure you'd enjoy a shopping trip. We could have an early lunch together before I go to my meeting.'

He expressed surprise when I declined the offer. 'You don't want to leave me here on my own in case I get into mischief,' I teased him. 'Besides I remember how long some of the meetings you used to have lasted. You might end up having to stay overnight in Glasgow.'

Reluctantly he agreed he'd be better going on his own. 'You're right. If we continue into the evening it might be too late to catch the last ferry.'

He went off early the next morning with strong warnings that I should be careful. 'I hope the circus has permission to leave the island soon,' he said. 'That will end your association with them.'

After he departed in a flurry of missing car keys and spectacles, I went out into the garden to sit at the table and have breakfast, though the seagulls hovering over the bay might chase me indoors with my meal. With regular watering and feeding the pots I'd bought from Mill Cottage had come into full flower. A decided improvement on the bare look of that part of the garden.

It was strangely quiet without Simon. I'd miss him when he took up his contract – we'd become so used to being together this last while. Nonsense. This is a good opportunity to write up those proposals you've been considering for ages, I told myself sternly. But not yet, a second voice inside my head said and I poured another cup of coffee. Work could wait.

My mobile lay on the table, inviting me to phone Maura. Surely there could be no harm in giving her a call and before I could think too much about it, I dialled her number hoping it wouldn't go to ansaphone.

She picked up at once. 'Hi, Maura,' I said putting on a cheerful voice. 'Thought I'd give you a quick call.'

'Sorry, Mum, I've been meaning to phone you but life has been so hectic since I came back. And you'll remember how much time three children take up – what with nursery and school and the numerous activities.'

'Yes, indeed I remember.' A pause then I said, 'And is all well?' I didn't want to ask her outright about Alan but she must know how concerned I was.

She sounded subdued as she said, 'It's a bit of a story but best I tell you when I have more time. How about I give you a call later tonight?'

In the background I could hear sounds of a disturbance, a loud thumping followed by a wail.

'I'll have to go,' she said. 'Noah and Connor are fighting. Speak later.'

And with that she was gone, leaving me staring at my phone. It sounded as if she might call me later with good news. If there had been continuing difficulties this would have been her opportunity to tell me. Our brief chat gave me hope though how I'd manage to wait until she phoned back in the evening I'd no idea.

I needn't have worried. No sooner had I ended the call to Maura than my phone rang. This time it was the police, wanting to speak to Simon.

'Sorry, he's in Glasgow. He should be back tonight or tomorrow at the latest. Can I help?'

It turned out I could. 'We'd like him to come in to look at some photos. He might be able to identify the man calling himself Damien who sold him the stolen boat.'

'I also met him,' I said. 'Would it be helpful if I came and had a look?'

'Fine. Any time today that suits you.'

With nothing else in prospect for the day, I decided to go over before lunch. And I might be able to arrange to catch up with Tara, who lived out at Straad. We'd been friends since working together on a history of the Rothesay Pavilion some years before but it had been a while since we'd been in contact.

Tara declared herself delighted to hear from me and free to meet up. 'The children are both at school now,' she said, 'which leaves me more time. Though I should be getting back to work.' She didn't sound happy at the prospect.

We arranged to meet at The Kettledrum opposite the Albert Pier in Rothesay and in a lighter mood I left for the Police Station.

Sergeant McQuoid wasn't there and I was left in the charge of the young constable, P.C Bevin, someone who took his duties seriously. My comment of 'Is this the Rogues' Gallery?' as he presented me with a set of photographs raised no more than a frown.

He had the script off pat. 'Take your time and go through the photographs carefully. While it's important to identify the correct person, we don't want mistakes.'

'You don't want to arrest the wrong person, you mean?'

Again this attempt at a joke fell flat and with a sigh I began to trawl through the pages of photographs, scrutinising each one carefully under the watchful eye of the constable.

Midway through my search I spied him. 'I'm sure that's Damien,' I said, putting my finger on the photo.

P.C. Bevin peered over my shoulder. 'Are you absolutely certain?' he said. 'You wouldn't want to make a mistake.'

'Absolutely. I'd recognise him anywhere.'

Again he hesitated. 'I don't think so.'

This annoyed me. 'Of course I recognise him. That black bushy beard and the slightly crooked nose mean I couldn't forget him.'

P.C Bevin looked puzzled. 'Mmm…'he said.

Now I was becoming impatient. 'You asked me here to identify Damien. This,' jabbing at the photo, 'is the man I recognise as Damien. What more do you want me to say?'

'That's the problem.'

I sat back and crossed my arms, wondering what he would say next.

'That's Tony Teller and he's been in prison for the past year.'

Could I be wrong? But Damien had been so distinctive with his large beard and crooked nose.

The constable sat down opposite me. 'You see, that's the problem about this man Damien. He can adapt his appearance so easily.'

'I can look through the photos again. Perhaps I made a mistake.'

The constable closed the book with a sigh. 'Let's leave it there. When your husband returns to the island we'll ask him to come over and have a look.'

There was no point in saying so but Simon was even less likely to be able to identify Damien than I was.

Saying, 'Thank you for coming in,' P.C. Bevin dismissed me and I left to meet Tara in a thoughtful mood. It wasn't pleasant to think that Damien, or whoever he was, might still be out there in some other part of the country continuing to scam people. But I'd been so sure I'd recognised the photo. I wasn't as observant as I thought, then.

THIRTY-EIGHT

Tara was in a cheerful mood as we settled into The Kettledrum for lunch. Lunch for me is usually a sandwich but frustrated by my experience at the police station, I opted for comfort food of fish and chips.

When I told the story of the boat scam to Tara over lunch she was sympathetic to the loss suffered by Simon but did agree with me that buying something like a boat unseen was not sensible.

'I thought Simon was happy to retire early,' Tara said. 'When does he start his new job?'

'He's gone to Glasgow today for a meeting. I'm not sure he'll manage to return tonight.' His latest text had suggested, as I'd suspected, this meeting might well overrun.

Tara listened in silence to my problems and expressed concern at how I'd manage when Simon took up his contract.

'I'll be fine,' I assured her. 'I'm considering pitching for a couple of commissions.'

'I suppose you've had lots of experience of being on your own because of Simon's job.'

'Exactly. Though I'll have to make the decision whether I should stay on Bute or try to find a home on the mainland.'

'You like living on Bute, surely?' As a Brandane Tara couldn't imagine anyone not wanting to make their home on the island.

'How are getting on with your job at the circus?'

she said, waving away the dessert menu, much to my disappointment.

As briefly as I could, I told her the story of the strange events at Kanzi's ending by saying, 'It looks as if there's not much hope of the circus continuing. Nicolas Gastrell is determined to sell. The only possibility is a reprieve so that the Glasgow part of the tour can take place but I suspect that's because he needs time to find a buyer and it's better to bring in some money rather than none. What's more he can showcase the company if there are live performances.'

We chatted about our families (though I said little about Maura), about the weather, about the problems with the ferries (always a hot topic) until finally she said, 'You'll soon be finished with the circus. So if you're looking for a volunteer job there are plenty of opportunities here on the island. For example…'

I held my hand up to stop her. 'Sorry, Tara, I've no intention of taking on another role as a volunteer. I've a few ideas I want to pitch – that will keep me fully occupied.'

'Don't become so busy you've no time to meet up again. It's been so long since we had time for lunch together.'

She leaned forward, a serious expression on her face. 'I'm glad you've decided to look for a new writing commission. There's something happening at Kanzi's and it's dangerous. That caravan fire – word is it was started deliberately.'

'Where did you hear that?' The story of the fire would be common knowledge but a limited number of people knew an accelerant had been used.

'Ah, so it's true. You're never sure with gossip.' She shook her head. 'Get out of there, Alison.'

‘Nonsense. I’m not in any danger. And yes, another couple of days and the circus will have moved on. The Meadows is needed for the next big event and the police have agreed the circus can leave. It’s not as if they’ll be far – only in Glasgow.’

‘It may only be a few days but be careful.’

‘Brannan was so helpful with the boat I don’t think I can back out now.’

We paid our bill and left. Tara had parked at the Albert Pier.

‘I can’t squeeze into any of the spaces there,’ I said. ‘They were designed for much smaller cars.’

‘I have a small car,’ Tara said, pointing to a Fiat. ‘Now when are we going to meet again. Let’s not leave it with the usual “I’ll phone you”. That way time drifts.’

‘Agreed. How about…’ I stopped in midsentence. On the other side of the street, coming out of the Print Point was the fair-haired woman I’d spotted at the circus. She turned left to hurry along East Princes Street.

‘Sorry, sorry, ‘I said. ‘I have to go. I’ll phone you, Tara. Promise.’

She looked startled as I began to run across the road and towards the Print Point, waving goodbye.

There was no sign of the woman as I reached Guildford Square. She must be in one of the shops. I stopped for a minute to get my breath back then made my way slowly along, peering into The Diner, then the hairdresser’s. Had she gone into the Co-op? The automatic doors swung open as a customer came out and I hurried in to look up and down the aisles. But this shop is small and it took only a few minutes to determine she wasn’t here.

I came out and stood gazing around. The only shops

left to try were the Cancer Charity Shop and the Pet Shop. Or she may have headed to Montague Street. I couldn't face going into every shop looking for her. I had to admit I'd lost her. Yes, I was anxious to know who she was but if I did find her, what would I say? Another foolish idea.

Whatever she'd been up to at the circus I wasn't going to find out this way.

As I turned to walk to where I'd parked my car, suddenly there she was again, coming down from Argyle Street into Guildford Square.

I stood and watched her, lurking behind a large Range Rover parked on the edge of the Square. Where was she going? It could do no harm to follow her.

Striding out determinedly she walked quickly past the row of shops and turned left onto the High Street.

As stealthily as I could, I began to go after her, dodging behind the Market Cross as I watched her continue past the Police Station.

Then I realised. She was heading for The Meadows. She must be going back to Kanzi's Circus. This time I'd confront her.

THIRTY-NINE

It wasn't easy trying to follow the woman up to The Meadows without being seen. Past the Police Station there wasn't much cover and once or twice I dodged into doorways. Anyone watching would have thought I was the suspicious person.

As we reached The Meadows it seemed as if she would go into the Rothesay Leisure Centre but she kept on walking towards the caravans before cutting across the field and through to the Big Top.

What should I do next? The site was quiet with no signs of life. My instinct was to find Brannan but how could I spend time looking for him without losing sight of this mystery woman?

And what could I say to Brannan? She might have a perfectly good reason for being here.

I'd have to find out more about her and decision made, I crept over to the Big Top and pushed aside the entrance flap. The Big Top was empty, cold, and dark without lights and music. How much of the atmosphere of the circus depended on the excitement created by the flashing lights, the noise, the applause, and the laughter of the audience. It was all an illusion – smoke and mirrors – and I reflected on how hard the performers worked to sustain this sense of magic.

But I wasn't here to reflect on the illusions created by the circus performers. The woman must be somewhere inside. If she wasn't in the arena she must have gone into the changing rooms at the back of the arena. Could I manage to catch up her without being spotted? This might prove difficult. She could be in any of the temporary rooms.

How foolish. This wasn't a job for me. Brannan must be about somewhere and I began to make my way to the main entrance. If he wasn't in his caravan I'd call him, ask him if he knew who this woman was. After all, he'd asked me to investigate anything unusual and my impression was this woman was nothing to do with the circus. If it turned out I was wrong and she was there legitimately then there was no harm done.

Suddenly there was a noise from the back of the arena. This might be my chance.

I crept along by the side of the arena, keeping close to the bottom row of seats. Intent on staying out of sight in case she should suddenly appear, I didn't notice the metal bucket lying beside the entrance and almost tripped over it. There was a loud clang and I stopped, holding my breath. Surely she must have heard me.

The flap to the backstage opened and Fabio stuck his head out. 'Who is there?' he said.

I slipped into the next row and waited, crouched down in the shadows, wedged between the first and the second rows, hoping he wouldn't spot me.

He turned to someone I couldn't see, saying, 'It's nothing. Something must have fallen over. I have to go. If you don't understand, it is not my fault.'

As he began to walk quickly across the arena a figure appeared, running after him. It was the woman I'd been following. Ah, that was the explanation. It must be someone Fabio knew and I remembered being told of Fabio's success with women. It wasn't Joffo she was involved with after all and it explained why she'd been lurking around the circus. And whatever had happened between them it was clear Fabio wasn't pleased to see her.

They stood together in the centre of the arena. Now I had a good view of both of them as she turned to face him. She was certainly attractive in a petite way.

'Do not talk to me about this again,' Fabio said. 'How many times do I have to tell you it is over. It was never much to begin with.'

The woman looked furious. 'No, that's not true. You promised I'd be your partner if anything happened to Melody Blue and did you keep that promise? No – you chose Chiara over me. Do you think I'm going to stand for that?'

There was something familiar about that voice. I'd heard it before. But where?

The argument continued and I tried to change my position, cramped as I was between the seats. My awkward position had made my left leg numb and I tried rubbing it to ease the discomfort.

Fabio laughed. 'You can do what you like. What would make you think you were nearly as good as Chiara? She's doing well – will be back soon. In time for the Glasgow performances.'

This was the wrong thing to say.

The woman took a step back, reached into her jacket pocket and drew out a knife. 'If you're not going to have me as your partner, you won't be performing at all.'

As she lunged forward, Fabio tried to sidestep but consumed with fury she was too quick for him.

Unable to watch this scene play out before me without taking action, I scrambled to my feet shouting, 'Stop! Stop!' almost falling over in attempting to move from my confined hiding place.

Taken by surprise, the woman turned in the

direction of my voice and in that split second Fabio was able to jump over and wrest the knife from her.

'You!' she hissed. 'Interfering again. This is nothing to do with you. I knew you were trouble.'

'It is as well Alison was here,' Fabio said in a shaky voice, clutching the knife to him.

I gazed at the woman with a dawning realisation. I recognised her. Or rather identified the voice because without the clown's make-up she looked completely different.

But there was no doubt about it. I was looking at Joffo.

FORTY

'I can't believe it,' Brannan kept saying over and over again. 'Joffo? Why did I not know? How could she have kept up that disguise for so long?'

'Because she was always in makeup except for when she thought she could escape from the circus, go off without being recognised.'

We were sitting in Brannan's caravan. He looked stunned by what had happened. Joffo or Charlie had been taken off by the police, screaming and raging, leaving a shaken Fabio to tell the story about what had happened. Once more I'd be a witness. I didn't like the way the sergeant said to me, 'So we meet again, Mrs Cameron.'

Brannan looked puzzled. 'But her name? When she signed up she had to fill in all the forms.'

'That was nothing to do with you. And it's not unusual for a woman to shorten her name. Yes, she was called Charlene Leetone but shortening her first name to Charlie meant you assumed it was a man you were dealing with. Though,' I said, 'on reflection her high-pitched voice might have been a clue.'

'So she was responsible for loosening the links in the chain. It was so deliberate. And the attack on Chiara.' He shook his head again in disbelief. 'Thank goodness she was interrupted or there might have been a second death.'

'And disposing of the programmes was a way of trying to get rid of me. She thought I might find out the truth. So if the programmes went missing I'd be blamed and told not to return to the circus.'

Brannan stroked his chin. 'I understand that. Do you remember that phone call where I asked you to help investigate? She or rather Joffo, came in in the middle of that – she must have overheard.'

'Thank goodness it was only stealing the programmes she had in mind. Little did she know I'd made no progress at all in finding Melody Blue's killer.' I shuddered at the thought.

Brannan continued as though I wasn't there. 'I know she'd experience of trapeze work – many of the performers have been in other acts and as I said in the end they are all athletes. But to kill just to be in The Flying Volantes? That seems improbable.'

'Not from what I heard. She was in love, obsessed, with Fabio – one of many from what you said. He promised her if anything ever happened to Melody Blue she'd be the replacement. Of course Melody Blue was never going to leave, though Charlie tried to persuade Fabio to sack her. He was stringing Charlie along and in the end she had no choice, or so she thought. And I suspect she intended Melody Blue to have an accident that would mean she couldn't continue as Fabio's partner, not to kill her.'

Brannan stood up. 'I'll have to call everyone together, tell them about this. Nicky won't want to go on with running the circus now.' He looked despondent. 'What am I going to say?'

'Have you had been in touch with Nicolas?'

'Not yet. We were to have a meeting this evening. I suppose I'll have to contact him before then. It's all such a mess.'

'I'd better be on my way, let you get on.' Then I said, 'What about Rhys? Was that her doing?'

'Yes. Rhys told me the full story. He caught her one

day without her makeup and decided he might be able to make some money from her.'

'Even though she was a killer? How awful.'

'No, no.' Brannan shook his head. 'All he knew was that Joffo wanted to keep his…I mean her…identity secret for some reason.'

This explained the fire at Rhys's caravan but right now, I was anxious to go home, to have time to myself. The past few hours had been fraught and there was no more help I could give Brannan now. It was up to him to negotiate with Nicolas about the future of the circus.

But I was wrong if I thought I could escape so easily.

'Not so fast, Alison.' Brannan grabbed my arm. 'I know this is a big ask but could you possibly wait for this meeting with Nicolas.'

'I don't think so,' I said, gently removing his hand from my arm. 'You know who was responsible for what happened. If you want the circus to go ahead it's up to you to convince Nicolas.'

He looked crestfallen. 'I need support,' he said.

'The circus performers will support you,' I said.

'You think so? We've already lost the Sixtus Troupe as you know and Timor is making noises about looking for another place.'

'I thought there were few circuses?'

'Here in Britain there are few but these people are happy to travel anywhere. If we lose our best acts there's no point in continuing. Audiences these days are discerning. They want excitement, something different.'

There was a knock on the door and Salome popped her head in. 'Did you say you wanted to see us?' Once again, out of costume I was struck by how ordinary these performers looked.

'Yes, yes,' Brannan said. 'If everyone could meet in the arena I'll be along shortly.'

He turned to me again. 'Come on, Alison. You've been with us so far. What harm can another few days do? Then we'll be packing up for Glasgow. Which may well be our farewell performance.'

Reluctantly I followed him out of the caravan and across to the arena.

Everyone was there, some in costume, some in their normal attire of casual clothes. Fabio was standing at the back and he'd been joined by Chiara. She had her arm linked through Fabio's. He'd have a difficult time disentangling himself from this relationship, I thought.

As we entered the Big Top the hum of chatter ceased and all eyes focussed on Brannan.

He cleared his throat and said, 'This is a difficult day for us. By now you'll have heard what has happened. How Charlie, or rather Joffo as we knew him…I mean her…I mean. Oh, well, Charlie anyway. How Charlie was responsible for the death of Melody Blue and for the attack on Chiara…'

'And for the attempt to kill me by burning down my caravan,' Rhys interrupted. He looked embarrassed. 'I should have said I'd seen Joffo without his makeup but…'

'Yes, that too,' Brannan said though clearly he was annoyed at his speech being interrupted.

'And I've not heard a word yet about compensation,' Rhys muttered, though Brannan ignored him and went on, 'I'm meeting with Nicky Gastrell tonight. It's not a special meeting – it's been planned – and we'll be discussing the future of the circus.'

‘If there is a future,’ Stoffo murmured, echoed by Boffo’s, ‘If there is a future.’

‘Come now, let’s not be too downhearted. This might turn out well in the end. Now that the killer has been identified we can get on with what we do best – providing amazing acts to delight and enthral audiences.’

At this a half-hearted cheer went up, though I noticed Rhys and Tegan didn’t join in while Fabio and Chiara stood looking sullen.

‘When will we hear what’s happening. If we have a job or not?’ This from Timor.

‘As soon as the meeting is over, I’ll let you know. Whatever happens the decision will be taken tonight.’

He turned on his heel and walked off, quickening his pace as he left and I hurried after him.

How I wished we hadn’t adopted Maura’s suggestion of asking Brannan to help with the boat. Now although Simon didn’t have a boat, I wasn’t yet free of my involvement with the circus.

FORTY-ONE

The meeting was to take place in the Stuart Hotel opposite Rothesay Castle, where Nicolas was staying. I'd been there before when I'd been employed helping with a group of American tourists. It had the advantage of several meeting rooms and Nicholas had booked one of these well away from prying eyes.

'I've learned that the walls have ears on this island,' he growled as he ushered us in. It was a small meeting room – simply furnished with a table, six chairs and a side table with an internal telephone. 'In case we need refreshments,' Nicolas said. 'But we won't.'

He'd no intention of prolonging the meeting by the sound of it and this suited me, anxious to return to the cottage and return to normal life. Besides, I was hoping there would be word from Maura by now. A sneaky look at my mobile from time to time had shown there were no messages but she might have been trying to contact me on the landline in the cottage. I could only hope.

Nicolas wasted no time in starting the discussion. 'Terrible news about the murder,' he said. 'Not a good advert for Kanzi's, is it?'

Brannan had contacted him then to tell him about Joffo.

'But I'm sure we can put all that behind us,' Brannan said eagerly. 'Everyone will pull together now, make sure this is the best circus in the world.'

Nicolas raised his eyebrows. 'That's an

exaggeration, surely.'

'Well, the best in Britain,' Brannan said.

'It's no use. This news is the final straw. No one will want to come now. Best not to delay.'

Privately I thought this news might bring more people to the circus but I didn't say so. I was there as an observer, nothing else.

'You said we'd be able to have the Glasgow run at least. You promised,' Brannan pleaded. 'You know how many advance tickets we've sold for those performances.'

Nicolas leaned over, thumping the table, making me jump. 'You're not listening, Brannan. I was prepared to give you the benefit of the doubt, to let you try Glasgow. But not now. And who would want to come along to a circus where they might be murdered?'

This was nonsense and Brannan knew it but it was perhaps unwise of him to say, 'The killer has been caught, Nicky. All that is over with.'

Nicolas got to his feet. 'Too late, Brannan. I've found a buyer.'

Brannan seemed to glimpse a ray of hope. 'Then the buyer might be prepared to continue…'

'No, no. You don't understand. The buyer wants the assets not the people. You're living in the past, Brannan, the circus is dead…'

The door to the meeting room flew open and a tall man, leaning on the arm of a young woman, came in.

'Not so fast,' said the tall man. 'I might have something to say about your plans.'

Nicolas went white and grabbed at the edge of the table before sinking down into a chair, gasping, 'Dad, what are you doing here?'

Brannan looked confused. 'Jonas? Is it you?'

The young woman guided Jonas to a seat. 'Yes, not

quite what you expected, is it Nicolas? You thought I was off the scene, that I was dead and you could do whatever you liked. Well, that's not going to happen.'

During this exchange Brannan had sat dumbstruck but now he managed to croak. 'What's going on?'

Jonas smiled. 'I've suspected for some time that my son was siphoning off funds. The private plane for a start. My fault. I should never have left him in charge of the finances. Especially with his track record.' He shook his head. 'But getting proof wasn't easy. I so didn't want to believe he was defrauding me.'

'But we thought you wouldn't recover – that you were in hospital and would die there.' Brannan stopped and put his hand to his mouth.

Jonas said, 'It's okay, Brannan. Everyone, including the doctors thought I'd had a fatal stroke. Turned out it was a severe case of hemiplegic migraine – it imitates a stroke and this one was particularly bad. Couldn't speak, couldn't move. But then they discovered what it was and I saw an opportunity to lie low and find out what my son was really up to.'

'No, Dad, you have it wrong. I was trying to do what was best. There's no future in circuses. My plan would have brought some money in. Money that would have enabled us to do something new.' His voice began to rise as he became more hysterical. 'Honestly, Dad, you have it wrong. Just let me explain.'

Jonas shook his head. 'There's a future for Kanzi's circus under the able management of Brannan here.'

'What will happen to me.' Nicholas's voice had dropped to a whisper.

'You're my son. Always will be. But I want nothing more to do with you. You'll hand over the company bank cards and go.'

As he saw the stricken look on Nicholas's face, he said, 'Don't worry. I'm not going to call in the police. But I never want to see you again.'

Without a word, Nicolas went into his briefcase and pulled out a wallet and passed it to his father.

Jonas made no comment as the wallet was handed over. Instead he turned to Brannan.

'This is Imogen Feinsby, my new accountant. She'll be taking over the finances of the circus but I'd like you to stay on as manager.'

Brannan's face lit up. 'How delighted I'd be to do that. I'll make sure Kanzi's circus is something you'll be proud of.'

In the excitement of this news, no one noticed that Nicolas had slunk away.

I felt delighted. Happy for Brannan and for the circus people but happy also for myself that it had ended well and I could leave Brannan and Imogen to discuss how they would take plans for Kanzi's forward. I suspected they'd get on rather well, if first impressions were correct.

EPILOGUE

The good news was that the circus would survive. Poor Melody Blue's killer had been found and now with Nicolas no longer in charge Kanzi's would go from strength to strength under the management of Brannan and Imogen.

And the police had finally tracked down the man who called himself Damien Loughty. He'd overreached himself by taking in a launch for repair which had been spotted by the owner on a yachting website when Damien tried to sell it. Sadly Simon's money was long gone but he was philosophical about it.

Everyone else's problems were solved but not the one which troubled me most.

Back at the cottage I sat in the living room as dusk crept in, too tired to put on a light.

Several times I lifted my mobile to phone Maura, but each time put it back down again without dialling. What was the point? I'd no control over what happened to any of my children. Those days were past.

If only Simon were here, I thought. He'd texted earlier to say he wasn't sure if he'd be back tonight. I'd be on my own.

Perhaps I should make some supper though I wasn't really hungry.

In the kitchen I rummaged through the fridge but there was nothing tempting. Then I remembered the lamb casserole Simon had made. There was plenty of that left in the freezer and it wouldn't take long to defrost. There would be too much for one person but we could have the rest tomorrow when Simon returned.

I'd no sooner put the casserole in the microwave and set it to defrost when I heard the sound of a key in the lock. Had Simon managed to leave his meeting in time to catch the last ferry after all? Thank goodness.

I hurried down the hall to the front door as it opened.

It was Simon and behind him was Maura …and Alan and the three children.

'Look who I met on the ferry,' Simon said with a grin.

I stood there speechless until he said, 'Are you going to let us in?'

'Of course, of course,' I stammered, moving back, unable to believe my eyes.

'Grandma, Grandma,' said the children, flinging themselves on me. As I attempted to disentangle myself, I said, 'It's lovely to see you…'

'Don't worry,' Maura laughed. 'We've booked one of the cottages at Kames Castle but we thought we'd drop in and see you first.'

'I'm starving,' Connor said.

Thank goodness I defrosted the lamb casserole, I thought, wondering if I'd enough potatoes for everyone.

Simon settled the family in the living room, thoughtfully putting on a television programme about polar bears to entertain the children while Maura followed me into the kitchen.

Now I had to ask her. 'Is everything now settled?'

She grinned and sat down on one of the kitchen

chairs. ‘Absolutely. I feel such a fool. I suspected Alan of having an affair with one of my friends, Bethany. He refused to answer when I asked him, except to say I should trust him. I’m lucky he’s so understanding. My suspicions might well have caused a break up. You were right, Mum, I’m so lucky,’ she said again.

‘So the idea of an affair was nonsense?’

‘Yes, Bethany is a travel agent and I should have put two and two together. Next year it’s twenty-five years since we first met at school. I hadn’t remembered that. Anyway, Alan wanted to celebrate in a big way. He’s been so busy and I’ve had to give up so much because of his career he thought it would be a good idea to plan a surprise cruise – something special. That’s why he was in contact with Bethany and he didn’t want to tell me till the arrangements were finalised.’ She looked ashamed. ‘I almost spoiled the surprise…and our marriage. I’ve no idea why I ever doubted him.’

‘How wonderful.’ I leaned over and hugged her. ‘I couldn’t have hoped for better news.’

‘Thing is,’ she began to trace a circle on the table with her finger before looking up at me. ‘Thing is, Mum, we wondered if you and Dad would look after the children while we’re away.

ACKNOWLEDGEMENTS

Grateful thanks to everyone who helped with this novel: Bill Daly, Joan Fleming and Joan Weeple for comments and proof reading and Paul Duffy and Rosemary Gemmell for technical advice.

Printed in Dunstable, United Kingdom

65730511R00163